DEATH IS SO KIND

DEATH

IS SO KIND

a novel of suspense

by L I A M   R E D M O N D

THE DEVIN-ADAIR COMPANY

New York 1959

Contents

DEATH IS SO KIND

Prologue

Poor Martin

Martin Coyne had chosen to hide in Malcolm **Street.**
Skinner MacCormack, who seemed to know almost everybody, knew a man who owned one of the tenements. Skinner
got him a top back room—with a skylight exit to the roofs. It
was Skinner too who managed to procure the greasy peaked
cap that seemed to lurch naturally to one side, the dark and
dirty suit, and the down-at-heel yellow pointed shoes. It
wasn't a bad place to hide, within easy reach of O'Connell
Street, where he could ease the evening hours away in one of
the cinemas. Not the most cheerful street in the world, of
course, grey-brown brick of decayed Georgian houses, as
melancholy as the grey mist that seemed always to be hanging around. But you become immune to most things. Coyne
was no longer bothered by the smell of decay in the drab
bare-boarded hallways, the grime on the broken glass of
graceful Georgian fanlights, or the corrosion of old ironwork.

3

On that morning the watery sun made patches of silver on the damp pavements. Coyne paused in the dark hallway. It was unwise to light a cigarette: and he knew it was unwise. Anyone watching would be put on the alert. But it made his hesitation seem more natural and it gave him a better opportunity to ensure that the street was safe. Besides, lately he didn't seem to care so much any more. You get like that.

A barefoot child, lingering on her way to school, was playing hopscotch on the far pavement; a milk-cart rattled disconsolately away down the street. Over in Nelson Road a shopboy was removing the shutters from a window. A muddy-faced, ugly, over-pregnant woman lumbered by. Coyne couldn't think what she reminded him of: a little man with a big drum maybe. But there was pain in her eyes.

With the cigarette dangling carelessly, Coyne tripped jauntily down the worn steps. It was best, he found, to give an impression of carelessness. The more brazen you were the less they seemed to notice. He was wondering about crossing the street when the two men came from under the archway. Just about the same time he heard the footsteps behind. Coyne gave little sign of his awareness, except that his pace quickened; and his hand strayed.

"Keep your hand in your pocket!"

He tried pulling the gun. But no good. A shot rang out that seemed to shake even the sluggish mist.

One of the men approached and bent over the inert body. The smoking cigarette still dangled from Coyne's lips. His fingers twitched. The man—unlike his companions, rather low-sized—bent down casually, took the cigarette and transferred it to his own lips. Then he fired another shot into Coyne's head. The slum urchin who had watched the scene with interest came slowly over. She looked up smiling.

"Eh, Mister, are you playin' soldiers? . . . Are you?"

4

1

Mr. Nolan

On that cold grey evening when Mr. Nolan fussed down the steps of the Four Provinces Insurance Company there was little to suggest, except on the newspaper placards, an atmosphere of terror. The street lamps were already lighting: and although it was nearly closing time and scarcely worth the trouble, some of the shop windows were beginning to brighten. Almost typical, Mr. Nolan blended diffidently with the other office menials who emptied themselves with humdrum haste on to the moist pavements. His bowler hat, frayed black overcoat and shiny striped trousers suggested a caricature of the office worker. Of course he had an umbrella, tightly rolled; and his shoes were excessively polished. At the street corner a newspaper placard was attracting some attention:

"TERRORIST LEADER SHOT DEAD"

Mr. Nolan's face revealed neither interest nor emotion: but he took his place in the queue. Having procured a paper he didn't bother pausing to read but folded it meticulously and put it carefully under his left arm. Then he padded his way down the main street, his middle-aged movement suggesting vagueness of mind and a gentle tendency to abstraction.

Near Wellington Park he viewed with the same singular disinterest another placard:

"POLICE BATTLE WITH GUNMAN"

Mr. Nolan ambled into the Park. The great trees were leafless and the little avenues deserted. He found a seat under an evergreen and with characteristic deliberation proceeded to make preparation for perusal of the journal. Having placed the newspaper on a dry section of the seat he extracted his spectacle-case from the inside pocket of his jacket. With dignified precision he took out the pince-nez with an attendant piece of chamois. Methodically he breathed on each side of the lenses, then assiduously polished each in turn. He put the spectacle-case back in his pocket before he fixed the glasses delicately on his nose. Taking up the paper again he unfolded it and began to read. The formidable black headline was nearly frightening:

"TERRORIST LEADER SHOT DEAD"

Police Battle in Dublin Street

"In an early morning battle with police Martin Coyne, notorious Terrorist Leader, was this morning shot dead while attempting to resist arrest. Coyne's death follows immediately on the Government's declared determination to stamp out subversive activity throughout the country.

"On Friday last the Minister for Justice introducing the People's Protection Act declared that 'the function of Government could not be usurped by any secret organisation.' In a vigorous speech Mr. Dirrane denounced the use of force by minority groups to end Partition as 'immoral and unchristian.'

"The People's Protection Act provides for the suspension of Habeas Corpus. It also provides for the setting up of Military Tribunals to deal with the crimes of 'illegal organisations.'

"Coyne had eluded capture . . ."

Mr. Nolan had not been unaware of the death of Martin Coyne. The information was conveyed to him with all necessary speed, but there was the possibility that he might glean some further detail from the newspaper account. There would be a meeting this evening. Better check on that. Meticulously again he folded the paper, this time making it sufficiently small to fit in his outer pocket. He replaced the pince-nez in its case, and the case in his inner jacket pocket. Meticulously he flicked a dust mark from his sleeve and smoothed the lapel of his coat. Bartley Moore would most likely be in Smith Street.

As Mr. Nolan got up from the Park seat his face relaxed a little of its mask-like formality. He had known for some time that Martin Coyne would be killed. Martin was well-intentioned, but he hadn't the steely core necessary. Martin was a dreamer. Mr. Nolan remembered that in the preparation for the War of Independence there had been many such as Martin, courageous in thought but insufficiently ruthless in action. Martin was the type that as the "troubles" became more than mere skirmishing either hardened or dropped away. Action made leadership so much simpler. Before the troubled times Volunteers had been indulging in all the same stupidly ineffective propagandising, enjoying their cowboy fun at midnight hours, painting slogans on street corners, broadcasting illiterate nonsense from ineffective little Pirate Stations, indulging themselves in all manner of schoolboy escapades, and finding the superb thrill in the occasional capture of a few archaic guns. Poor Martin was the religious type! He had read too much of the New Testament. He dreamed himself a crucified martyr.

Mr. Nolan remembered now with satisfaction the drab hours he himself had endured in that sordid room night after night, year after year, thinking forward in preparation for this day. Cold, passionate, unshakable determination was the hall-mark of successful Revolution. The time had not been wasted, he was sure of that now; the agony had been made worth while. Of course they didn't all like him: Skinner MacCormack was all right—and Walshe. But Joe Corcoran—Joe was a weakling: enough ability and too much vanity, that was the trouble.

On the far side of the Park Mr. Nolan found himself in a narrow murky street. He maintained his middle-aged, vaguely abstracted ambling gait, but his little grey eyes were active. In the old days he had learned always to be on the alert, without ever giving that impression. The casual turn to spot a possible shadow had become second nature; his keen-eyed search for danger around every corner was merely habit now.

Revenge was a sweet incentive. Success was revenge. There were times when he had doubted the propriety of such sentiments. In the old days it had not seemed so. Mr. Nolan's mind relaxed in remembrance. He thought of old comrades, some of them Senators now, some Ministers in the Dail. Their photographs appeared in journals giving hearty handshakes, brisk smiling fat men, all comfortably optimistic. He remembered other days when they were less

8

self-possessed: raw-boned yobs, whose accents matched their manners, firing antiquated guns from behind a hump of ditch, and some of them not too good at that itself. Sweet incentive! Curious, all the same; in the old days they deferred to him—"Better ask Nolan." Now with their fleshy wives and formal dress they sped through the city in sleek cars. Compromisers! Mr. Nolan wondered if they ever thought or spoke of him. Laughter was a good defence. If he was mentioned at all some funny-boy would probably laugh uncomfortably and make an effort at derision. "The Diehard"! But occasionally, standing at the grave of an old comrade who had sacrificed all for the ideals they betrayed, they must be needled by the voice.

The gutter was lined with fruit and vegetable barrows. It was the end of the day, and the screeching shawlies divided their time between packing up their wares and making a final sales effort. The street was littered with vegetable refuse giving off a mild stench of decay—cabbage waste, onion peel, and over-ripe tomato. The stench was not offensive to Mr. Nolan, but he felt unhappy urging his way through the raucous shawlies, his ears assailed by irreverent screeching:

"A penny each the bananas, sixpence a pound the tamatas."

"Eh luv, what would you like for your tay?"

A wrinkled harridan grabbed his sleeve, thrusting a grey chicken carcass under his nose.

"Hey, Mister! Lovely chicken to take home to the wife. Look at that breast, Mister! That one could go on the movies."

He shoved doggedly on. Bartley Moore would be outside Fagan's.

Mr. Nolan had made his plan carefully. The design had taken shape slowly after years of brooding. Sometimes, as he wandered in the rain, a thought had come, was nurtured, developed, and fitted into the main trend. In the solitary,

9

cold, early morning hours he had put aside a book of Kropotkin or Lenin to wonder how some detail of their practice could be used in his Movement. He wouldn't introduce any changes immediately. He wouldn't let them perceive his genius or the dream of a vast New Revolution he had conceived. He'd give them the impression that he was just carrying on where Martin Coyne left off. Only gradually would they become aware of his capacity, his ability to encourage the right man here, the right idea elsewhere. At the moment the Movement's most valuable asset was the tacit sympathy of the people. That sympathy was associated probably with the people's inherent distrust of Government, a hangover from the British regime: but it was essential that it be assiduously nurtured. It would be necessary to maintain the Pirate Station, but it was equally necessary to get a worth-while transmitter. Their friends in America would help in that. Sonny Coughlan, the engineering student, should be encouraged—another Martin Coyne, too much of the visionary; but he might be tempered by work and danger.

There were two immediate problems: the development of the Movement in country districts and the procurement of small arms in worth-while quantities. Corcoran's cajoling of an occasional Thompson-gun from a Regular Army man was ludicrously cumbersome. In radio propaganda it was important to keep hammering the Partition issue, emphasising that Six Counties of Ireland were still in bondage to a brutal British garrison, that in those Six Counties there was freedom neither of thought, speech, religion, or political belief. The Six Counties must be the eventual battleground. That should not be forgotten.

Mr. Nolan knew that within six months he would have an organisation which would be of dominant importance in shaping the future of the country, and which must eventually take over the reins of Government. Allowing his mind to luxuriate ever so mildly in dreams of the future, he seemed to hear the echoing tramp of marching men as the People's Army ascended to freedom.

He heard the voice of Bartley Moore before he saw the old man. Bartley was standing in the gutter outside Fagan's Public House, a bearded patriarchal figure in tattered scarecrow clothes:

"Some died by the glenside
Some died 'mid the stranger
And wise men have said
That their Cause was a failure
But they loved dear oul' Ireland
And never feared danger.
Glory O! Glory O! to the Bould Fenian Men."

Mr. Nolan didn't particularly care for Bartley. The old ballad-maker was in the Gaelic tradition of Blind Raftery, but his self-conscious awareness of that tradition and his mawkish sentimentality were embarrassing. However, the important thing was that he was blind. Even if tempted into disloyalty he couldn't identify members of the conspiracy.

Mr. Nolan dropped a coin into the greasy tweed cap.

"Good evening, Bartley."

"Good evening, sir, and blessings."

Bartley Moore's red-rimmed eyes seemed always to be looking out over the world. There was curious nobility in his gaunt bearded face.

"Your voice," said Bartley, "is one I know. If you're the one you'll know the word."

Mr. Nolan appreciated the necessity for passwords, but on this occasion he found it irritating.

"Comrade!"

"Mr. Nolan! Ah yes, the meeting is at half-past six in Number Sixty-seven. Martin Coyne is dead."

"I know."

"They'll kill you too, maybe."

Mr. Nolan smiled. He was no dreamer like Martin Coyne.

"Do they all know?"

"All but Joe Corcoran."

Again Mr. Nolan felt a sense of irritation. It was difficult to deal with Corcoran. He was never late or absent from a meeting without some tidy excuse for inexcusable untidiness. Probably drinking now. But Corcoran had ability —nobody could deny that. His broadcasting scripts, though facile, were ideal propaganda. If he could possibly learn discipline he might be a brilliant revolutionary.

"Do you think he was arrested?"

"I do not then."

"That's something."

"It'd need the Dear Lord Himself and a regiment of saints to round up that fellow. Saving your presence, Mr. Nolan sir, he's as slick as an eel in a bucket of snot."

"Quite so." Mr. Nolan's lips were tremulous with distaste.

"I've tried to find him. I have and that's the living truth. There's one place yet but."

"Do your best."

"I'll do that. I'll do that, Mr. Nolan, sir. I'll find him for you."

2

Joe Corcoran

It was wise for any member of the Movement as prominent as Joe to be always on the alert, but he wasn't afraid. The greater the tension the keener the thrill so far as he was concerned. Joe liked Kelly's, an obliging pub, one of the best houses in Dublin. Skinner MacCormack said the cellars ran under the Liffey, but then you'd never know. Certainly they served the best pint of draught in the city: though some of the other publicans tried to make out that Kelly dosed the stuff with baking soda. Ah, but that was only a story. A pint in Kelly's was a poem in itself, the froth as smooth as cream: 'twas a joy the way it stuck to the glass on the way down.

Joe Corcoran didn't drink stout much, but he liked to lace them occasionally. Whiskey was Joe's drink, clean and sharp as a baby's tooth. Of course it wasn't only for the drink he liked Kelly's. It was comfortable and old-fashioned

13

without being dreary. There was a share of sawdust at the base of the counter, right enough, and he knew the oak veneer wasn't even a good painter's job; still he preferred it to the chromium-plated kips with all the loud tarts and phoney talk. One advantage of Kelly's: it was bright enough without being too bright. Sitting in the sort of alcove, his face almost in darkness, he could keep an eye on the men coming in through the door, or back from the lavatory.

Another thing about Kelly's: the barmen were decent. Joe Corcoran watched the little raggedy man with the urgent voice talking. He had a copy of the *Evening Herald*. Amazing! There were the headlines about Martin Coyne glaring from the front page and the little man was talking about football. Poor Martin! Funny, the way a man dies. You like him or you don't. You think you could never do without him or that he's just a bloody nuisance, and then he's gone—just like that. The Unexpected Absolute. Poor bastard! The way he used to recite poetry in the bars when he had a few jars.

All he ever wanted was to die for the People. Well, he had his wish. Decent skin, God rest him. It'd be joy to land a shower o' lead in the guts of the bastard that got him. Might too. Seemed almost impossible to carry on. But that's what they thought when Goulding was got. Terrible to think they'd be at the mercy now of oul' Narky Nolan with his ferrety Civil Service mind. However, the Movement was bigger than them all. They'd carry on. He wondered about Martin. . . . Sensitive poor bastard. He, too, must have known the lonely bewilderment.

A man came from the lavatory door; there was an entrance behind there too. Joe wasn't afraid but he had to be careful. He felt sure he wasn't being trailed; but all the same . . .

He wondered if Martin ever had a woman. Bitch of a

14

thing that no one seemed to escape. Martin was a little fond of Anna, maybe, the way he used to look at her, how conscientiously he'd praise her. Hard to know. Of course religion was a help, though how he managed to reconcile being in the Movement with going to daily Mass was a bit of a stickler: a Jesuit up in Gardiner Street, they said. And then off to Communion of a Sunday morning: coming down the aisle, hands joined, and his angel eyes stuck down in his chest. That made it easier, maybe.

Joe took another sip. He hated the stuff really. Extraordinary about whiskey: nobody could say it had a nice taste. It gave you a slight lift, but nothing to talk about. He'd just have one more and then go. The Meeting was at half-past six. He could cut out drink if he wanted to; if he hadn't had such a bad night he wouldn't be drinking now. Besides if you want to do business you have to drink. The important thing was that he'd managed to get the Tommy-gun from that little twister up in Griffith Barracks. It'd be marvellous to cut it out completely: get on to a really strict discipline of hard work. Sixteen hours a day. To-morrow morning he'd get up at dawn, work four hours, get a humdinger script ready for the broadcast, and then down to business. Work was the thing that mattered. What the Organisation needed was disciplined hard work. . . .

Joe raised his hand to get the barman's attention.

"Same again."

"Same?"

"Stout and a large Irish."

"Right."

Anna was back from the office now. She'd have that turquoise housecoat on, flurrying up and down the corridor, laying the table and getting the tea. Even hunched over the greasy sink, Anna seemed somehow always radiant. She had grace, that was the word: the delicate grace of an infinitely gentle wild thing. Her lips too had that unfixed, tremulous, mildly alert expectancy.

Amazing the others thought her so inaccessible! "A cure for bad thoughts. I wouldn't try doing a job on her." Skinner MacCormack leered. "She'd want you to write a pamphlet on it first. 'The Importance of Orgasm in the Coming Revolution.'"

There was a time when Joe thought her cold too. That first time he ever saw her, the night Brian Goulding was hanged: after the riots in O'Connell Street, when the crowd gathered in the College Hotel. She came in dressed all in black, and her face was pale: compelling attention without effort she moved with quiet repose across the room. At that moment her pure and austere beauty seemed to synthesise all the compulsive idealism of the Movement.

Two docker types, typical pint drinkers, shoved through the swing doors and shambled to the bar, their faces grey with coal dust, peaked caps settled precariously on the Kildare side. Joe watched the tall lean barman with the priest's face as he moved down the counter. The two men, standing motionless, staring at the infinity of bottles, seemed unaware of his presence.

"What can I do for you, gentlemen?"

The taller one gave the question a degree of thought: his face masked in contemplation, endeavouring to choose from all the exotic drinks in the universe.

"Two pints."

The barman moved away to engage himself in the slow process of pouring. Still they were quiet enough. The small one shuffled a step, rested his hand on the counter, coughed wheezily and spat into the sawdust. Joe knew there would be no hurry, the longer the preparation the sweeter the flavour.

16

The night of her twenty-first birthday, wasn't it, Skinner MacCormack made her drink the three glasses of champagne! She became a little over-gay then: chattering too much and telling everybody that champagne had absolutely no effect, absolutely no effect. Reaction probably! Afterwards when it was all over and the last drunken shout had died down the stairs she looked despairingly at the chaos—and laughed; laughed joyously and recklessly, as though the porter stains on the carpet, the overflowing ashtrays, and half-empty glasses were all palpable proofs of success.

"Now I know the joys of anarchy."

While she opened the windows, clearing the lingering smoke, and emptied ashtrays, he took a final double for comfort and stretched out on the couch. Extraordinary how quickly she could tidy a room. She was methodical of course. And for a declared Revolutionary she had an inappropriate fondness for order.

"Well, it certainly was some party."

"I think they enjoyed themselves."

"Certainly did. Me too. I'm limp as a rag."

"You're tired," she said. "I'll turn off this light."

After an eternity of concoction the barman had come back with his offering, placed two creamy pints on the counter before them—the rich froth overflowing. Silently the tall one gave him some coin. Still they did not drink, seeming deliberately to ignore the luscious black foam-topped tumblers.

"Shockin' about that this mornin'."

"What? What was that?"

"That fellow, what's his name, Coyne."

"Oh yeh. I read about that."

"Shockin'. It goes to show."

"One of them diehards, wasn't he?"

"So they say. Oh, it only goes to show."

"Jesus, the country is bad enough without that fella makin' a ballox of it altogether."

"I wouldn't say that."

"You what?"

"I wouldn't say that."

The small one seemed about to stretch for his pint but decided instead to lapse back into silence.

She came to him silently and stood by the head of the couch.

"You were awfully good, Joe. I could never have managed."

They chatted a while, recalling the crazier goings-on at the party, remembering affectionately poor Skinner Mac-Cormack's efforts to maintain dignity without sobriety. Her laughter died and there was silence. He somehow sensed a tension. Should he go? His heart, for no good reason, was pounding. He took another slow gulp and had just let his head loll back—when she bent over quickly and kissed him softly on the lips.

"I've wanted to do that for a long time."

The big man stretched out and lifted his pint. The other followed suit. They drank long and hungrily. When they put them down again the glasses were half-empty.

A pause.

"After all what was he fightin' for only what we've been tryin' to get for seven hundred bloody years. Freedom, that's what. Not for twenty-six mangy counties but thirty-two. It's not wrong to want what's your own, is it?"

"That's all right."

"What's all right?"

"It's different now."

"What's different?"

"We've had too much bloody fightin' in this country. What good does it do?"

"Divil a much. God knows."

That austere, coldly modelled face gave so little hint of emotion that passion seemed incompatible with her nature. Her kiss was like no other woman's kiss, cold and soft and infinitely tender. Love, he knew then, was a holy thing, cleansing their bodies of evil, transforming every gesture to unheard-of loveliness. When he stretched out his arms to draw her down she was trembling.

"If I only had known that I could have hoped."

Taking her head between his hands he kissed her, first slowly and tenderly, then long and passionately. Their bodies drifted in an eternity of loveliness. Her lips parted. And her body seemed to dissolve in gentle tremblings.

"Lie down beside me."

Silently she obeyed.

The couch wasn't wide but they found room enough, their arms and thighs in close contact. Gently he showered her with kisses, on forehead, lips, on cheeks and chin. When he kissed her eyelids it seemed to make her calm. . . .

"Another thing."

"Yeh?"

"Things is different. We have our own Government now. If there's any fightin' to do let them do it. We've had too much bloody fightin'."

"Is it that crowd?"

"Why not?"

"A crowd of prime chancers. Makin' a lot of cushy jobs for theirselves and their friends. Is it that crowd?"

"They're our own, aren't they?"

"That crowd!"

Together they stretched out again, lifted their glasses and ferried the remainder down their gullets.

"Are you havin' another?"

"Wait till after."

They shambled towards the swing doors and shoved out into the air. . . .

She too must have known that consummation was inescapable, that they were the helpless happy instruments of an eternal Design.

"I love you," he said. And she kissed him again. His hand groped for her breast and she relaxed. Her flesh was velvet soft. He stretched across and brought his lips down to caress that warm sweet whiteness.

"Oh, oh, oh—" she moaned softly. "It isn't right to be so happy. It isn't right to love you so much."

He kissed her again and she in turn smoothed his forehead with her fingers, and let her lips rest delicately on his eyelids. He found her pressing closer and her hand moving sensuously over his body. Again he felt little shame. Her pleasure pleased him most.

"Does that make you happy?" she asked.

"Yes, darling."

He kissed her again, a full moist open-lipped kiss, and let his hand drift.

"Oh darling, darling," she moaned again. "It isn't right— but I do love you."

"I know. I love you too."

"We have too many clothes on. We'll go to bed darling. We'll go to bed."

"Yes, sweet."

She rose quickly, smoothed her clothes a little, bent down to give him a quick smiling kiss.

"I'm not a virgin you know, Joe. I loved a boy in England."

"Don't tell me any more."

He remembered her words, and was troubled. "I loved a boy." How many had she loved before they met? How many since . . . ?

Incredible the others never seemed to suspect. Of course they didn't care a lot for her. "Frigid as a dead fish," Skinner said. Commiskey didn't like her either. "Keep the goddam women out of it. More interested in how *they* look than in how the Movement looks." Bitter bastard, Commiskey. Wouldn't care to be at the wrong end of his gun. That poor woman of his must have had a hell of a time. No wonder she skipped. That's what made him bitter, most likely; though they say he was bitter enough before. All the same . . .

Commiskey was crazy. Everyone in the Civil War was a little crazy after. CARRY THE WAR INTO ENGLAND was Commiskey's idea. Sabotage power stations, blow up bridges, bomb reservoirs. The fellow was looney. Surely he knew that world sympathy would disappear overnight. The dream of freedom for a United Ireland would become a shameful nightmare and the hopes of countless generations would be darkened for another hundred years.

Joe smiled dreamily as he thought of his own plan—to engineer a rising in the North. Need careful planning! IN ONE GLORIOUS NIGHT to smash all communications,

21

capture the radio station, occupy the principal buildings, surround the barracks. A magnificent conception, daring enough to be possible, simple enough to be successful. No exhibitionist parades through the cities. Silently in the darkness of the night each town . . .

When Charlie Horgan opened the bar door Joe felt a mildly paralysing heaviness in his limbs; and he knew that his forehead was wet. It was the unexpectedness! And after a bad night you lose your grip. Charlie's lips were upturned in a Buddha-like smile: and he walked with the delicate care of a pleasantly drunk man. Joe shouldn't have been afraid, he knew that. They had nothing on him, at least nothing they could prove. Besides, Charlie was an old friend, not even stationed in Dublin; he wouldn't be such a louser. It was just the unexpectedness! He watched Charlie intently as he manoeuvered round the corner, wondering would he notice. He raised the glass to his lips. The alcove was dark, he should be all right. Charlie swayed slightly as he sailed towards the table.

"Well, if it isn't Joe Corcoran! How're you, Joe."

Joe wasn't afraid any more.

"Charlie Horgan! Where did you drop from?"

Charlie hadn't aged well. His face had fattened and coarsened, and the line of his mouth was hard.

"What are you havin', Joe?"

"Not just now, thank you. Have to be on my way."

Fervently Horgan gripped his hand—and turned, shouting.

"Hi, Udolphus, hurl us up a basket of stout. Come on Joe, what'll you have? A large one?"

"All right, but I'm in possession," Joe said quietly. "It's my order."

Curious to think of Horgan as a lush. In the old days he was careful, almost mean: never the first to buy and then slipping off unbeknownst when things looked like getting rough. Amazing how people changed! Horgan dragged over a chair and plomped down. He was tidier now anyway; at least his clothes were clean. Joe remembered the greasy black overcoat that had been a byword in the Dramatic Society: food stains on the lapels, and a smell of stale sweat that made the girls edge away. His clothes were still crumpled, but at least they looked clean. The little smiling barman hurried across, wiping his hands.

"A large one for me," Joe said. He turned to Horgan. "I thought you were stationed in Cork. What are you going to have?"

"The same." He pulled his chair closer to Joe, clapping him on the knee. "Sure I was. But the bastards couldn't do without me. You can't keep a good man down in Cork." He laughed gaily at his little joke. "By God that's good, Joe, isn't it? You can't keep a good man down in Cork. They brought me up to supervise that shipment of arms from Sweden. I'm an inspector now," he said beaming, pleased and seeming surprised. "Dammit Joe, it's good to see you." He clapped Joe on the knee again. "Brings back old times. We saw some good days together. Remember the walks we had in the hills? Remember the night—? Do you ever see any of the Dramatic crowd? What happened to Jim Fortune?"

Joe was thinking about the shipment of arms.

"Still in the Corporation."

"Mad as ever, I suppose. And Jack Casey?"

"No idea where he is."

"That little twirp Leary is still around."

"Yeah. Acting in the Gaiety. I always thought you'd take it up yourself, Charlie; as a profession I mean."

"Me?"

"Yeah. Why not?" Joe felt more comfortable now. Charlie

had always been vain about his acting. "Will you ever forget the first reading of 'The Shaughraun'? I thought I'd burst my sides laughing. You could have gone anywhere, Charlie. I was aways stuck with the soppy parts, leading juv."

"Fair enough." Charlie's boisterous gaiety seemed to desert him suddenly. He stared sadly into his drink. "You got the girl. That's all they want to know. Who gets the girl?" He seemed almost as if he were about to cry. "Funny man never gets the girl. They clap the comic. They don't have to be afraid. He never gets the girl." He brightened magically. "You're not married, Joe, are you?"

"No. How about you?"

"Loveliest little missus in the world. Here, wait till I show you." He fumbled in his inside pocket, scattering papers as he dragged out a bulging wallet. "Loveliest little missus this side of Bray." He pulled open the wallet. "Look at that. And the two God forbids."

Behind the cellophane screen was a snapshot of a mousey-haired unsmiling woman and two young children.

"That's charming."

"Isn't she nice?"

"She's lovely."

"And the two kids. A boy and a girl; what you call sharp-shooting, eh Joe?"

"What are their names?"

"Sean and Lily. Ah, they're a caution, that's what they are, a caution. You should settle down yourself, Joe."

"You couldn't tell but I might."

"It's the only life. Dammit that's good whiskey. I can feel it oozing into my four bones like the Grace of God. By the way, how's the Movement?"

"What movement?" Joe was suddenly, but not noticeably, alert.

"Ah now Joe don't try that stuff on me. Sure every little

24

dribbley-nosed sergeant from here to Bray knows you're in the Movement."

"What are you talking about?" He tried to suggest that he was mildly mystified, but his tone was petulant. Horgan was talking again. He bent over confidentially, wagging an impressive finger.

"And I'll tell you something more," he whispered. "There's a share of us wouldn't mind being in it ourselves. No names, no pack-drill." He glanced round the pub, afraid of being overheard. "After all what kind of a muck-up have we now? God save the Southern Part of Ireland, three quarters of a Nation once again. What's the sense of talking about bloody Freedom and the country still partitioned? Am I right?"

"I'll go bail."

"An' another thing."

"Yeah?"

"There's no good, me oul' segocio, in takin' down the Union Jack off Dublin Castle an' puttin' up the Tricolour. England will still rule you, oul' son. She'll rule you through the Banks, through her usurers, through her property owners—"

"Personally," Joe said, "I don't give a bugger one way or the other."

Horgan didn't seem to hear. He gulped down his whiskey and banged on the table.

"Eh, Michael Angelo," he shouted. "Hurl us up another couple of the same."

"No thanks, I have to be going now."

Horgan plomped down again, exaggerated disappointment on his face.

"Ah now Joe, we're old friends. In memory of days gone by."

"I'm afraid not."

"For auld lang syne."

He seemed about to break forth in song, but Joe interrupted.

"I'm sorry," he said. "I have to get back to the digs. The landlady's a bit of a hoor. But I don't want to spoil a good thing."

"O.K. Joe. No offence. O.K., whatever you say. Till we meet again."

His hands closed over Joe's fingers in a firm embrace. "Listen Joe. We were good friends. You did me many a good turn. Don't think I'm forgettin': 'Blow blow thou winter wind.' Remember, Joe, if you're ever in trouble, mind you I mean this, always remember Charlie Horgan—I'm tellin' you now."

"I'll remember."

"A friend in need," Horgan said intensely. He took Joe's hand again. "Good-bye Joe. We'll meet again, God willin'. Good-bye old friend." He seemed inclined to burst into tears, but instead his expression changed. "Hey, what are you doin' to-night, Joe?"

"I don't know yet." Joe hesitated, searching. "Probably I'll have to work."

"Nine o'clock to-night . . . Jumpy Jordan's Bar. I'll be there, don't forget."

"O.K. I must be going now, Charlie."

"Good-bye Joe. A friend in need. Jumpy Jordan's Bar at nine o'clock."

3

Anna Quin

Joe slipped out the side door into the laneway. The cold air, striking viciously, reminded him that he had had more than enough to drink; if he was going to the meeting he'd have to give an impression of sobriety. He glanced to the right. Nobody in sight. Pulling his hat more firmly over his eyes and buttoning his overcoat to the neck, he turned left, away from the main thoroughfare. His face took on the cultivated blank expression that looked at nothing and saw everything. Best make his way through the maze of laneways over to Anna's place and scrounge a cup of coffee. She'd be thrilled to see him, he thought with a complacent smile: and so unexpectedly!

Before he reached the corner he heard the whiney voice of Bartley Moore meandering through one of his ballads. And when he wheeled to the left, there, sure enough, was the old blind ballad singer, in the gutter as usual, almost opposite the door. Ordinarily Joe could tolerate the senti-

27

mental droolings, but this evening somehow he didn't feel up to it. For all his Gaelic pretensions Bartley could be so goddam insensitive.

Joe studied again the location of the flat. There was no quick getaway, and it could be watched without difficulty from the Park. But then, if you got half a break you were over the railings. Half a break . . . The house was out of alignment with the others, set back a couple of yards: which meant that you could be pounced on in no time. The back exit was worse, opening on to a small garden hemmed in by factory walls: gaunt and hopeless as a prison yard. A death trap!

The street was nearly deserted and his hob-nailed boots seemed to thunder on the pavement. Passing Bartley, he tried disguising his footsteps. It was no good.

"Joe!"

"Yes, what is it?"

"What's your hurry, lad?"

"No hurry. I've got business to do, that's all."

"There's a meeting."

"I know."

"Half-past six."

"At Sixty-seven. MacCormack told me."

"Martin Coyne is dead."

"You don't say."

"It's true."

"Well what d'you know!"

"You're makin' mock of me, Joe. Why would you be wishin' to make a mockery of blind Bartley? Are you afraid, Joe?"

"Afraid? What have I got to—"

"Don't be afraid, Joe. The time might come when your word, if it was brave and strong, could lift us all out of the mire. Don't be afraid, lad, no matter what."

28

"What the hell—"

"A man need never need to fear that's sure he knows what's right."

"Ah, go to hell."

"Wait, Joe. How is the mother takin' it?"

"What mother?"

"Martin's."

"Oh! How the hell do I know?"

"His pain was quick; 'tis she will have the long sorrow."

Joe turned quickly away; Bartley's ponderous droolings were heavy going.

The apartment-house hall-door was open as usual. He hurried up the stairs, finding the long climb a bit of a strain. Joe tried analysing the peculiar smell, something related to hot cats and stale cabbage. . . . Strange, he hadn't remembered that Martin had a mother. Somewhere down in Kildare. A kindly woman she'd be surely; it would have been from her that Martin got his gentleness. Curious he had forgotten and Bartley remembered. Her eyes now were rimmed red with crying. Bartley was right. 'Tis she would have the long suffering.

On the top landing Joe noted again the thin steel bars across the skylight. He had intended suggesting to Anna that she have them removed. Just in case! He rang the bell, four short jabs to let her know. Inside, a door banged and he heard laughter and gleeful voices. He realised too late that he should have phoned. Hurried footsteps echoed in the corridor. It was obvious when Anna opened the door that she was perturbed.

"Joe! Where did you drop from?"

She slipped out to the landing, drawing the door behind her.

"What's all the excitement?"

"Sonny Coughlan's inside."

"So what?"

"Well, I'm never sure whether you want to meet these people. He's on his way to the meeting. Would you like to come in and talk to him?"

"Better not."

"All right then. Into the bedroom. I won't be long getting rid of him."

She opened the door again and Joe hurried down the corridor. It was a relief to escape from the cold. The electric fire was on, and the room, as usual, pleasantly tidy. A moment's relaxation could do no harm: the confusion of whiskey and stout had left his mind muzzy. He must pull himself together. Taking care not to soil the patchwork quilt, he stretched out lazily. Anna's excitement was unnerving. What harm if they did meet? Right enough he liked to be secretive, but it wasn't of world-shaking importance. It almost seemed as though she had a sense of guilt. Surely she wasn't afraid he'd be jealous of that little twirp?

A door opened and Joe heard Sonny's wavering high-pitched giggle. Anna's easy good humour was a pleasant contrast to that embarrassing uncertainty. Good at his job but the same Coughlan: once he started fiddling with a transmitter his whole character changed. His gauche irresolution vanished and he became a capable craftsman; useful to the Movement too: though his romantic conception of Revolution was almost as embarrassing as his giggle.

The outer door closed.

"Come out, Joe. It's all right."

Anna was standing before the fire in the sitting room, smiling her welcome, her arms outstretched.

"Joe darling."

"Hello dear."

It was cheering to see her face, sunny with affection. His wondering about Coughlan had been silly. She was Joe's woman, only Joe's. Urging her body unashamedly against his, she wound her arms around him, her moist lips brushing endearingly over his face.

"Joe my sweet, my darling love."

"Anna, Anna. Kind Anna."

"Wasn't it terrible about Martin?"

"Terrible."

"I can't bear to think of it."

"Yeh, I know."

"What happened? I thought he had the perfect hideout."

"There's no such thing. They shot him like a dog. Bastards! Never had a chance."

"Poor boy."

"I wouldn't mind getting my hands on the bastard that did it."

"What'll happen now?"

"How d'you mean?"

"About the Movement."

"We'll carry on, don't worry. It won't be easy, things are getting a bit tricky. But it'll work out O.K."

"Will they get the Coercion Act through, d'you think, the Government, I mean?"

"Hard to say. A lot of their own crowd don't care for it."

"Poor Martin. The best are always the first to die. He was a saint really."

"I suppose so. Maybe."

"I'll never forget that time in Bodenstown, the way he could quiet a crowd with the fire of his words."

"Damn good poker player. You should have heard the fire of *my* words the time he got fours twice in the one night. And me with two good-looking full houses."

"Don't tease, Joe. Martin was noble. He made the Movement seem splendid and holy."

"Who said it wasn't splendid and holy?"

31

"Now, now, don't tease."

"Anna!"

"Yes?"

"If you ever happen to come down to earth again would you ever get us a cup of coffee? I'm wore out."

"Certainly, darling. It's right here on the tray. We were having some."

He noticed again with pleasure the elegance of the embroidered tray-cloth and the simple charm of the china. Anna's fingers danced daintily from plate to coffee-pot. Without looking up she murmured, almost casually:

"Joe, you've been drinking."

"So what?"

"Nothing."

"Two drinks just. I was wore out. You've no idea." Joe allowed his head to slump forward and his body drooped. He flopped on to the couch. "That crowd thinks I should be at their beck and call day and night! D'you think Joe should we do this and d'you think Joe should we do that?' I wouldn't mind but half the time they're good judges to ask me: when they do make a decision they make a bloody hames of it. As much savvy as a duck in a thunderstorm. And then there's the other crowd that just can't knuckle down to a bit of work. Anything to escape from the job. It's all right. I don't mind giving them a hand now and then, but honest to God it's gettin' me down. I'm like a wet rag most of the time, takin' care of other people's troubles. I won't be able to stick it, that's all. That's all there is to it."

"What have you been up to now?"

"Oh—the usual." He hooshed himself up off the couch and paced uneasily about the room, turning swiftly and halting to mark an emphasis. "Up to Lurgan Thursday week: Snatcher Maille is tryin' to organise a private little Revolution all on his own. Thirteen meetings in two days about. In the end I had to tell the Snatcher that if he doesn't toe the line I'd blow the bejaysus out of him. The others weren't much help either: more interested in usin' the Movement for their own good than takin' part in a Revolution. A lot of land-hungry no-good bastards that think the Movement is an excuse for grabbin' another acre. Then off to Newcastle where John Joe Mulligan has a scheme for buying arms from Tangiers, using Spanish trawlers for transport. Not bad either. Might work. Down to Wexford on Wednesday where I managed to organise another circle."

"Marvellous!"

"Not bad if you got half a chance, but it has me wore out. Such goddam stupidity! Half the energy and half the time is spent tryin' to get them to see things straight. Jesus, you couldn't believe it. Then all last night I spent tryin' to wangle a Tommy-gun from a little twister in Griffiths' Barracks."

"Did you get it?"

"Oh, I got it all right."

"That's fine."

"But what the hell! I had to ply the chancer with whiskey for two hours. Christ, there's nothing I hate so much as too much whiskey. The cost of that alone is nearly more than the gun is worth."

"Oh, I don't know, I wouldn't say that."

"It has me wore out anyway. I can't go on like this. Working sixteen hours a day and no thanks for it. Just the opposite. The more you do the more they take it for granted; it'd kill you. I wouldn't mind but they're all so goddam smug. Think there's no end to what you can do. No, I'm near the end of my tether and that's a fact. I'm getting jumpy and that's no good. You have to have your wits about you when the bullets start flying. I'm not sleeping at night and my mind is in a whirl all the time." Swaying un-

33

easily he paced wearily back, eased himself down to the couch, and sat hunched on its edge, a picture of despair.

"There, there, darling. You're just tired, that's all. And you're lonely. Did you miss me at all?"

"Of course I did, sweet."

"Lie back on the couch now. You've only got a few minutes."

Soothed by her assuasive voice he allowed himself to lie back contentedly.

"Take your coffee now."

"Thank you. My darling tranquiliser."

It was a cosy room. Joe wondered if he should tell Anna about Charlie Horgan. Any association with Horgan implied danger, but he felt tolerably sure that he was capable of handling the situation. Anna sometimes jerked so quickly to a flurry of apprehension. At the same time there might be equal danger in concealing the contact.

"You'll never guess who I met."

"Who?"

"Horgan."

"Who's he?"

"Charlie Horgan. The G-Man. Inspector now. Used to be down in Cork."

"Oh?"

"You remember. He was in the dramatic class years ago."

"Yes, you told me. I remember."

"Walked into the pub, drunk as a fiddler's bitch."

"Didn't say anything, did he?"

"Nothing much. Something about an arms shipment. Might be worth following up."

"An arms shipment! Where from?"

"Sweden, he said."

"How interesting."

34

"Poor Charlie. He was slobbering drunk. I was wondering could we use him."

"Too high-up, I'd say."

"Useful if we could."

"Need careful handling."

"Well, we'll see how it works out. Maybe better not to bother."

Lying at ease on the couch, looking up at the pale blue ceiling, Joe allowed himself to luxuriate in the homeliness. For the first time in weeks he didn't have that vigilant dread of every casual sound. Made him feel like a child, romping in the shelter of the all-embracing trees. A baby in the womb, free of the knowledge of danger, had the best of life. What stupid vanity made him think he could help people, when he was so incapable of helping himself? What sweet contentment to be a bank clerk or a civil servant: out in a fluster every morning; a lazy day's routine; small hatreds and small rewards; back to the garden and the kids at six; a couple of quiet pints; and then into bed like a rabbit with the missus.

"Anna!"

"Yes, darling. A moment now. I just must tidy the place."

"Anna, did you ever think that this is all only a bad dream?"

"How unflattering."

"This haunted life I mean."

"Frankly no. I quite enjoy it."

"I'm expecting any moment to wake up with a sigh of relief to find it's all been a silly nightmare."

"If you do, darling, I hope you find yourself in bed with a thoroughly disgusting old hag. I can be jealous, my sweet love, even of your dreams."

"Anna, wouldn't it be wonderful if we both woke up

together, lying on the sands of some island in the sun, where there are no meetings, no shootings, and no Special Branch Police: where nobody wants too much out of life: a little sun, a little fruit, a lot of love and a little sleep: and where we might escape at last from this cruel agony of the mind."

"Poor love, you *are* tired. I always know when you go sailing away in that Pink Ship."

Softly she came to him. For a moment she paused, seeming to study with concern the weariness in his eyes. Then, kneeling she bent over, taking his hand lovingly in hers.

"You've been working too hard. You'll be better when you get some sleep. It's all our fault. We depend too much on you."

"Don't be silly. I was only joking."

"I thought maybe you were. But it's true. You mustn't get depressed, Joe. We could never carry on if you were to weaken. There would be no Movement without you, no matter what the others may think."

"Nonsense."

"I know you don't like me saying things like that, but it's true. You've more brains than the whole lot of them put together."

"Anna sweet, take it easy, can't I relax for a few minutes without you making a tragedy of it."

"Of course, love."

"Oh dear, I'd better be going, hadn't I?"

"I suppose so. You're late already. Where's your hat?"

"Over there."

"Now darling! Do I or do I not get my dutiful kiss?"

When she pressed her body against his he could feel the first mild stirrings. Resting his lips on her moist warm mouth he thought forward quickly. The meeting would be over by eight or half-past. Should he go down to Jordan's? It'd mean more drinking: dangerous too, but then again he might learn something about that arms shipment. What time could he get back?

"Did you miss me at all?" he asked.

"What do you think?"

"I wouldn't know."

"Darling, I love you so I sometimes feel I've no shame left. Tell me you love me a little too."

"Of course I do."

"And you missed me?"

"Lonely as a lost cloud."

"Sweetling. When am I going to see you?"

"Maybe I'll call in to-night."

"Do. I'll have some supper for you."

"Oh no, don't bother."

"No bother. You must run now. They'll be annoyed."

"Let them go to hell."

In the corridor he kissed her again, a playful au revoir. She held the door while he buttoned his coat.

"Joe!"

"Yeah?"

"I want you to do something for me."

"Anything you say."

"It's nothing much. Just that I want you to keep an eye on Sonny Coughlan."

"How d'you mean?"

"See that he doesn't get into any trouble. He's a little impetuous, you know. Doesn't mean any harm."

"Needs a little cooling down maybe."

"Be nice to him Joe. He's sweet really. A little over-blessed with enthusiasm, that's all. He might easily do himself—and the Movement—a lot of harm."

"I get you. A touch of cold reality is the cure for that kind."

"Don't be rough with him, Joe. He's really rather a pet."

"O.K. Anything for you darling. Good-bye."

"Au revoir."

What was the little twirp doing smelling round Anna? As he hurried down the stairs Joe could not repress a surge of fury. It was uncivilised, he knew that, and it stemmed from the most despicable of emotions. But it was impossible to subdue. What did the little bastard want? Joe's lips tightened. A touch of cold reality was the cure. Cold reality! Better try thinking of something else.

4

Meet the Boys!

Skinner MacCormack knew a red-bearded genius, Aloysius MacSwiggan, who had founded the Sandymount Existentialist Society. Skinner arranged to get their offices occasionally for after-hour meetings. It was a perfect cover, the annex at the back of an elegant house in a thoroughly respectable Georgian square: and in case of embarrassment there were three slick getaways.

Had Mr. Nolan not been indifferent to environment he might have been impressed by the fantasy of the scene. The heavy curtains on the back window were discreetly drawn. Meagre light from a naked and anaemic table-lamp shone on the faces of eight or nine mostly young men: students, labourers, shopboys, and professionals. The thin light revealed only vaguely the grotesque sculptures and weird pictures which provided a background of fantastic unbalance.

39

Mr. Nolan was not sensitive to atmosphere, but he could not avoid an awareness of the tension. It pleased him, made him glow a little with a consciousness of his own composure. These good-natured visionaries expected that every minor crisis was a death-blow. How little they realised that, compared with those of the future, this was merely a slippery stepping-stone. Crises fortunately might be utilised. Tension made these youngsters more capable of effort —more amenable to calculated suggestion. To that extent poor Martin need not be classed as a failure. His death had evoked an intensity of emotion he never seemed able to evoke in life. Each grim little face contained its own memory of Coyne, its own story that would swell the legend, building a featureless figurehead into a mighty hero. What matter, so long as the lie and the legend provided a buttress for their courage.

"I propose"—Dermot Walshe seemed to enjoy the ritual —"that Mr. Nolan take the chair."

"I second that."

"Very well, very well. Thank you, thank you. Are we all here?"

"I think so."

"Good."

"All but Joe Corcoran."

"Ah yes."

"Wonder what's happened to Joe?"

"Think he was run in?"

"Not Joe."

"Joe could smell a G-Man at forty yards."

"Joe'll be late for his own funeral."

Mr. Nolan found it difficult to control his irritation but he appreciated the inadvisability of asserting his authority. Only gradually would it be possible to refine this crude material into a disciplined and effective conspiracy. Corcoran's mentality was symptomatic of the general flabbiness. Mr. Nolan pulled his chair to the head of the table.

"We were just talking about poor Martin when you came in." Smiling his most intimate, Skinner MacCormack grasped Mr. Nolan's arm. "A great bloody character all the same. I don't know what we'll do without him."

It would be proper to rebuke MacCormack for his untidy lack of respect: but again Mr. Nolan was aware that restraint was imperative. MacCormack was just one great lump of vanity; his overfamiliar approach was a form of exhibitionism. Mr. Nolan perceived that he would have to handle Skinner with care. It wasn't that he meant any harm; just that he found too much enjoyment in being a conspirator. However, perhaps the sentimental reference to Coyne could be utilised.

"Gerry Baker here?"

A flabby-faced student leaned out of the darkness. Habitually self-effacing, Gerry was a more than efficient intelligence officer.

"I think it is desirable, as soon as possible, that you let us have a report on the killing of Martin Coyne."

"Certainly, sir."

"Barefaced bloody murder."

"Hear, hear."

"You have your own methods, Gerry, we realise that, and we don't enquire into them. However, I suggest that it shouldn't be difficult to find out who precisely fired the fatal shots." Mr. Nolan was speaking calmly and factually. "When we have detailed information available I propose that we hold a court, that the particular police officer be charged with murder, and if found guilty that he be sentenced to death—and that that sentence be expeditiously implemented.

41

An eye for an eye, a tooth for a tooth, and a life for a life should be our motto."

Mr. Nolan meant every word he said, and it was gratifying to feel the responsive glow. But he was vaguely afraid, too, that the crudity of his tactics might be apparent.

"Now let's get on with the meeting."

Dermot Walshe was on his feet. Dermot was not an ideal Revolutionary, but he was useful. A briefless barrister, he appeared to enjoy the discipline of committee procedure.

"As you realise, this is an extraordinary rather than an ordinary Council meeting." He smiled in his curiously enigmatic way. It was difficult to know how his mind worked. "As Second-in-Command," he addressed Mr. Nolan, "you are now automatically Leader of the Movement. The only essential business of the evening is to elect a new Second-in-Command in case—" again he smirked "—in case anything might happen to you."

Mr. Nolan smiled in turn. "I have no intention," he said, "of being killed for just a little while yet."

There was more ease in the atmosphere now. Only the melancholy fanatic face of Hughie Commiskey retained its tension.

Mr. Nolan felt a kinship with Commiskey. Though he looked less than middle-aged, Hughie was a veteran of the National Revolution; and though he couldn't have been more than a youngster at that time, the legends of his bravery had grown and multiplied. Having experienced every ecstasy of near-dying, Hughie seemed somehow never again to find contentment in mere living. His personal life, subsequent to the Revolution, had been so darkened by failure that he had become a bitter introvert. However, he was still a good soldier. There was determination in the thin line of his mouth and the cold passion in his eyes.

The chairs creaked as they relaxed into new positions.

42

Somebody giggled. Mr. Nolan glanced over, noticing Sonny Coughlan for the first time.

"Ah," he said, pleased to change the subject, "before we proceed with the business of electing a Second-in-Command, I should like to welcome Mr. Coughlan to the Executive."

"Hear, hear," from MacCormack.

Sonny was embarrassed; he smiled, scratched the side of his neck, and blushed.

Mr. Nolan made a mental note that he must remember to impress on Coughlan the necessity for secrecy. He, too, was a weakling—the dreamy type, like Coyne, but more so. Young enough to be a killer, but insufficiently animal.

"You will report to the Studio to-morrow, and it might be as well if you transferred that Thompson-gun from its present resting-place."

"Yes, sir."

"Well now, you all know the purpose of this meeting. Our leader has been killed. As Second-in-Command I now take his place at a moment of great challenge. I am confident we can meet that challenge because I know that the Movement has your unquestioned loyalty." Mr. Nolan was doing well. His voice had the impartial tone which makes its own drama. "The immediate purpose of this meeting, as Dermot said, is to elect a Second-in-Command to take my place should anything happen. Now, who do you propose?"

In the silence Mr. Nolan again felt his domination. It wasn't important who would be elected, yet he sensed embarrassment. He knew that MacCormack would be the first to speak. Skinner would probably like to be Second-in-Command himself.

"I propose Dermot Walshe."

Mr. Nolan knew that MacCormack knew that Dermot was unsuitable. Walshe was the ideal secretary. Impossible to improve on him. But he was too cynical to inspire loyalty. MacCormack's proposal was merely a means of drawing attention to himself.

"The organisation is in sufficiently bad shape without my ruining it altogether," Dermot smiled. "What about yourself, Skinner?"

Mr. Nolan knew that Dermot Walshe knew that Mac-Cormack would be unsuitable. Because he was a fool, and a genial fool, he had everyone's friendship and everyone's contempt. There was banter in Dermot's tone, but MacCormack would never see that.

"I'm afraid I haven't much time to spare," Skinner said hesitantly. His tone cajoled persuasion.

"I doubt if he could be spared," said Mr. Nolan.

"What about you, Hughie?" Dermot Walshe asked.

Hughie Commiskey's face was almost in shadow.

"I'm not the man," he said.

He spoke with a simple deliberation that left no invitation for discussion. Mr. Nolan was regretful.

"What about Joe Corcoran?" Skinner MacCormack asked.

There was something damned irritating about MacCormack. He'd say anything for notice. Mr. Nolan knew that his Second-in-Command need have no authority; still, he would have wished for somebody with whom he could discuss plans before taking them to the Executive. Commiskey, if he were a little more intelligent, would have been useful, but not Corcoran. Mr. Nolan had a mild suspicion that Joe didn't altogether give him his due respect. Besides, Corcoran could be so positive.

"Possible," Walshe said.

MacCormack was pleased that his suggestion was not unfavorably received. He brightened. "He couldn't do a lot of harm," he said.

"No?" Walshe raised a quizzical eyebrow.

Mr. Nolan felt he should say something.

"I understand he's been drinking a lot lately."

MacCormack became tenacious.

"Maybe. I don't know. But after all you can't condemn a man because he takes a few jars. If that was the way," he laughed at the absurdity, "I shouldn't be on the Executive myself. No, I know Joe. I've worked with him on and off for a few years now. We've been in a few tight spots, believe you me, and I can tell you Joe is a right good guy. You can go through hell with a man you know for sure will never let you down. And that's Joe."

"Quite so," said Mr. Nolan.

"May I say a word?" Dermot asked.

"Certainly."

"I'd like everybody to know that I'm very fond of Joe. Like Skinner I've been in a few tight spots with him and I know he's got guts. He's a good friend; if I was ever in a real jam I think Joe is the man I'd go to; I'd know for sure he wouldn't let me down. He has a damn good mind too when he bothers to use it. But Joe is a funny genius. One day he's all up in the air with enthusiasm, and next day he's a different man entirely. I wonder if that temperament is the best qualification for leadership. Now don't think I have anything against him." Mr. Nolan decided that he might have to revise his opinion of Dermot. Those suave tones were edged with something approaching cunning. "Maybe he's like that because he drinks too much, but after all a man who lets alcohol affect his character to that extent mightn't be our best choice. I dunno. He's a hell of a good man in a lot of ways."

"All right, he takes a few jars." MacCormack wasn't going to be silenced. "That's how he makes his contacts. Look at the work he does. Organising Circles all over the country. You can't do that kind of thing without getting your man at the other side of a pint. He didn't get that Tommy-gun by mail order, did he? You may be sure he had to do a quare lot of talking before he got to the point."

"Perhaps."

"What do you say, Hughie?"

Dermot was shrewd. He knew that in a curious way Hughie Commiskey's attitude would have some influence on the others.

"I'm again him."

MacCormack wasn't going to be put off.

"I suggest we take a vote." If only Joe had been there. Some of the boys though would most likely pass on the word. "Joe is intelligent, one of the best organisers we have; he's an all-round man. He can write a radio script, organise a Circle, or outline a plan of action as well as any man I know."

Mr. Nolan was satisfied that Joe Corcoran would be elected. It would be unwise on his part to be openly antagonistic. He must remember to discipline MacCormack.

"I suggest we take a vote," Skinner said again.

"Very well. Let me have your proposals."

"I propose Joe Corcoran." Skinner was delighted with himself.

"I second that."

Sonny Coughlan had spoken. Mr. Nolan raised an interested eyebrow.

"Any other proposals?"

It was ludicrous. He knew that there would be no other proposals. Best get it over. It was apparent that there were underground antagonisms of which he had no knowledge. He'd learn in time. MacCormack was everyone's confidant because he was a fool, and Joe was equally obviously a favourite because he was hail-fellow-well-met. Running a Revolution was no sinecure. However, Corcoran could do

46

little harm, and he might be encouraged by the seeming confidence of the Committee to a greater sense of responsibility.

"Joe Corcoran proposed by Harry MacCormack, seconded by Sonny Coughlan. Any other proposals . . . ?"

The short silence was peculiarly embarrassing.

"I take it then that Joe Corcoran is elected. Very well."

"I think you're making a mistake," Hughie Commiskey said.

Mr. Nolan ignored the interruption.

"Now, Dermot, what's the next item?"

5

Reluctant Leader

Now it was dark. The hustle of rush-hour was over, leaving the pavements subdued and lonely. Huge street lamps, like giant caricatures, poured dim silver on the roadway. Looking up at the star-brightened sky, Joe Corcoran thought of all the people everywhere talking about poor Martin, arguing rights and wrongs over shimmering firelight, praising and grumbling in remote and dreary pubs. The clink of Joe's hob-nailed boots echoed along the pavement. Better get rid of them, now he was back. Police were on the alert. He could imagine the grim-faced yahoos above in Headquarters, hovering round the squad-cars, wondering about reprisals. And to think it was all on account of Martin Coyne that hardly opened his gob when he was sober and couldn't keep it shut when he was jarred. It'd be no worry to sink a bullet in the bastard that got poor Martin. Might too.

Joe wondered would the election be over. He hoped

they'd make Dermot Walshe Second-in-Command. Walshe was at least civilised. There was the danger of MacCormack. Skinner was a hard chaw and decent enough, but in a position like that he'd make a terrible gom of himself. Commiskey was the unpredictable possible. There was the chance that he himself might be elected. He was curiously flattered by the thought. How should he react? Probably wouldn't make much difference one way or the other but it might help to ease his position; lately he had the suspicion that he was held in slight disfavour. Of course he could always make the gesture of refusing. That would be interesting: spare him a share of worry and gain him a modicum of respect. What if they insisted?

Coming around the corner into the square, Joe found himself buffeted by a blustering wind. A quick scrutiny assured him that all was clear. His pace firmed and quickened. It was exhilarating to meet the challenge of the turbulent air. He felt confident again, if it proved necessary, to cajole and master his little audience. Briskly, but without ostentation, he climbed the steps.

The guard inside the heavy door greeted him cordially.

"The great man himself. Delighted to see you again, Joe."

" 'Evening. Has the meeting begun?"

"About ten minutes, sir."

The rumble of hob-nails on stone flags reverberated down the hallway. Making no effort to minimise the threat, Joe curved aside from the gracious stairway and entered the long narrow corridor. Only when he found himself outside the blacked-out glass door did he feel a momentary tremor. His knock was answered by confused scurrying and scraping of chairs.

"Who's that?"

"Corcoran."

MacCormack opened the door.

"Jesus, Joe, you near scared the hell out of us. We thought you must be God Almighty coming with a search warrant."

"Sorry. My apologies for being late."

Always sensitive to atmosphere, Joe was able, even in that uncertain moment, to relish the quaint grimness of the scene. Only Mr. Nolan had remained seated. The others, looking like startled animals, fierce and fighting, were bunched loosely together, beyond the reach of the feeble light. They seemed somewhat shamefaced as they returned to their places.

"Had me pissin' in me britches."

"Glad to see you back, Joe."

"How's the hard man?"

"He came down that corridor like a tank on a holiday."

Joe glimpsed Commiskey slipping a gun back in his pocket. It wasn't the thing to carry a gun in Council. But Commiskey never could remember rules.

"Sorry, lads."

"Won't you sit down, Joe?" Mr. Nolan's smiling diffidence was the appropriate mask for self-complacency. "We were just wondering what had happened to you."

"I was delayed, I'm afraid, by a cumpulsory exchange with a policeman."

"What! Did they pull you in?"

"What happened?"

"Did they run you in, Joe?"

"How did you get away?"

"Nothing so untidy. An old friend, Charlie Horgan, we were on the stage together. He was half-jarred and insisted on me having a drink. Somehow I have a feeling we might use him."

"Interesting."

"Good man, Joe. That's the stuff to give the troops."

"Good man."

"Yes. Quite so." Mr. Nolan almost purred when he smiled. "It could be a little, shall we say, precarious, but I'm sure we all know we don't have to tell Joe that."

"Joe's bloody well able to look after himself," MacCormack declared.

"Ah yes. Indeed yes."

"Joe, wasn't it terrible about poor Martin?"

"Sad. But," Joe added sententiously, "he's gone to join a goodly company."

"True."

"I was talking to him," Skinner mourned, "only last night down by Milltown Cross. And to think—if I could nail the bastard that—"

"Take it easy, Skinner," Dermot Walshe interjected. "We can talk about that afterwards."

"Sorry."

"Let's get on with the meeting. You will be interested to hear, Joe, that we have just done you the honour of electing you Vice President of the Executive."

"Wha—? Well, that's very good of you." Joe's feelings were confused. The honour was a welcome reassurance, but its acceptance would imply increased responsibility. Besides, it was poor tactics to accept honours eagerly from incompetents. "I am indeed honoured. My only fear is that my health may not be sufficiently strong to bear any additional burden just now."

Mr. Nolan affected concern.

"I'm sorry to hear that, Joe. You haven't been well?"

"No, I'm afraid not." Joe was pathetic. "I don't know what's the matter with me. Feel terrible lately."

"Working too hard probably."

"Yeah, you're looking a bit shook all right," from Mac-Cormack.

"Don't say you've stopped drinking, Joe."

"That's tough, Joe. You'd want to take it easy."

"I see." Mr. Nolan had the unctuous benevolence of a parish priest. "Well, let us, shall we say, leave the matter for the moment. We'll have a little talk about it together later, Joe, you and I, and if you feel as time goes on that you wish to have the matter reconsidered, then we can always put it before the Council at another time."

"Fair enough."

"Good man, Joe."

"Find yourself a chair, Joe."

"There you are, oul' son."

"Anything else on the agenda?"

"Let's get on with the meeting."

"Where were we?"

Joe dragged a chair awkwardly across.

"Don't let me waste any more of your time."

"Quiet please. Mr. Nolan has the floor."

"I was just emphasising that we are the only legal Government of the Irish Republic until such time as our country is unified and the connection with Britain is finally broken. As such we are tremendously honoured with a terrifying responsibility, an honour which demands from us, if we are to appreciate it, the highest perfection of discipline. The murder of Martin Coyne is an indication that the Satellite Government set up here is frightened, because they know that the only authentic voice of the Irish Nation . . ."

Joe had heard all this before, a thousand times. Having made a successful entrance, and finding his audience tolerably accommodating, he felt that he could reward his mind with an allowance of relaxation. His mind unhappily was not decently responsive. Once free of discipline it slipped, slithered, and tumbled away to confusion.

". . . murder of Martin Coyne is a threat and a warning, a warning that if we are to survive we must utilise every separate grain of cunning. Secrecy is our essential and deadly weapon. What guarantee have any of you of your neighbour's good faith? What makes you sure of your acquaintance? Who said your friend was not a spy?"

Joe's thought blurred numbly into an easy mist and Nolan's naked voice became only a dreamy monotone. . . . Anna would be pleased. . . . By the wall-cupboard on tiptoe she stretched up in a pale pink silky nakedness, climbed, stretching to the top shelf for her blue new nightie, laughing, her breast lazing sidewards. . . .

". . . Martin Coyne is dead and his hideout must have been revealed. The only guarantee of survival is the ever-present awareness that even our closest comrade may be an Informer. . . ."

The needling voice drilled relentlessly, insisting, demanding the rights of reality, dulling memory. Joe tried dividing his mind, to salvage a little of both worlds. It wasn't easy.

". . . extra precautions when going to the Studio, to parades and meetings. The Government and the police will be ruthless in their efforts to wipe us out, particularly if they get this Coercion Act through. . . ."

Remember Inishdarragh in the sun: the druid mountain's mystery! By the lake edge they poised together: nakedly free, exultant as the wind. . . . Her gliding body in black water was pale gold. . . . The cold rock was thorny. . . . But under eternal heaven they caught communion. . . .

". . . Later we shall initiate negotiations with countries abroad to get supplies of arms for the training of members, the defence of properties, and carrying out those minor 'jobs' which are part of the natural growth of a Revolutionary Body. Now, if any of you have any ideas in this regard I'd like to hear them."

Silence was broken by MacCormack.

"I have a source in France, as you know. Takes time but. Have to make another trip."

"Quite so."

"Not worth the risk."

"Not for the amount you can take back."

"How about America?"

"We'll depend on America to help us with the bigger shipments. Our friends there are eager, but we mustn't abuse their enthusiasm."

"How about the Army here?"

"You managed to get that Thompson-gun, didn't you?" Mr. Nolan queried. "Joe! You got that Thompson-gun, Joe, didn't you?"

Joe raised his eyes. With his elbow on the edge of the table he had cradled his forehead between thumb and outstretched fingers. A tenuous note in the adroit tones needled him, but for the moment he did not change his position. It gave him an opportunity to put order on his thoughts. And it could be subtly disconcerting.

"Yes, I've got it," he said deprecatingly. "For what it's worth."

"Good man."

"Yes, indeed. Very creditable. But that method is expensive and, shall we say, a little cumbersome. Takes such long talks—and drinks—to reach the point."

"How about planting some of our lads in the Army?" MacCormack asked.

"Getting them to smuggle the stuff out, you mean?"

Honeycomb the whole bloody Army, that's what I mean."

"What the Fenians did."

"That's a thought."

54

Smiling benignly, Mr. Nolan turned to Joe.

"You seem to be pondering this problem deeply. Would you like to let us have the results of your cogitations?"

Again the suave phrasing was a warning. Joe stared fixedly at Mr. Nolan, his mind, it would seem, to judge by his silence, concerned with greater issues.

"I was thinking."

"Ah good, good. That's fine."

Joe raised his head slowly without speaking, until his gaze was fixed on the top left-hand corner of the room.

"I suppose it couldn't be helped, but it's a pity adequate notice wasn't given that this matter would be raised to-day. I wonder if it isn't a problem which could be dealt with more appropriately by the Military Council. To my mind it isn't so much a question of ideas. We all have our ideas, I'm sure, and most of them are probably workable. But the problem—at least to my mind—is scarcely worth discussing until we are agreed on our terms of reference."

Joe had spoken with quiet and kindly authority. Now he paused to allow MacCormack to wonder about "terms of reference." When he spoke again the intonation was that degree sharper.

"What class of arms are required? In what precise quantities? When is it essential that they be made available? And what risks in money and men's lives are we prepared to take to make them available? With these facts clearly in mind it will then become merely a question of selecting and editing the schemes suggested."

"Sounds to me like we're getting somewhere," MacCormack announced.

Joe had the knack of putting words together, and pronouncing them in such a manner that they appeared to have profound implications. In the silence that followed he kept his gaze fixed still upon that remote dark corner. He knew

55

Mr. Nolan must feel that he had been rebuked: and he was satisfied to leave it like that without exactly provoking enmity.

"When we have time and money available there should be no difficulty—to my mind—in getting any supply of arms we may require through Tangiers. That city, as you realise, is a Free Port and probably the most notorious smuggling centre in the world. Having purchased the arms, the question of transport will arise. Again I am satisfied that the problem is not insuperable. You know that Spain is across the Mediterranean from Tangiers. A Spanish fishing boat could slip into Tangiers without suspicion. These Spanish boats, as you know, come up every week, year after year, trawling the west coast. The crews are ill-paid and always ready to ease the burden of life with 'danger' money. As a matter of fact I have had an opportunity of talking personally with a number of the Spanish skippers, and I'm assured—I'll say no more—that when the time comes we'll be able to make a deal. I mention this particular idea more as an illustration than anything else. Its implementation, as I have emphasised, would require money and time, but it probably would be an inexhaustible source. On the other hand if we require only small supplies immediately and without the risk of vast expense I should think it might be advisable to examine the possibility of intercepting the Swedish shipment."

A pause during which Joe unfixed his gaze, and permitted that lofty far corner to take care of itself. Silence followed his speech. Joe looked around almost accusingly.

"Why not?"

Dermot Walshe had the courage of his ignorance.

"I'm sorry," he said, "but I am rather in the dark. What shipment is this?"

56

Joe was surprised. "That stuff the Army is getting in," he said.

"Yeah, I heard something about that," MacCormack ventured. "From Sweden, isn't it?"

"That's right." It would be foolish to bewilder them too much. "I haven't bothered to go into the matter thoroughly. Frankly, as you understand, I haven't had time, and besides I expected you people would already have a certain amount of information. But it might be the sort of scheme Mr. Nolan seems to visualise, a limited consignment which, if we are enabled successfully to intercept it, would be ideally suited to the purpose specified. There are drawbacks. There would be little expense so far as money is concerned, but there could be expenditure of lives on a large scale. The consignment would obviously have to be intercepted between the Port and the Barracks. It would probably be travelling under heavy guard. Nevertheless, if the action was planned with a careful eye to timing, there is no reason why it should not be successful. But even with the most astute intelligence, the most thoughtful planning and disciplined execution, the success of this enterprise would depend in the end on individual daring. In that respect it presents certain welcome opportunities to us all. It's about time we threw away the talking machines and took out our guns again. This organisation, to my mind, is rotten ripe for action."

"Hear, hear."

"That's the bloody talk."

It was too easy. Even the suggestion of action was like a gift from God. Joe slackened in his chair.

"Just the thing."

"When does the stuff arrive?"

"Get on to it quick."

"How many lorries, d'you think?"

"Good man, Joe."

Even Mr. Nolan's smile of pleasure appeared genuine. "Yes indeed. It sounds the sort of scheme we want. But as Joe rightly points out it's probably a matter for the Military Council. You've been very helpful Joe, very helpful indeed. Thank you. Thank you, Joe."

6

Jumpy Jordan's

Jumpy Jordan's customers were creatures of habit who liked an occasional game of bagatelle. When Joe shouldered in the door and sidled round the makeshift partition he was intrigued to see the same moronic faces he had known there years before. The warm blue haze seemed to catch and carry the white light to the men's faces, giving them a peculiar paleness. Jumpy, a keen-eyed crafty little man, turned as the door opened.

"Hello, Joe. Haven't seen you for an age. Where've you been?"

"Oh, here and there. Haven't been drinking much."

"What's your medicine?"

"Bottle of stout. By the way, d'you know a fellow be the name of Horgan, Charlie Horgan? In the Police."

"Yeh, sure. He's there behind you, drunk as a fiddler's bitch."

Joe glanced round and there sure enough was an empty scarecrow figure, huddled behind the partition. Joe was amused that Horgan had chanced on the most strategic position in the pub. Without being seen himself he could watch the entry of each new customer.

"How're you Charlie?"

"The hard Joe. What're you havin'?"

"Just ordered a bottle of stout."

"Hey, Jumpy! What about the bloody customers? Hurl us up a basket of malt."

The babble and clatter of voices was drowned in loud clapping. A pleasing voice called, "One for the loser." And there was more clapping. The clink of glasses and a shuffling footstep portended the arrival of Jumpy.

"Sit down Joe. Take the weight off your feet."

While Jumpy was pouring, Joe manoeuvred to a seat behind the crude table. Slowly Charlie pulled from his pocket a mud-coloured big handkerchief with which he proceeded to make floundering efforts at removing the stout slobber from his chin.

"What are you having, Charlie?"

A share of Horgan's vitality seemed to have deserted him, and he looked even more dishevelled. His overcoat, hanging open with collar upturned, was crumpled about him helplessly.

"Large one."

"A large whiskey."

"And I don't want any of that ammoniated bloody nitric acid you gave me last time." Charlie eased the hat back off his forehead. "Put that stuff back in the lamp."

"Right." Mock-saluting, Jumpy skipped back across the bar and under the counter-flap.

Charlie allowed his head to slump forward again and a soft drool stole from the corner of his hanging lower lip.

"That fellow'd sell his mother," he pronounced gravely, "for a pennorth of piss." Slowly struggling, he shoved back the obstinate handkerchief into his pocket.

"They're the one breed, publicans are, everywhere."

"Did you remark the slanty eyebrows?"

"And the shifty smile."

"All the oul' talk too. 'Where have you been since? You're lookin' well.' A hell of a lot that little gobshite cares, except for the few bob he's missin'."

"A louser. I hate them all, seed, breed and generation. They're no good, that's a fact, publicans aren't."

"No lie. No lie at all."

"Hey! Jumpy! What's keepin' that whiskey? Are you writin' away for it or what?"

"Comin'."

Flaunting his false teeth, Jumpy Jordan elbowed up the counter-flap and came smiling across.

"I brought you some water. To-day's delivery."

Without bothering to turn his head Joe gave him the money: and he skipped away again, smiling still. Joe and Charlie stared solemnly at their drinks. The smell, from the coke stove stuck in the middle of the floor, was offensive. A meaty-faced burly-looking man in a peaked cap came waddling in. He joined a nearby table. "Did you hear anything?" he queried merrily. The stove crackled vexedly and a gasp of grey smoke circled upwards. Bending forward Joe gripped the glass of stout.

"Good luck."

Charlie stretched out questing fingers.

"All the best there is, oul' son."

The stout tasted good, smooth and sharp. Joe gaped at the thin line of overcoats along the counter and the dark bulk of bodies around the bagatelle.

"I dunno what brings you into this place."

"I suppose not." Steadying his elbow on the table, Charlie edged his lips towards the brimful glass.

"A tawdry job."

"Aye. Right enough." A fair-sized gulp and Charlie lurched slowly back. "D'you know what I'm goin' to tell you Joe?" Charlie's shirt was open and his right hand went searching and scratching across his chest and under his armpit. He swayed gently forward. "D'you know what I'm goin' to tell you, oul' son, and you're goin' to be surprised. I kinda *like* this place."

"Aw, for cryin'—"

"I'll tell you why. Puts me in mind of me poor oul' father, God rest him." He lifted his hat in tearful reverence. "He was a hard oul' bastard."

"Your father?"

"Now don't inerrup me."

"I wasn't interrupting."

"Listen here to me, Joe. Wait till I tell you. Listen."

"I'm listening."

"Wait till you hear. When I was a young chiseler down in Kildare the father used to take me out walkin' the land of an evenin' to see that the beasts was comin' to no harm in the back meadow. I used always look forward to that, I don't know why. I remember lookin' across at them bullocks grazin' away for further orders and thinkin' how much more contented they were munchin' away without thinkin' and never botherin' their arses to wonder what was goin' happen the day after to-morrow. Well, when I came to Dublin I sorta got into the habit of comin' here, d'you know. Kept wonderin' what it was I liked about it. And damned a bit could I make out why it reminded me of the oul' fella. Then one day it struck me fair and square that them yobs suckin' their porter aren't different much from the beasts

62

grazin' the back meadow. They have the best of life, Joe, and that's a fact, wantin' little and wonderin' less, the best of life. Drudgin', eatin', coortin', drinkin' and never botherin' their arses."

"You've got something there."

"Hey! Jumpy! Is there a drink in the house? Will you have a short one, Joe?"

"Suppose I may as well."

"Two large ones, Mr. Jordan." Charlie's obtrusive roar topped the clatter. "Do you hear me?"

A couple of overcoats turned from the counter. An anonymous face grinned commiseration.

"Are you lookin' much?" Charlie challenged.

The overcoats turned smiling away.

"Ah, the father was a character."

"Is that so?"

"A great character."

"He's dead now is he?"

"Who?"

"The father."

"Oh, dead and rotten."

"You're glad to be back I suppose."

"Back?"

"In Dublin."

"Dublin. Oh, I wouldn't say that."

"You liked it down there?"

"Where?"

"In Cork."

"I did."

Jumpy slipped over unobtrusively, lodged two large ones on the table, quietly.

Charlie's foraging fingers plunging down his pocket came grasping back with an array of coin. Blearily he offered

63

a clutching palm. Jumpy dipped daintily, extracted four shining silver discs, held them up for inspection before he turned, skipping silently away.

"Ah, Cork isn't the worst."

"I daresay."

"All the best."

"Good luck."

"It's easy-goin', that's what I like."

"So they say."

"I like that."

"You can't be so easy-goin' up here."

"Ah, I don't know. Everything's easy if you take it slow."

"After all it's the capital. You're in Headquarters now."

"Ah, don't give me that. Look at Funky Farren, the man over me. Terrified to take a step out of line, that's Farren; bleedin' the bejaysus out of the men below for fear of the men above."

"What did you bother comin' back for so?"

"It's the wife, Sadie, one of the Plunketts of Cabra. She likes it here."

"I see."

"Still, it could be worse. I can't complain."

"How d'you get on with the Army?"

"The who?"

"The Army crowd. You have to deal with them on this Swedish job, don't you?"

"Oh them. They're a caution. Did I tell you about them?"

"No. I don't think so."

"Are you sure?"

"Not that I remember."

"Oh they're a caution. Did I tell you? You wouldn't believe it. Are you sure I didn't tell you?"

"Not that I remember."

"Oh you'll die when you hear. Wait till I tell you. When I

came up to the office the first day, there was Funky Farren peerin' out from behind thirty-five telephones on half-an-acre of desk. 'Get in touch with General Factotum,' says he, 'in the Army,' says he, 'and see about that Swedish shipment.' So I got on the buzzer. 'I'm the Guards' Liaison,' says I, 'and I want to see you about that shipment.' 'Right! One o'clock Gresham Hotel,' says he, very businesslike. Are you sure I didn't tell you?"

"Not a word."

"Well I polished my boots, straightened up my tie, and went along to the Gresham. And what d'you think? There was the General in full canonicals, stuck up on a high stool in the Bar, knockin' back large ones goodo. 'What're you havin'?' says he. 'Whatever you're havin' yourself,' says I. Well, in the words of our dear and gentle Saviour, no bird ever flew on one wing. We had a bellyful there, meandered into the Grill, swallowed a couple of steaks, and nothin' would do him then but back to the Officers' Mess above in Portobello. The crowd up there is a caution. I needn't tell you one drink borrowed another and in the heel of the hunt it was home in the small hours. Next day there was Funky Farren up behind the big desk. 'How are things progressin'?' says he. 'Another conference to-day,' says I. So, on to the buzzer again. One o'clock Gresham Hotel, into the Bar, down to the Grill, back to the Officers' Mess, home in taxis, nicely thank you. It went on like that for five solid days till I was feelin' frail as an oul' one. Came Thursday. I remember it well. On to the yoke. 'Gresham Hotel, one o'clock,' says he. 'Pick me up,' says I, casual like, 'at the office on your way down.' 'Right,' says he very businesslike as per usual. So he drops into the office with the Angelus bell, lookin' like death on a holiday. 'Sit down there,' says I, 'till we get a little bit of business settled. When is the stuff comin'?' says I. 'Twenty-third,' says he, 'Wexford Harbour, *Merry-*

oak.' 'Right,' I said. 'The Guards will be responsible only for the supervision of the stuff from the boat to the lorries, but will post special men along the route,' says I. 'Is that all right?' 'Fair enough,' says he. 'What route are you takin'?' 'The old Military Road,' says he. 'It's your funeral,' says I. 'What about a drink?' says he. So off we went down to the Gresham, into the Bar, down to the Grill, back to the Mess, home with the milk. And be the hokey I haven't been sober since."

"What do they want taking the stuff by the Military Road?"

"Search me."

"That oul' road isn't fit for man or beast."

"Ah, it's a sort of tradition, I suppose. What's the use of havin' a Military Road if the Military never uses it?"

"Sounds crazy."

"Ah, what the hell! But remember, Joe, what I've told you is strictly entre nous, sub rosa and all that sort of thing. Keep it under your hat."

"You can trust me."

"Hey, Jumpy! Hurl us up a couple of gargles."

There were more people in the pub now, thronged tight along the counter and down around the bagatelle. A wisp of grey smoke from the chesty stove curled upwards, mingling lazily in the blue haze. The garrulous drone hurried on in subdued delirium. At a nearby table a pale-faced frightened little man sang "Love Thee Dearest" in a wavering high pitch. His friends, with pints in hand, stood in a semicircle, their faces listening sadly, murmuring praise.

"Lift it, Jem."

"Gorgeous voice."

Jumpy Jordan rubbed hurriedly with a wet cloth along the far counter.

66

"What's wrong with that little bastard? Hey? Jumpy! Jumpy! Hurl us up a basket of malt."

Charlie's raucous bawling subdued still more the garrulous drone. The overcoats turned again, unsmiling. The little singing man looked still more frightened. A growl came from the crowd.

"One voice only, please!"

"One voice only!"

Charlie swayed upwards.

"Eh, Joe! What kind of a kip is this? Hey! Jumpy! Hurl us up a basket of malt before I tear the place asunder!"

The singer stopped. The meaty-faced burly man came slouching over. Joe eased his position so that his hands were free. The table was screwed down. Pity.

"Why don't youse go home?" the meaty-faced man suggested. "Youse make the place untidy."

"Eh, Joe! Who's this buff? Does he think he owns the kip?"

Silence now in the Bar: all eyes turned in their direction. Jumpy had disappeared.

"A friend of mine," the burly man went on dispassionately, "Jack Riordan over there, was singin' a song. A lot of us were gettin' a bit of pleasure out of it. You've no call bawlin' like a jackass while no friend of mine is singin'."

"Ah, go to hell! I don't give a bugger for you or your friend."

"Is that so?"

"What about me ball o' malt? Eh, Joe, what about me gargle?"

"It's all right, Charlie. I'll get it."

With the help of the table Joe eased up lazily. It gave him a fair position. The meaty-faced man laid his hand on Joe's wrist.

"Sit down."

Joe looked into the other's eyes. "I'm a peaceable man," he said, "and I don't want any trouble, but you're just a little too free with your hands."

"Sit down."

Joe caught him a short right jab on the point of the jaw, and he went down like a skittle. Joe tried grabbing the bottle then, but before he had a chance the others were on him. The first blow knocked him sprawling; but an adroit upward kick as he went sent his assailant howling back, spread-eagling the crowd.

Hedged behind the table Charlie was helpless. "Lorry him up," he shouted gaily. "A kick in the crotch brings the highest man low."

Joe fell to the side, and the bottle with him. He grabbed by the neck. Smashing the bottom on the stone floor he came up like a light to face the crowd, the jagged weapon held before him.

"Now, who's next," he challenged. "Come on, you sons-of-bitches. Come on till I murder you."

Jumpy Jordan came fluttering through, his face grey. "Jesus, Joe, what are you after doing? They'll have me license on the head of this."

"Tell that bunch of bowsies not to try anything on Charlie Horgan. He's a friend of mine."

"All right Joe. Whatever you say. Gentlemen, will you for God's sake have a little sense. Lift up that unfortunate man, God help him. Are yiz gone mad or what that I can't stir a foot without holy hell breaking loose? Can't you see the poor man has a drop taken?"

The crowd growled morosely, shuffling back to their drinks.

"Did you see him give that right hook?" Charlie was ecstatic.

68

"For the love and honour of God will you put that bottle down Joe, like a good decent man," Jumpy pleaded.

Joe watched the crowd back to their places. Reluctantly, it seemed, he put down the bottle.

"Did you see that right jab? Ah, man dear it was a honey. Did you see it Mr. Jordan?"

"I did not then, Mr. Horgan. And I think you, an officer of the law, should have a little more to do than starting brawls in a respectable house. What about me license?"

"You and your so-and-so license. Will we pull the place asunder, Joe? Will we tear it apart?"

"Let's go."

"Ah, you're right Joe. You're always right. Let's get the hell out of here. I don't know what possessed us," his voice rising, "to come into a dirty low-down hooligans' kip the like of this. Come on Joe."

"For the love and honour of God—"

With the support of Jumpy on one side and the partition on the other Charlie groped his way to the door. Keeping a wary eye on the background cluster, Joe slouched slowly after.

"Eh Joe! Come out. Come out man! Eh, for the love and honour of God, Charlie, d'you want to smash me gorgeous plate-glass winda?"

On the pavement outside Charlie was making hazardous efforts to maintain his uprightness, with Jumpy dancing in terror.

"Don't worry, I'll manage."

"Maybe the amber street lights were responsible for the freak effect; but, as they tacked fitfully towards Hargrove Lane, Joe inclined to suspect that he was more drunk than he had thought.

"Well, that was great, Joe." Charlie sighed luxuriously. "That fellow never knew what hit him."

"Brightened up the evening anyway. Will I get you a taxi?"

"Brightened up the evening! Dammit you're a caution."

Across the way a herd of human animals, vomited out of a cinema, spread-eagled on the sidewalk. A motor-cycle exploded. Faraway a train shrieked.

Charlie halted. His expression hardened to a formal rigidity.

"You did me a good turn Joe," he pronounced gravely. "I won't forget. You did me a good turn."

"Ah sure 'twas nothing. Will I find you a taxi?"

"Thank you. Thank you Joe." He grasped Joe's hand. "Yes, do. Do that for me."

As they staggered towards Barrington Street, Charlie ventured a few bars of a song about a pale moon rising; but he didn't seem to remember it too well. He halted again at the corner.

"Joe. You're my friend. Is there anything I can do for you?"

"No. Not at all. I don't think so."

"Are you sure now? You did me a good turn you know."

"Sure I'm sure. Come on now Charlie, there's a taxi over there."

A misty half-thought dangled! What did Coughlan want anyway hanging around Anna? A little cooling down was what he needed! A touch of cold reality!

"Are you certain sure? You've only got to ask."

"I don't think so. Come on, Charlie."

"You don't think what?"

"I don't think there's anything."

"Don't be afraid to ask. I'm your friend, remember. You can trust me."

Horgan trusted him. Even a tit-bit of trust might well pay off.

70

"Well—"

"Well what?"

"Ah, nothin'."

"Come on oul' son, tell us."

"Ah it's a silly thing."

"Well, what is it?"

"It's nothing really, just there's a young fellow, Sonny Coughlan is his name, needs a little cooling down . . ."

"Sonny Coughlan."

"Yeh. Needs a little cooling down."

"That's all right, son. You just tell me what to do. . . ."

7

Sanctuary

Now it was warmer. A shower had softened the air. Down the street, away to the east, was a grey-black mountain of cloud. Overhead it was clear more or less, except for a quixotic line of scud, like hard wads of cotton waste, stretched high across sky centre.

Even the drudgery of being on the alert had a kind of kick to-night. That footstep creeping up behind could mean a Webley in his ribs. That shadow lurking on the corner . . . Always walk on the edge of the path, that was the drill; never get caught 'twixt the kerb and the wall. Across the way a car screeched to a halt. . . . Crowd on their way to a hooley.

He couldn't get over the big fellow's yelp when he got him in the knackers. And the poor slob that started the row doesn't know what hit him yet. He should've taken the whole pub on, scattered them left and centre. Good to know, anyway, he could still use his mitts.

Incredible about Horgan: like a gift from the hand of God. Took a hell of a time getting to the point but, oh boy, was it worth it! Shake the starch, so it would, out of Mr. Snotty Nolan. Arriving on the twenty-third! That'd give them time enough. *Merryoak,* Wexford Harbour: two lorries. Strange about Horgan! Part of the brain-pan was sealed off. With most people after a few jars you can feel into their minds. With Horgan it was different, like talking to a "queer."

One wispy half-thought! Coughlan, Sonny Coughlan . . . Charlie swore his Bible oath 'twould all be all right. He'd just pull him in for a couple of hours, give the lad a bit of a fright, throw a scare into him . . . The hovering half-thought lingered. Every wrong in his life had been done after too many jars. He'd never have met Horgan, of course, if he hadn't gone to Kelly's. Cut it down, that was the answer, drink beer and stout just, maybe an occasional glass of wine. Horgan was too jarred to remember anyway.

Anna! He knew her every crevice, mind and body. She had no guile. She would be waiting, bathed and perfumed, clean as a crocus. Pity: it wasn't that he was jarred, but always after a day like that he hadn't the finesse. Whiskey was the bad man. A snipe of champagne and he'd finger a tune that'd wheedle an angel. Of course nothing-at-all was as bad as too much, with him anyway; drained him of the courage to make the gallant stand, or made him edgy enough to jump the gun.

Love made every man a slave, and woman too: the priest even behind the door flogging the bishop. When pussy passed by and the little dog laughed, pimps and presidents were all as one. Three weeks without and the thought was enough.

73

Sex at first sight. When I hear the word freedom I reach for my sex.

He elbowed in the door. Languidly he began the smelly climb. Wanting to please, Anna would offer him a drink, unwillingly. She too, even she, Anna of the Incorruptible Dream, was a creature of clay when love tickled her fancy. Camouflage, that's love. Nature's bait to catch continuance. Why be so prodigal, Mr. N., of so precious a bait? Why so anxious?

He didn't look forward now so much to this session with Anna. Wouldn't want to see her again for a while. Anna the All-enveloper: inhale ten men in one paroxysm . . . His drowsy mind dreamed away to a small lithe passive thing, inviting envelopment.

Joe paused on the landing, leaning relaxed on the bannister, resting a moment, allowing the muzziness to move away. Vague odors of sweat uprising from the floor closed in around him from the cold walls, and from the sky. Fumbling, he fixed his hip under the bannister, letting his body slump forward, at ease. . . . It would pass, the nausea. . . . Nothing, nothing more devastatingly sick-making than a big-boned big-breasted woman smiling sweaty invitation from a naked couch. It was the eagerness was wearying, the smiling, self-assured, uninhibited eagerness.

That book of Skinner's. What was it? Erogenous zones. Talk, touch, titillate, and tantalise. *Sex Technique* or something. Make it gradual was the thing. Words without thought, action without energy, emotion without feeling. Seventy-ninth performance at this theatre. She'd never know but, she'd never know.

Joe straightened his body grimly, shook the cobwebs from his mind, and turned briskly. Bars on the skylight. A death-trap.

He rang the bell and the light went on in the corridor.

74

"Hello Joe. I was hoping you'd drop in." The blue night-gown swished slyly through the skirt of her housecoat.

"What d'you know for sure?"

"Nothing for sure. Go ahead. Make yourself at home. Put your coat there anywhere. I have a fire in the bedroom."

"Am I entitled to a kiss?"

"Of course, darling."

"What lovely perfume."

"Do you like it?"

He kissed her gently, almost formally. It was part of a ritual they both understood; but to-night he was more consciously detached. Liking to prolong the preliminaries, she affected a little aloofness.

There wasn't much room between the bed and the grate but Anna had managed to place a low cushioned chair on either side: and a tiny table, attractively laid, on the hearth-rug between.

"Sit down, Joe, won't you? I hope you're not too hungry, I just made some sandwiches."

"That's fine."

Anna's was an easy presence; the room was friendly, and the fire comforting. He hadn't known he was so tired. Now as he lounged back wearily he perceived again dimly his lonely bewilderment; that this was his only haven of peace, his only escape from uncertainty.

"Like coffee or a drink?"

"What would you like me to like?"

"That's up to you."

"Think I'll have a little coffee."

"Sure it won't keep you awake?"

"Shouldn't think so."

"You're welcome to a drink, you know."

"Yes, I know."

"Heavens! You're still wearing those horrid boots."

"I'm afraid so."

"I'll see can I find your slippers."

"Thanks."

Crouched on her hunkers, a posture at once unflattering and obscene, she fussed noisily in the bottom shelf of the cupboard. Joe bent over, untying his laces.

"I still can't believe poor Martin is dead. Seems so unreal."

"Yes, I know."

"You knew him well, didn't you Joe?"

"I suppose so."

"Must have been an awful shock."

"Yes, maybe. I learned a while back to keep a rigid mind, put my emotions in cold storage. You get like that from talking to undertakers."

"What was he really like?"

"Ah, a hell of a nice fellow. Bit dreamy you know."

"Yes, I could see that. There you are, my sweet. Slippers with a smile."

"Thank you, darling. May I have the pleasure of presenting you with one chaste kiss as a small token of my esteem?"

"Don't be silly dear. No one ever took pleasure in a chaste kiss. Coffee. Black or white?"

"White please."

"Sugar?"

"Yes please."

"Help yourself to the sandwiches."

When she leaned over he could see the first soft incline of her breast. Knowing her love was his gave Joe a tremor of joy. Unexpectedly he was overcome by a sense of guilt, guilt at being there at all, a pretender at the holy shrine. . . .

"Like the radio?"

"Don't bother, I'll do it."

A string orchestra was playing a Schubert selection—the

76

appropriate unobtrusive background. Returning to the fire he felt obliged to dally a while by her chair, letting his fingers drift through her hair. She took his hand in hers, kissed it fondly.

"How did the meeting go, darling?"

"Not too bad."

"How about Mr. Nolan? Think he'll work out all right?"

"Hard to say. Bit of a dark horse. Good Revolutionary though."

"Who did they make Second-in-Command?"

"Me."

"You?"

"Yes. What's so surprising about that?"

"Nothing at all. I'm just thrilled, absolutely thrilled, that's all. Why didn't you ring me?"

"I don't know."

"Why, that's wonderful!"

"What's so wonderful about it?"

"Darling, it'll mean that you'll be able to use your real ability instead of always being stuck with the drudgery."

"Don't worry: I'll still get stuck. It just means five or six extra jobs."

"Silly darling! It's about time you put your foot down and told them where to get off. The Organisation wouldn't mean a thing without you. And they know it."

"Oh, let's forget it. Do you mind? I'm sorry."

"I understand dear. I still think it's wonderful. . . . Shall I move that table?"

"Thanks. . . . It's just that this is the only place in the world where I can get away from it all."

"I know. Of course darling. I understand."

When she had moved the table he slipped down on to the hearthrug. It was expected of him.

"Do you mind if I sit here?"

"Not at all."

"Read a little for me."

"What is it?"

"Omar Khayyam."

"Reading is surely your job. 'The Golden Voice of Revolution.'"

He opened the book, selecting her favourite stanzas. His voice now had a sonorous, almost caressing quality.

"Come, fill the cup, and in the Fire of Spring
The Winter Garment of Repentance fling:
The Bird of Time has but a little way
To fly—and Lo! the Bird is on the Wing.

"Here with a Loaf of Bread beneath the Bough,
A Flask of Wine, a Book of Verse—and Thou
Beside me singing in the Wilderness—
And Wilderness is Paradise enow."

"That's beautiful, Joe. Thank you."

"A kiss to show you're truly grateful."

She stretched over and kissed him softly on the lips.

Quietly he put his arms around her. His fingers played delicately along her spine.

"Naughty!"

"D'you like that?"

"I like it too much."

She took his hand in hers and they sat together leaning back against the end of the bed, their feet stretched towards the fire. Playfully she fondled his hand, smoothening his palm with her fingertips. The skirt of her housecoat had fallen aside; through the flimsy covering he could glimpse dimly a pale outline.

"Anna! Did anyone tell you that you look lovely to-night?"

78

"No."

"It's true."

"I must be in love. . . . Joe!"

"Yes?"

"You'll think I'm selfish."

"Why?"

"When I heard about Martin I was glad."

"Glad—"

"That it wasn't you. Is that wrong?"

"I don't suppose so."

He let his hand lollop carelessly on to her knee. A little while and dutiful fingers were squeezing, petting, exploring.

"Kiss me Joe. I want you to."

Long and lovingly he pressed his lips on hers. It was a calculated effort. Gradually, under pressure of his embrace, she sank slowly back.

"Joe!"

"Yes, darling?"

"Don't let them take you from me."

"No, darling."

"D'you think will you be pulled?"

"No, they've got nothing on me."

"Will you have to go 'on the run'?"

"Shouldn't think so."

His right hand was under her head. His left hand meandered caressingly over her breasts, down around her waist and smoothly over her heavy hips.

"Kiss me again."

This time her lips were hot. He touched them softly, ventured peacefully away to moisten her closed eyelids, nibble tenderly at her ear-lobes, and rest a score of baby kisses on her glowing forehead.

"Kiss me, Joe." Her lips were parted. "You've too many clothes on. You'll stay, Joe, won't you?"

79

"I've a script to write for the broadcast to-morrow."

"You can do it here. It'll give me a chance to study it."

"All right, Miss Golden Voice."

"Kiss me again."

While she was in the bathroom he undressed hurriedly, turned off the radio and slipped into bed. The sheets were ice-cold. He shivered slightly and crouched, waiting. Gradually his body-heat had a mildly thawing effect. From the bathroom he heard the flush of the toilet. Soon after Anna came hurrying back.

"I'm frozen."

She switched off the light: and he could see her, in misty silhouette, slipping out of her housecoat and wrestling her nightgown over her head. He lifted the covers.

"Quickly, before I freeze to death."

"Oh, darling, you're lovely and warm."

The first quick contact was always exquisite.

"Am I freezing you?"

"Not at all."

He let his lips rest tenderly on hers. Even then they seemed to catch a strange communion. It seeped swiftly into his consciousness, and he was pleased, that the formula was no longer necessary. Unthinkingly, he had drifted into a pleasant groove, the gay swirling eddying tide of desire. He was strong again, his mind a cheery servant now, no longer ruling. To-morrow he mightn't even remember. Tragic thought. Creation without existence.

"Anna!"

"Yes darling?"

"This is how I want to spend eternity."

"Yes, love."

"For ever and for ever."

"And for ever."

"With my two lips on yours, touching."

"Yes, sweet my love."

His right hand was under her head. His left hand fondled her hair, stroking it easily, rhythmically. Softly again with moist lips he touched her eyelids. His hand moved caressingly down over her silky shoulder to her breast.

"Don't do that. Puts bad thoughts in my mind."

She squirmed, shuddering a little; and he kissed her again on the lips, now warm and moist. Tightening his embrace he crushed his lips almost brutally on hers.

"Oh Joe, Joe," she moaned. "God is good."

In a quick swirl of passion his lips brushed hurriedly over her neck and shoulders down to her breasts.

Her body was trembling now.

"Come to me, Joe. I want you."

They were startled when the telephone rang.

"What's that?"

"Only the telephone."

"Hell of a time to ring."

"Better answer it I suppose or it'll go on all night."

She slipped out of bed. The telephone was on the wall near the door. He could see the grey outline of her body.

"Hello . . . ? Yes . . . ? Who's that . . . ? Who? I see. Yes, of course, darling."

"Who is it?"

A pause. Her hand muffled the mouthpiece.

"Sonny Coughlan."

"What does he want?" Joe's voice was drowsy.

"Oh, he's just being silly."

"A little cooling down is what he wants."

"Hello—hello! Yes, I'm listening. What? Yes. To-morrow night will be all right. What? About eight o'clock. Whatever you say, dear. Very well, I'll see you at the Studio. We'll talk about it then. What time? Half-past one and two. Very good. Yes, I'll be there before you. Good-night.

Yes, that's all right, Mr. Nolan will be there. We can arrange it then. That's a good boy. Good-night."

She hurried back to the bed and climbed in quickly.

"I'm frozen. Put your arms around me Joe."

But Joe was sleeping peacefully.

8

Sonny Coughlan

He was low-sized, slight in body. Perhaps it was the open white collar made him seem even younger than he was, or the look of wonderment. Sonny knew it was essential to appear natural, as though nothing unusual were happening, but, coming down from the Lecture Theatre, he found it difficult to mingle casually in the hectic palaver.

In the main hall the others gravitated to the radiator. Ten past one, the clock said! No more lectures now till Monday. He had promised to meet Mr. Nolan at the Studio before two. Time enough! With a throwaway "so long" Sonny detached himself and ambled down the further corridor. The lockers were in a dark corner down the stairs near the toilets. Sonny tripped jauntily down. Bart Mulligan banged out through the glass doors.

"Hiya." Bart bounded up the stairs.

"Hiya." Sonny fingered his pocket, searching for the key. If only Bart knew!

The basement light was off, the lockers almost in darkness. He glanced round—and paused listening—before he bent down and inserted the key. He pulled gently. The warped steel was difficult. He tried again, this time more forcefully. No good! Lift it a little and ease it out. That's better. A quick jerk. The cramped door gave way with a shattering clangour. He waited breathless. No! Not a sound! No one apparently around! With trembling fingers he reached in and opened the violin case. Everything in order: the Tommy-gun, dismantled and neatly packed, exactly as he left it. He closed the case quickly.

Hurriedly he fumbled on his trench-coat, seized the case in a firm grip, and banged the locker shut. He slipped his hand into the pocket. The automatic was there, safe and sound.

In the Main Hall Jimmie Kavanagh, with two giggling girls, was lounging against the radiator.

"Anybody buy an oul' fiddle?" Jimmie shouted.

Sonny's lips twitched uneasily in a weak smile. Joe Corcoran would have been marvellous in a situation like that. Exactly the right answer!

Outside the sun shone brightly in a white sky. There was a feeling of resurgence in the air, a remote gentle stirring that seemed to brighten and strengthen the strolling people. Sonny's step was light as his heart. It seemed as though he had been to Confession and cleansed his soul of all its sins. Not since his schooldays when, yearning for priesthood, he had pictured himself following Christ on the path to Calvary, did he feel the same exaltation. At last he had found his true vocation, to take his place with the unnumbered martyrs, the bright-eyed youngsters of every generation who had gone out with their cheeks pale and their red lips apart to give their lives for Mother Ireland.

A policeman was standing at the corner of Glentworth

Street, gazing vacantly into the clouds. Sonny found the violin case rather weighty. That was something he hadn't foreseen; a Tommy-gun was so much heavier than a violin. He would have liked to change the case to his other hand; but that might draw attention. The nearer he approached the weightier the case seemed to become. His heart was pounding. . . . The Guard was bound to notice. With a sudden shudder he realised that he was carrying the case in his right hand; and the automatic was in his right-hand pocket. He'd have to drop the machine-gun to get the automatic. Safety-catch was on too: that'd take more time! And he wasn't even sure if there was a bullet in the breech. . . .

Sonny sighed with sweet relief to find himself at last beyond the reach of that great relaxed statuesque monster. He changed the case to the other hand.

He was first in the bus queue, but only just. Two professional-looking gentlemen were quick to join him. One was tall and heavy with thick sensuous lips, a smiling contented face, and balding forehead. He wore no hat. He had a white carnation in his buttonhole. His companion, a dainty young man, minced fussily beside him. "Good gracious me," Sonny heard the tall man say. The dainty man was prattling away.

"Mary and I drop in for tea every Friday to that *dotie* little place off Dawson Street. I can't imagine what *possessed* me to invite her to the pictures. She looked positively *enormous;* I could have taken a Bible oath it was twins. It wouldn't have been so bad but, my dear, the picture was all about *doctors* and *hospitals.* And then *right* in the middle of the most thrilling part she said, 'Percy,' she said, 'I've got a pain.'"

"Good gracious me."

With little footsteps a frail old lady padded her way towards the queue. Her wrinkled face was softened by a kindly half-smile. She had a red nose. Sonny watched her warily. There was something exaggerated about her feebleness.

"'. . . Don't dream of such a thing,' I told her, 'I'm not the *teeniest* bit embarrassed.' Anyway I got her into the foyer. *Every*body, my dear, simply *every*body was there, all looking at *me*, as if it was *my* fault. 'Get a taxi quick, Percy,' she said, and *in* with her into 'Ladies.' "

"Good gracious me."

Two more men joined the queue. They were the obvious policeman type, too much so: simple dishonest faces—farmers or cattle dealers up for the Market. Sonny wondered what he should do with the violin case when he got on the bus—take it with him to his seat or put it in the cubbyhole under the stairs.

". . . I had the wind up in *gales*. When I said I wanted to go to the *maternity* hospital he made a coarse remark. I could have slapped his face, the nasty thing. Then he got the idea that if I wasn't the *mother*, I must surely be the *father*. My dear! Positively *revolting*. He was such a coarse man. . . ."

Sonny placed the violin case securely under his left oxter. In the trench-coat pocket his right hand enfolded the automatic. Nice comfortable feeling. Two-gun Coughlan. "With blazing guns Sonny Coughlan, bravest of Ireland's heroes, stood alone against the enemy. His gun barked twice. . . ."

". . . Then out came the usherette. And *was* she in a flap! *My dear!* 'You'd better get that taxi quick,' she said. 'The waters is broken.' What *could* she have meant? But that was only the beginning. Wait till I tell you, darling, what happened in the taxi. It was *shattering*. . . ."

The bus had arrived.

"Hold tight please. No standing."

86

It would be wisest to remain on the lower deck. If there was trouble he could make a quick getaway. Percy Precious fluttered upstairs close on the heels of his gracious friend. The little old lady followed Sonny on to the lower deck: but that was only to be expected. The two burly men went upstairs. On the lower deck there was only one seat and that completely empty. It was at the front: tactically not a good position; but Sonny had no alternative. He couldn't repress a slight shiver when the old lady sat down beside him.

"Fares please."

"Twopence," Sonny said.

"I think I'll have a tuppenny too," the old lady beamed, fumbling.

Sonny knew she would speak. He hadn't long to wait.

"I see you're a musician."

"Only a student."

She smiled, sighing. "It's nice to think of someone to-day learning the violin. In my day every young lady was expected to play. Sad."

Sonny didn't think a comment was necessary.

"Nowadays everyone is so busy. I don't think, somehow, when I was young we were all in such a hurry. I hope you have a good teacher?"

"I have."

"It was a Belgian who taught me. Professor Van der Velde —charming old man. I remember he used to say, 'It's more important that I teach you to love music than that I teach you music.' Wasn't that interesting? My poor husband used to play the clarinet."

"Did he die?" Sonny asked awkwardly.

"Ah yes . . . the War you know, 1917, in France. I'm glad in a way he didn't live to see the unpleasantness here. He was devoted to Ireland."

87

Sonny said nothing. The violin case, cradled in his arms, was a little cramping.

"You really must love your instrument. You are so careful. Would you like me to help? Perhaps—"

"No. It's quite all right. Don't bother at all. I'm quite all right."

There was a pause during which her mind seemed to climb far away into the tower of its own thought. After a while she was back again.

"Have you any favourite tune?"

Frantically he searched his mind. " 'Erin the Tear and the Smile in Thine Eye.' "

"Ah yes, Thomas Moore. Moore's Melodies. So seldom you hear them now. Archie used to sing a little song called 'Annie Dear.' I remember he sang it for the Lord Lieutenant. A pity isn't it, Dublin has changed so much? But perhaps you were not displeased to see the British go?"

"I don't remember it at all."

"Of course. You were too young. I am silly. I'll never forget the pageantry of Dublin in those days. The Castle Balls were so charming. Everyone dressed so beautifully. And the carriages . . . I often feel it was a mistake for the Lord Lieutenant to go away like that, no matter what those nasty men said. Don't you agree?"

"I never meddle in politics."

"And very wise you are too. Nothing but trouble comes from politics."

As they approached the terminus Sonny and the old lady were the only passengers left in the lower saloon. She got up at the second-last stop.

"Good-bye now," she said. "This is where I must leave you."

"Good-bye."

The conductor assisted her on to the pavement, and,

as the bus moved on, Sonny watched her cross to a walled garden.

At the terminus he got off quickly. He heard someone above, but didn't think it wise to wait. Sonny turned sharply into Hazel Avenue. It was a cul-de-sac, and the house used by the Organisation was the second last. The avenue was deserted. When he reached the gate he glanced back, to make sure he was not being followed. Joe Corcoran was watching from an upper window. Mr. Nolan opened the door.

"Ah Sonny, you got here safely I see."

Sonny smiled.

"And I do declare you've brought your little message."

It was a large vacant house. Mr. Nolan took the case and preceded Sonny up the wide staircase. Their footsteps echoed ominously on the bare boards. Mr. Nolan purred pleasantly.

"Yes. Indeed yes. A most successful broadcast. Good script. Should be effective. We're sending it out now. Anna's in great fettle. . . ."

Mr. Nolan guided him to a front room on the first floor, where Joe Corcoran was lounging by the window.

"Welcome to Elsinore," Joe murmured gravely.

"Hiya."

It was a high spacious room, thickly carpeted: but there was a minimum of furniture: a few crude chairs: and in the corner a cheap desk. Part of the room was cut off by a glass partition. Sonny could see Anna, script in hand, working away at the microphone. Her voice, sweetly subdued, came through on the monitor.

". . . The British murder gangs no longer have to waste their bullets fighting the separatist ideal. They can get Irish murder gangs with ruthless Coercion Acts to fight it for them. They don't have to waste their precious British lives main-

89

taining Partition. They have two puppet governments and a thousand vested interests, willing to maintain it for them, and to fight with every iota of armed strength any movement which seeks to represent the Soul of the people. At the present time the Satellite Government in the South is attempting to pass what it calls a People's Protection Act. . . ."

"Now Sonny," Mr. Nolan said benignly, "let's see what you know about radio. Perhaps you'd like—"

"Hold it!" Joe cut in. "We're being watched."

Mr. Nolan darted to the window.

"Better keep back," Joe said. "That's Clancy and Mac-Namee, two Castle G-Men."

About that time, so far as Sonny was concerned, everything seemed to become unreal. Across the road to the right in the mouth of a laneway he could see the two heavy farmer types. It looked as if they were arguing. It occurred to Sonny that they must have trailed him, but he hadn't time now to think. The talkative one kept turning and staring and turning away, half lifting his hand, pointing.

"Sonny, you stand by the window. If they stir give us a shout."

"Right."

Mr. Nolan didn't reprimand him, nor did Joe. As though in a dream, Sonny found to his surprise that he was vigorously alert. Joe dragged a gun from his pocket and released the safety-catch. The way he did it didn't seem exciting. It was a different Joe, happier somehow. Mr. Nolan was talking.

"If they start anything I'll hold them here. The bus on the main road will take you down to the dump. Be careful of the transmitter."

"Right."

Joe was bundling things into a large leather case; Anna was fussing in and out collecting cable. Across the way, the

90

men had stopped arguing. It was silly but Sonny couldn't help wondering which was Clancy, and which MacNamee. Yes, they had stopped arguing all right. They were both tall, but one was taller, and the face of the smaller one was cruel like a monkey.

"They're crossing over!"

"Have you a gun?"

"Yes." Sonny pulled the automatic.

"Not that. Here." Mr. Nolan grabbed a Colt .45 from a drawer in the desk. "It's ready loaded." Again, as in a dream, Sonny found himself balancing the gun and releasing the catch. "Don't use it until you have to."

From a holster under his arm Mr. Nolan pulled a large Webley. He broke it, spun the chamber, checked the ammunition. Sonny couldn't help but admire Mr. Nolan's cool command.

"They're at the gate now. They're coming in, I think."

Joe and Anna were hustling on to the landing, the transmitter between them. With the butt of his gun Mr. Nolan smashed the lower pane of glass. He crouched at the corner of the window. Still in a haze of incredulity, Sonny saw his lips tighten. And there was something about Mr. Nolan's grey eyes that reminded him of Commiskey. It occurred to Sonny, he didn't know why, that maybe Mr. Nolan was mad. But then it was all vaguely unreal and Sonny was only mildly surprised to find himself blending into the unreality. He hadn't time to get his thoughts in any kind of order when the first deafening shot rang out. Mr. Nolan's thin lips curled.

"That'll give them something to think about."

The men had dived below a low cement wall. It was disturbing to keep wondering which was Clancy. There were the yellow flowers in the grass and a little snow still lingered. The sun was bright in a steely sky. And it was two o'clock in the afternoon. Clancy was the big man probably. A decent skin if you met him in a pub, or went with him up to the house.

"They'll likely creep along behind that wall. Keep your eye on the gate next door."

Mr. Nolan hadn't finished speaking when Sonny saw a hand gripping the pillar. As the big man darted, he fired.

"Did you get him?"

"I don't know." Sonny no longer felt any fear, only a tremendous exhilaration. He was surprised at his own daring, so overcome that he was taken unawares when the second man darted after the first. He fired again, wildly.

The first shot from the G-Men seemed to come from nowhere. It smashed the glass above them. A flying splinter cut deep into Sonny's hand.

"Are you all right?"

"Yeh, sure."

"We should have smashed it ourselves. Always too late! Flying glass can be dangerous. What are they up to now?"

"Don't know. Probably get into one of the gardens further down and creep back."

"I doubt it. Likely gone for help."

Two more shots in quick succession jabbed into the brick and ricocheted away, leaving spurts of dust.

Mr. Nolan stretched up cautiously to get a better view. Another shot! Even when he saw the look of surprised annoyance and pain Sonny didn't somehow relate the shot to Mr. Nolan.

"Go on boy, fire back."

Sonny fired two shots. Then he heard the thud. He looked around. Mr. Nolan was crumpled on the floor. A slow trickle of blood oozed from his left temple. Sonny knew before he bent over that Mr. Nolan was dead.

9

Merely Incidental

It was always so on Sundays. Even MacCormack's hair was smoothly subdued. Ludicrous that these starched characters with their shiny faces were the leaders of a conspiracy . . . Sunday was so innocent a day, the afternoon sun so boldly bright. It made fun of the fantastic drawings and macabre sculpture, made delightful fun of everything except the atmosphere of tension—which could neither be derided nor suppressed.

"Is it audacity on our part," Joe asked, "to seek to represent the Soul of the People? Perhaps! It is a question which must have troubled many men in many centuries. Had those men in other generations felt self-conscious on receiving so singular a call, the Irish Nation to-day would be as drab and dead as a Manchester laneway. What right have we to lay claim to so high a heritage? We do not set ourselves up as great men. We are mostly poor and many of us are ignorant. We lay claim to our heritage because we are the one Organisation which to-day gives unquestioning loyalty to the same unsullied Separatist Ideals. Each one of us has sworn, if necessary, to lay down his life for Ireland. And during the past three days two of our Leaders have proved with their warm blood that that oath was no empty formula."

The low growl was meant to be encouraging.

"God rest them," MacCormack whispered.

There was an insinuation of terror at this, the second emergency meeting within three days. Behind the bulk of flesh-and-blood that was Joe Corcoran each member could see the smiling shadow of Mr. Nolan, who had moved with such suave confidence, only two days before, into that same position. Joe's high rhetoric was invigorating, the very words to brace their spirits.

"As yet we are only an infant Movement, but the foul murder of our two Leaders shows that the Satellite Governments set up here know we are dangerous. In the next few days we may—any one of us—be confronted by torture and death. With all solemnity I say—that if any one of you has a particle of doubt as to his ability to face that trial, then *get out now*. If there is any one among you who you think will prove unworthy, then I say—*throw him overboard*. And do it now! No matter who it may be! If you think *I* am unworthy—then it is your duty to yourselves, to Ireland and to the dead generations to *throw me overboard*. And now."

Every Irishman is born three small whiskeys below par and Joe had taken just that. Even while speaking he sensed the pathos of his situation. Confused and apathetic himself he still had power to revive their courage. Joe had spent the morning in muddled conflict, struggling to decide if he should accept leadership and, if not, how he

94

could ease himself out without embarrassment. He was plagued, too, by other uncertainties: wondering particularly if Horgan had betrayed him. A bad hangover hadn't helped.

"On Friday you did me the honour of electing me Second-in-Command. Ordinarily it is understood that the Second-in-Command automatically becomes Leader. However, that election was made under duress of a distressing crisis. It was made hastily; and it was agreed between Mr. Nolan and myself, as you know, that it would be subject to further discussion. In these circumstances I have decided to resign my right to leadership and to ask for a formal election."

Joe sat down feebly to a bemused mumble. He had milked the cow and then kicked over the bucket. Even as he leaned back he realised his mistake. Enthralled and strengthened by his earlier heroics, the Council was shaken by this unexpected irresolution.

Dermot Walshe grumbled something about the Constitution.

"Bugger the Constitution," MacCormack blustered. "Let's elect him again and get it over. What the hell!"

"Hear, hear!"

"Before you do that," Joe said quietly, "I'd like you to consider seriously if somebody else might not be more suitable."

"Not at all."

"Don't be silly."

Hughie Commiskey's basalt tone cut the gabble.

"Are you afraid or what?"

Joe turned coolly.

"You should know."

"Easy, Hughie."

"Take it easy."

"This is no time for acting the maggot," Commiskey stood up. "We spend so much time wondering how we're doing in this glorified Kindergarten that we never do any-thin'."

"That's telling them, Hughie."

"It's not fair."

"Just a moment." MacCormack fancied himself as a mediator. "Whatever else we do let's not play into the hands of the enemy by fighting among ourselves. I don't think for a moment that Joe is afraid. And I don't believe anybody else thinks so either."

"Certainly not."

"He merely feels that, as this is a particularly critical occasion, you might like to endorse your decision by some-thing in the nature of a vote of confidence. Am I right Joe?"

"Precisely."

Hughie Commiskey's lips twisted contemptuously. "Cut the smarm. This Organisation is pledged to physical force. Let's drop the airs and graces and get down to straight shooting."

"I agree." Joe stood up to face Commiskey. "I completely agree. But let me tell you and the whole bloody lot of you that I am not going to lead this or any other organisation unless I have the unquestioned loyalty of every member. I am not going to be stabbed in the back by any bastard who thinks he could do the job better himself. And I am not going to have the Movement stabbed in the back either. That goes for the whole lot of you."

There was silence when he finished. Joe was surprised at the ferocity of his own attack, and more surprised when Commiskey sat down meekly. Hughie's nature was remote and unpredictable. Joe had been as much bewildered by the viciousness of his attack as he was astonished by his own reaction to it.

"I'm sorry. Maybe I'm a bit on edge. As Skinner said, this is no time for argument." He spoke coldly. Joe found it hard to gauge his sincerity. "May I have the honour of proposing our friend Joseph Corcoran as President of the Council?"

"Hear, hear!"

"Seconded."

"I second that."

A chorus of voices cried out support.

"I take it," Dermot Walshe said smilingly, "that Joe Corcoran is unanimously elected."

"Hear, hear!"

"That's the boy, Joe."

Now that the decision had been made Joe was not displeased. During the hours of struggle, when he could banish his irresolution, he had allowed his mind to range over the immense possibilities. Such casual dreaming leaves, always, the temptation to action.

"Thank you," Joe said with simple sincerity. "Thank you, Hughie. Now let's get down to business."

He was a good committeeman. When challenged, his mind was incisive and he liked to encourage and direct initiative, rather than dominate. MacCormack was elected Second-in-Command. Joe might have preferred Dermot Walshe, but he was not unhappy. Skinner could wreck the Movement in a week but, Joe thought grimly, if that happened he wouldn't be there to worry.

It was decided that, for the present, all parades should be restricted to locations in the city with a high percentage of safety. In this matter Joe made a point, without ostentation, of seeking and deferring to Commiskey's opinion. Skinner guaranteed to find, within two days, suitable premises to replace the Hazel Avenue Studio. Joe made a point too of avoiding all reference to the previous day's debacle. The effect of the discussions—and the helpful proposals arising from them—was to re-create a feeling of friendly enthusiasm, and a determination to face the crisis unflinchingly. The meeting appeared to be coming to an easy close when Commiskey cut in again.

"May I ask a question?"

"Certainly."

"What do you intend to do about the threat to wipe out the Organisation?"

"How do you mean?"

"I mean what I say. Already within three days two of our Leaders have been murdered. What do you intend to do?"

Commiskey made little effort to conceal his hostility. There was weary resignation in Joe's reply.

"I wonder if some members of this Council have any appreciation of the respect due to their elected Leader."

"Answer the question."

"Easy, Hughie."

"Take it easy, oul' son."

"I'll answer the question." Joe was controlled. "But I won't be browbeaten. And I warn you that if your attitude doesn't change I shall have to consider suspending you from the Council."

"I'm sorry. I'm worried, that's all."

"Thank you." Again Joe doubted the sincerity of the withdrawal. "It's understandable that you should be anxious. But it would be wrong to allow anxiety to drive us to hysteria. This above all is a time for cool heads and dispassionate thought."

"True."

"The situation is hazardous. I am aware of that. But however much my friend Hughie would wish to elevate me to the position of Dictator, I must point out that this is a democratic body, and that policy is decided by the freely elected Council, not by any one person."

"Fair enough."

"The most I can do is to make a suggestion."

"What do you suggest, Joe?"

"I suggest we take the offensive."

"But how?"

"By implementing my plans for the capture of the Swedish arms shipment."

"That's an idea."

"The situation isn't as black as it might seem, and I believe that with a little adroit timing we can twist it to our advantage. The killing of Martin Coyne and Mr. Nolan has made the Organisation appear weak in the eyes of the people; but it has also increased public sympathy, because the people realise that we are the only upholders of the separatist ideal. By taking the strongest offensive action as soon as possible and disproving the contention that we are weak, we can turn the Government's coercion policy to our advantage, and probably find ourselves for the first time in a really dominant position."

"Sounds good to me," Commiskey muttered, reluctantly. "Think we can do it?"

"I am, shall we say, reasonably optimistic. The stuff arrives in Wexford Harbour on the twenty-third of this month, on the good ship *Merryoak*. Two lorry-loads of rifles. Gerry Baker was able to establish yesterday that there will be an armed motor-cycle escort of a dozen men with each lorry. Guards will be posted at certain points along the route; but I don't think we need worry too much about them."

"What route are they using?"

"The old Military Road. Through the mountains."

"Funny."

"Appropriate but stupid."

"It won't be a simple action. I'll go into the plan of attack later with the Military Council. I've tried to avoid all possible loss of lives. But there are bound to be grave risks, a need for intense discipline and daring. However, if we are suc-

99

cessful we will not only have countered the Government's offensive but will have achieved a considerable victory. Have any of you got any alternative ideas?"

From the quality of the silence Joe sensed that he not only had edged out of a tricky spot, but had achieved a minor triumph.

"Personally," Dermot said, "I think you've supplied the answer."

"I agree," Commiskey concurred.

"Good. We should arrange a meeting of the Military Council as soon as possible. However, I cannot help thinking this meeting has gone on long enough. Nothing is achieved by exhausting ourselves unnecessarily. I suggest we bring it to a close. . . ."

Joe went first, accompanied by MacCormack. They slipped out the back into the laneway and moved away in the direction of the Quays. Darkness was gathering. MacCormack was in his sentimental mood.

"Let me take your hand, Joe. It's a great day for the Movement, a great day for Ireland."

"Bollax," Joe said. "Have you a mouth on you?"

"I wouldn't say I haven't."

"Let's have a gargle."

"I could be led with a halter of snow."

"Where'll we go?"

"There's a sailor's kip down the lane."

"That's our dart."

"Clutcher Keogh's."

"I know him. Louser of the first order."

"I know! Afraid to give you the itch for fear you'd have the pleasure of scratchin' it."

The pub was empty of customers. Mr. Keogh, a big inoffensive-looking man, welcomed them courteously.

"Good-day to you gentlemen. How are you, Mr. Mac-Cormack?"

"Can't complain. What'll you have, Joe?"

"Pint o' stout."

"Two."

They settled down at a remote table, two heroic pints before them. For a while they were silent, ignoring their drinks, faces masked in abstraction, each mind isolated in secret thought. At length Skinner leaned forward and lifted his pint. "Ah well." Raising his arm, elbow high, in a quaintly formal pose, he held the drink in mid-air. "Good health."

"Slainte." Joe stretched forward.

Pursing his lips, fish-like, Skinner drank deep.

"Begod Joe," he said, "that was a smashin' speech. You've a great gift of the gab."

"Didn't say anything I didn't mean."

Skinner's mind wasn't the brightest, and he was fascinated by Joe's adroit juggling.

"You scared the pants off me with all that talk about resigning. I don't mind telling you I wouldn't stay two minutes in the Organisation if you didn't take over."

"I'm next on the list. You'll have to take over then."

"Don't say that! Jaysus, I still can't believe that Martin Coyne is dead. And Mr. Nolan! Poor Martin! That was a decent skin. The only time he caused sadness was when he died. Things are getting hot Joe. I wonder if we shouldn't lie low for a while."

"Ach, I don't think so. Things aren't that bad." Joe was off again. With only doubts about his own strength he *would* push forward to inject strength into others. "The margin between success and failure is always narrow. At the moment maybe we're in trouble. But the Government's coercion policy is having a boomerang effect. Sympathy for the

Movement is on the increase. Important thing is not to get rattled. Things can change very quickly."

"You're right, Joe. Of course you're right."

Skinner took another long slug.

"Joe!"

"Yeh?"

"There's a couple of things I wanted to talk to you about."

"Go ahead."

"First of all—now you won't mind me sayin' this?"

"You haven't said it yet."

"Well—it's just that I think you ought to be more careful. Walking around the city and that. Makes it too easy for them."

"Maybe; they've got nothing on me yet, you know. Nothing they can prove."

"Doesn't matter. They'll be after you now anyway. They don't have to have anything to pull you in."

"True."

"There's another thing."

"Yeh?"

"You're going to be annoyed with me now for saying this, I know that. But don't you think you ought to cut down on the beer for a bit?"

"Begod that's good. That's coming from you that'd suck it off a sore leg."

"Oh I agree. I admit that. But all the same! I suppose it's all right to say it now that he's dead, but I had a tough enough tussle on that score with oul' Nolan before you arrived the other night. He talked like you were a bloody drunk."

"Don't worry. I can carry a couple of jars."

"I don't mean that. Everybody's entitled to a couple, so long as they don't overdo it. Once you start overdoing it is where the harm starts."

102

"What are you having?"

"The same again."

There was genuine gaiety in the laughter as Joe collected the glasses. He sauntered up to the counter. Mr. Keogh emerged from the back.

"Large Irish and a pint."

"Right. I'll bring them down."

"Where's the toilet?"

Pointing without looking, Mr. Keogh lowered his eyelids, whispering.

"In that door. Down the stairs."

The creaky door was reluctant. Joe peered blearily into the murk. A faint gurgle of water and the stale stench of ammonia gave encouragement. He groped for the steel rail and edged down the narrow flags. Elimination, the Americans called it. ARE YOU HAVING TROUBLE WITH YOUR ELIMINATION? In Ireland the body was a heresy, only the soul a reality. Lavatories, hidden in the back cellars of pubs, need never be clean, should never be lighted. Time spent there was maybe a delusion, maybe a reminder from God of the Animality of Man.

The unshaded bulb, dim and dirty, gave a modicum of light. With feet apart and head high Joe watched the impact of his ghostly breath on the brick wall. Somewhere behind the clouds he had become lost, drifted into a sidewater, away from the clear rhythm. There was a time long ago he was part of the outflow, eddying contentedly in the womb of the water. Now he was hazy, drifting in a maze of tired needs. Must it be this way always? Overcome by strange yearnings he glanced up at the murky ceiling as though he might penetrate stone wall, slate roof and clammy sky to catch communion with that Omnipotent Spirit Who made humanity His puppet. Momentarily he felt an impulse to fight back to an elemental state where life was not always an

103

effort, not always a pretence. Memory of other prayers, un-answered, deadened his lips. He shivered convulsively, adjusted his clothing and turned away.

Over the wash-basin was a murky glass. Smoothing his tousled hair Joe examined without prejudice the mirrored image—the mildly smiling cynicism of the whiskey addict! Skinner was right, he should give it up. Life should be at all times lyrical, a pattern of happy ever-changing movement. Even pain need not be anguish if one had sufficient zest. Black porter and stupefying whiskey were the enemies of the idyllic, knocking the pattern all awry.

The telephone booth in the corner reminded him. He searched in his pocket. Better hurry! MacCormack would be restless. He pushed the pennies in the slot, and dialled.

"Hello!"

"Hello! Anna? Joe here."

"Oh, hello Joe."

"I just thought I'd ring and tell you about the meeting."

"That was kind. I've just been hearing about it."

"What?"

"I've just been hearing about it. Sonny Coughlan."

"Oh! I see! Well, better not talk on the phone anyway."

"Maybe. Joe!"

"Yes?"

"When am I going to see you?"

"Well, that depends. I'll have a lot of extra work now."

"Come over soon, Joe. I'm all excited."

"Yes, as soon as I can."

"It's wonderful. I can't tell you how thrilled I am."

"I'd better go. There's somebody waiting."

"All right."

"Good-bye."

"Good-bye darling."

It didn't matter. Joe had always been contemptuous of jealousy, an animal instinct, irrational and base. Now, as he felt his mind clouding, he tried recapturing the arguments. Why should Anna account to him? Obviously she had friends—and lovers too—before they met, and would again. Anna was so naïve, that was all, so easily deceived. The truth of the matter was she needed guidance. It was impossible, though, to protect her from every casual encounter . . .

He hurried back to the bar. . . . Skinner was already halfway through his pint.

"That took a long time."

"Sorry. Had to make a phone call."

"Oh!"

They drank deep and relapsed into unself-conscious silence, each busied with his own thought.

"You were lucky," MacCormack said at length, gettin' away so easy."

"When? Yesterday you mean?"

"Yeh."

"I was. Funny, the two of us blunderin' through the hedge. And the transmitter between us."

"You got a bus easy?"

"No trouble. You'd imagine it was waitin'."

"God takes care of his own."

"And the Divil takes care of Joe."

They laughed lightly, and again for a while they were silent.

"Nolan died well."

"He proved his worth."

"The best way a man can."

"Did you remark Coughlan at the meetin'," MacCormack asked, "with the glove on his hand and the bandage stickin' out?"

"I saw that. Queer he wasn't caught. How'd he get away, I wonder."

"Hard to say."

"Commiskey is right. There must be a leak. What's his story?"

"Whose?"

"Coughlan's."

"Oh, you know! The usual. Hell and blue murder. Guns to the right of me, shots to the left of me. You'd think it was a bloody regiment with tanks and artillery."

"I see. Funny business."

"D'you think he was followed?"

"Might be. They didn't lick the information off the ground."

"Right enough."

"We had the meeting Friday." Joe's lips clipped tight and a frown darkened his eyes, as he sought to place the events in perspective. "Nolan gave his instructions. To shift the Tommy-gun. No one knew but the Executive, and even they didn't know where was the dump. Very funny! They didn't lick the information off the ground."

Though he had no conscious desire to do injury, Joe knew that he didn't share the suspicion he was creating. Perhaps it was that circumstances of late had been unkind, and he inclined to react against the symbol of that unkindness.

"You don't think—?"

"What?"

"You don't think—?"

"I haven't said a word. Not a word."

"Begod Joe, would you believe it, it never struck me. Never struck me for a minute. Can you beat that!"

10

"Why Didn't You Tell Me?"

Only a wispy gauze hung about overhead, but away to the east he could hear the hoarse wheeze of foghorns—a melancholy sound—the sad wail of danger ahead. The dark trees, arms held high, seemed strangely shameful in their nakedness. They stood, like gaunt tearful prisoners, under the silhouette of the terrifying houses. He was remarking how blearily the street lamps reflected in wet concrete when the Ford Custom glided by. Joe became watchful. There was a narrow laneway across the road: better make for that if there was trouble. He heard the footsteps coming behind but didn't somehow think them dangerous till he felt the jab in his spine.

"Keep moving."

A tiny click and a touch of steel on his wrist: it was done so adroitly he hadn't time to think, or maybe the whiskey had blunted his mind. When he turned to look he found himself handcuffed by the left wrist to a bitter-looking little rat-faced man. On his other side was the man with the gun."

"What's all this?"

"Keep moving. You'll learn."

Joe recognised the two detectives, Lehane and Mac-Guirk. Paddy Lehane, the little fellow, had a name for brutality. MacGuirk was supposed to be harmless.

When they reached the car the engine was purring and the back door open. MacGuirk frisked him, but Joe wasn't heeled. MacGuirk got in first.

"All right," he called.

With a pretence of indifference Joe followed. His sudden drag on the handcuffs might have been accidental.

"Take it easy, y' sonavabitch."

"Sorry. Didn't know you were so tender."

"So you want to get rough, d'you?" Lehane dragged the door shut. "Go ahead, Jem," he ordered the driver. "You'd like a little fun, heh?" With his left fist he gave Joe a neat jab to the point of the jaw. He delayed till the glaze was clearing before he followed with an uppercut.

"Now, little boy, what'd you like to play, heh?"

They hadn't turned. Joe was numb and dizzy, but he gathered that they were moving towards the outskirts, in the direction of the mountains. With a raucous warning the car hurtled over the canal bridge and wheeled shuddering to the right along a strait-laced suburban avenue. Might be taking him to an empty house, or up the hills, like the other crowd did with Noel Lamont. There was a cross there now, a stone cross marking the spot.

"Where are we going?"

"You'll find out."

Beat him up first, they said, trying to make him tell. Got the pincers then, pulling the hairs out of his moustache.

Comical character Noel. Most times he never stopped talking. Tried burning his eyebrows, but he wouldn't budge.
Pulled his teeth out. . . .

"Keepin' it a secret?"

"Anything you don't know will stay a secret."

. . . Nobody could hear him up there miles from anywhere. They shouldn't have got frightened. Couldn't stick
the screaming but. Shot him in the end. Some say they cut up
his body, but others make out 'twas the rats did that. He
never told. . . .

"Aren't you the brawny heroes! Two to one against a man
in handcuffs and there's no stopping you."

"Aw, shut it, can't you. You look nicer with it shut."

. . . The oul' mother afterwards, got up in mourning
clothes, traipsing through fern and heather, looking under
gorse bushes for the bits. Little enough left in the end but a
rotten memory . . .

The driver acknowledged the blind crossing at Appian
Way with another threatening hoot, but didn't slacken. A
double-decker bus rasped to a halt, and the Ford shot
through the beam of headlights.

"Jaysus Jem, you're a hawk at the wheel," MacGuirk murmured. "That driver's prayin' backwards for you."

Outwardly Joe was calm. But his mind, tensed by danger,
was active—eager to snatch at escape. . . . Familiar set-
tings were coloured by fear to nightmarish horror. Ranelagh,
a tawdry suburb where he once had digs, seemed now a
place of unquiet apprehension. The neon lights, green and
amber, of Sandford Cinema, gaped loutishly into the murk.
Casuals wandering the pavements, crawthumpers intent on
Devotions, lovers skulking to the movies, a lone woman walking her dog, were all creatures of a ghastly dream. Suppose
he were suddenly to scream? Near Marlborough Road a
clutch of youngsters tricked on the sidewalk! A callow
109

couple wrestled lustily. Shrill laughter of girls in season! She slid to the ground screeching protest!

Incredible that none seemed aware of his fear!

At Eglinton Road a giant pantechnicon lumbered over. A vicious grinding jolted the Ford to a halt.

"Where the hell do you think you're going?" Lehane roared. "These fellows think they own the road."

The pantechnicon lumbered sedately on.

The sudden jolt calmed Joe's nerves. No harm at all if they had an accident! Grab the gun. Shoot the others. How to get rid of the handcuffs but? The thought was sedative and tonic. Better die fighting.

"So you're the new Chief are you?"

"Chief of what?"

"Chief of the Movement of cut-throat gun-bullies pledged to confusion and bloody murder by sticking a bomb up the arsehole of reason."

The big man giggled.

"Be the holy," says he, "that's massive. Isn't Paddy a masterpiece with the words?"

With another harsh screech the car bumped over a humpy bridge and turned again.

"Can I have a cigarette?"

"Can he have a cigarette, Paddy?"

"Ah, I suppose so." He gave Joe another jab. "But don't try anything."

Joe brought out the cigarettes. Silently he offered the open packet. Lehane took one. MacGuirk stretched greedily too.

"Have you a light?"

"Eh, what d'you think we are, a charitable institution?"

MacGuirk produced a lighter.

The car was running more smoothly now, along a tree-lined avenue of characterless brick houses. Joe recognised the Wolsley Estate, a recent conglomeration of barrack-like buildings. They turned left and left again. Joe wasn't sure whether to be pleased or sorry when the Ford wheeled round a circle of trees and scraped to a jerky stop.

"Open the door, Jackie."

They had stopped outside one of the smaller houses. MacGuirk got out first and opened the door. He stood by, gun in hand, while Lehane dragged at Joe.

"Come on Garibaldi. On your bike."

The bulging end of a cul-de-sac! Nobody around! If he wanted to make a break he'd have to be sharp. Joe noted the figures on the gate. No. 13.

"You go ahead," Lehane ordered.

"Right."

The big man slipped the gun in his pocket and creaked open the gate. A granite bird-bath, austere in white outline, was revealed by the light from the window. A sullen-faced maid opened the door.

"Tell him we've come."

MacGuirk slouched in and stood, gun in hand again, between the stairway and the wall.

"Come on. Inside."

The front room was carelessly comfortable, a peacefully faded blue carpet, a confused assortment of lazy chairs and a heedless scattering of books. Over the fireplace was a shiny reproduction of Van Gogh's "Sunflowers." This and the featureless "Still Life" were evidence that the owner at some time had the culture bug.

"Where's your man?" Lehane asked.

"She's gone to get him."

Joe was relieved when Lehane produced a key and proceeded to remove the bracelets. He glanced nonchalantly at MacGuirk. The big man fingered the trigger, his body tense.

111

"How does it feel," Lehane's upper lip receded, "for the chief of the gun-bullies to find himself at the business end of a wipe-out?"

"Harmless enough."

"Sit down."

An unexpected jab unbalanced Joe into a wing-back chair. He tried struggling back, and got another abrupt crack on the jaw. The dividing doors rolled noisily back.

"Cut that out." The voice was loud with anger. "What the hell d'you think you're doin'?"

"Sorry, Inspector."

Charlie Horgan came into the room.

"Christ Almighty will youse never learn. I told you to pick him up and bring him along, not drag him here."

"Yes, Inspector."

"Go on. Get the hell out of here."

Joe should have been able to relish the unexpected reversal, to gloat on Lehane's discomfort and MacGuirk's shamefaced shuffling. But he was too sick.

"Come on. Make it snappy."

They shuffled awkwardly out, and the door closed softly.

"Are you all right?" Horgan hurried to Joe. He stooped slightly, resting a hand on his shoulder, peering. "Are you all right oul' son?"

"I'm O.K."

Still numb from shock Joe couldn't just get things in focus. Charlie's lower lip was hanging loose, his eyes were goggling, and his peering face was a mask of stupidity. Peculiar too to see Charlie in baggy corduroys: and his homespun jacket was too long and bulky. His head was too big.

"You've no idea what I'm up against, Joe. No idea. I warned them fellows to take it easy, not to try anything.

Jesus, I might as well be talking to the wall. Are you sure now you're all right? Are you sure, oul' son?"

"Yeh, sure."

"Look Joe. I had to see you." His voice was urgent. "I had to talk to you. If I'd pulled you into the Station I'd only be walkin' you into trouble. Are you sure now you're all right? Would you like a drink?"

"I don't mind."

"That's the man. I have a bottle here." He darted away to the corner by the big bureau. Stooping to grab he glanced back again, the look of pain still tightening his face. "A good stiff brandy is what you need. Where's that glass?"

Joe wished that Charlie wouldn't move in such uneasy spasms. "I had to see you, Joe. Boy, did you have me worried. Why didn't you tell me, Joe?"

"Tell you what?" Joe's fingers trembled as he took the drink. Horgan's self-pitying lilt drilled on.

"Why didn't you tell me that the little bastard, what's his name, Coughlan, was on his way to the Studio? If I hada known it woulda been all right. Why didn't you tell me, Joe? I only did what you said. You told me to pick him up. Jesus, Joe, I thought I was only helpin' you. Why didn't you tell me, son?"

Joe wanted to jump up and denounce Horgan, accuse the ugly rat of letting him down, betraying their friendship, being a dirty double-crossing bastard. Joe suggested pulling the lad to teach him a lesson, not having him trailed through the city. It'd be nice to grab Horgan, shake him like a rat, smash his fist into that pudgy flesh till the outsize body crumpled. . . . But he couldn't. . . . He couldn't do anything. Joe knew only his own guilt, that the monotonous accusation could never be obliterated, never submerged. Stupidity and carelessness had created a com-

113

plication, alive with danger, neither to be excused nor explained. He only knew that he was guilty probably of the death of Nolan, and that that guilt was too troublesome to be forgotten. It'd come hurrying always to torture him.

"And to think of them killin' poor oul' Jamesy Nolan; I haven't slept, thinkin' of it. And him with a wife and three kids. Jesus, Joe, I wouldn't've had it happen for the world. I wake up in the night thinkin' of it. And the worst part of it is I can't help feelin' it was my fault. But sure I couldn't do a thing like that. Sure Nolan was one of the old crowd. He did his bit. Him and the Minister was in Mountjoy together. Yeh. 'Course they were. Sure weren't they on hunger strike, Paddy Derrane and Jamesy Nolan. Nobody wanted to kill him. Why didn't you tell me Joe?"

"How was I to know?"

It was all Coughlan's fault. He hadn't wanted to admit even to himself but he knew at last without doubt that he hated Coughlan, hated him with a deep unquenchable loathing. And in the extremity of his agony he could admit that hatred had helped him to tell Horgan about Coughlan. Joe took another gulp. His hands were trembling. He wanted to hide them away so that Charlie wouldn't see. But it wasn't easy.

"I'm not blamin' you Joe. Whatever happens I wouldn't want you to feel bad. It's what I'm up against all the time, I tell you. Stupidity, rank bloody stupidity! That pair of thoolermawns Clancy and MacNamee, they're the ones I'm after. Joe, you've no idea. Tryin' to do the smarties. You give a man an order, tell him what to do. 'Pick up the little fellow outside the College one-fifteen.' All right. You'd think that'd be enough. Oh no. Not with that crowd . . ."

Joe took another sip but the stuff didn't have a taste; it scorched his gums but didn't taste, didn't even give him a lift. Why was Charlie so restless? He kept darting around

114

closing drawers and fiddling with things and books. If he hadn't been tanked up the night he met Horgan it would have been all right. One thing was certain: if ever he escaped from this jumble he'd never touch another drop.

". . . They have to start doin' the big stuff, playin' Mr. Bloody Sherlock Holmes moryah! Trailin' the little bastard from one end of the town to the other. That's what I'm up against all the time, Joe. If only I hada known it woulda been all right, Joe. You might at least've told me."

Again Joe felt that desperate urge to tower up and lash Horgan, tell him he was a fool, a blunderer, he'd made a bloody botch of everything. . . . But anger is energetic and Joe was drained of energy. Slowly, with painful effort, he dragged himself up from the chair.

"Do you mind if I go now?"

"Won't you finish your drink?"

"No. I don't feel like it."

"Are you sure now?"

"No. I don't feel too good somehow."

"Whatever you say, oul' son."

Slowly, with the heavy movement of a sick man, Joe moved to the door. Horgan gaped curiously, stretched out hesitant hands, about to help. Joe was glad when he didn't.

"Listen, Joe, you and me could work together. There's no reason why we shouldn't. We're all Irishmen, aren't we? We're all fightin' for the same thing. The Government wants to end Partition as much as you and me. Only they have to be careful; they can't come out in the open. We're all fightin' for the same thing, Joe. You want to use the gun and we want to use our heads. Dammit Joe if you and me could only get together we'd shake the world. We'd have this little country free in no time. Don't you agree?"

Was it a voice other than his own that answered weakly!

"Yes, Charlie, we'd shake the world."

115

"I'm terrible sorry about all this, Joe. If only you'd told me. Never mind but. You and me can do it, Joe. Workin' together. You and me. We'll set the place on fire, the law and the prophet.

"That's right Charlie."

"We'll meet again soon Joe, won't we?"

"We'll do that."

"In the next few days."

"Fine."

"I leave it to you, Joe. You get in touch any time. . . ."

The melancholy whine echoed in his brain as he moved down the path. The night was darkening now and the air was sweetly cold. A few drops of rain moistened his cheeks. He raised his head to catch the bitter pain. There were stars in the sky and a new moon looked shyly on the world. Up there somewhere, maybe a million miles away, were Orion and Plough, and beyond an incomprehensible infinity and Inscrutable Face. Away to the east the foghorns still wailed wheezily. Nearby a small wind shivered among leaves.

It'd be nice to walk.

11

She'll Be Comin' Round the Mountain

Joe's plan was a double ambush. The initial problem was the separation of the lorries from their escort. This was the assignment of the First Section—under Hughie Commiskey—concealed among trees high up in the valley. The plan was to allow the Convoy to come on a level with the Section, within short range of the hidden Volunteers. A tree-trunk across the road would compel a halt. The Volunteers had orders to withhold fire until the enemy had removed the tree-trunk. The escort, separated from their machines, would find themselves at a disadvantage under fire. Their first instinct, Joe reckoned, would be self-preservation. But he was prepared to gamble too on an effort being made to get the lorries away. Orders had been given to direct fire at the escort rather than the lorries, and the importance of incapacitating the machines rather than the men had been emphasised.

If things worked out as planned Joe felt certain that the unescorted lorries would press on down the Valley to the bridge, where they would come under fire of the Second Section. The forest in the vicinity of the bridge was less dense, but there were more boulders. Cover from fire was better but cover from view was less good. This was not necessarily a disadvantage. There was no longer the same necessity for surprise, and the position had many natural advantages. The road cascaded in a hairpin bend over two small bridges. As soon as the lorries were across, Coughlan had instructions to blow the bridges, cutting off attack from the rear. The road ahead would be obstructed by a second tree-trunk. The operation, from then on, should be simple as sin.

As the last straggles of night were slinking away Joe stood on the summit of Killeen, crouched in the shadow of a Cromlech. The hours of darkness had alternated between frantic preparation and sleepless vigil, but he was not tired. With the aid of binoculars he scanned the white road that went wriggling away to the sky's end. A fresh wind, whistling over the glen, rumbled among the tops of trees and frisked between fern and heather. Low feathery clouds, under a pure blue canopy, scrambled across the sky. The clean perfume of pine was lifted up on the edge of the wind.

Joe's feelings mingled apprehension and exhilaration. There was the threat of unforeseen danger, a detail forgotten, the fear that a Volunteer would reveal his position, and the uncertainty of the final gamble—that human beings would react as expected. But these apprehensions were merely tests of his resource, containing within them the seeds of exhilaration. Action was joy. Even the anticipation had its own elation. Joe found joy in the battling wind, the cold air burning his skin, flapping the skirt of his trench-coat, compelling resistance. It was pleasant, too, to find himself again among the hills, and to recapture something of the peace he had found there as a boy.

A darkening silhouette on the skyline caught his eye. The Convoy was rounding Tullish Mountain. As he lowered the glasses he heard a series of low whistles. Hughie Commiskey! Anna had word from the scouts! Joe scrambled down to the hump of ditch, vaulted the barbed-wire and raced across the marshy heather.

"We've had word from Ballygaraun."

"Yes?"

"Convoy just rounded Tullish."

"I know. Any idea what speed?"

"Fifteen an hour about. Close formation."

"How long does that give us?"

"Half-an-hour at most."

"Right. Prepare for action."

With Commiskey close behind, Joe blundered down the sheep-track. As they approached the forest-centre he could hear the laughter and murmured gabble of the men. Their indiscipline was annoying; but this was no time for reprimand. Besides, who better than he could understand how effectively laughter can camouflage uncertainty. Near the edge of the clearing he saw Anna readying her radio equipment. The men, sprawled around in scattered groups, seemed to sense the imminence of danger. Their chatter died abruptly.

"All right, men," Commiskey barked. "Prepare for action."

The order was a relief. They were smiling now, checking ammunition, tightening their belts, retrieving rifles.

"Just a moment," Joe called.

Halting, they turned, then hesitantly gathered forward, their faces vivid. For them this was no skirmish of a terrorist body but the re-enactment of a ritual made holy by

119

countless martyrdoms. Each one faced death with the knowledge that he was fighting for a good cause and that, if destined to die, the holiness of his sacrifice would be acknowledged. Joe was surprised to find his own thought chastened and uplifted by their faith. His dream had once been pure as theirs. For a moment he would have wished to wonder where the corruption had begun.

"You all know your positions. They've been selected carefully and afford excellent cover. Remember to avoid all unnecessary movement. The slightest stirring—even the muzzle of a rifle—can reveal a position. Be sure when moving forward or retreating not to crowd. In case of confusion take your orders from the nearest leader. Remember particularly that under no circumstances is a Volunteer to show himself until action has commenced. And it's essential to hold your fire till you get a clear signal. That's all. Good luck now."

As he moved away their cheery voices echoed his good wishes. Joe turned to Commiskey.

"All set?"

"Yeh. Everything O.K."

"The lorries are waiting over the hill for the getaway."

"Right."

"And good luck."

Turning quickly Commiskey followed the others. There would be no compromising friendliness. Joe smiled.

He had reached the edge of the clearing when he heard Anna's voice.

"Joe!"

Curious he had forgotten! She stood a little way off, fastening her rucksack, her lips parted slightly, her eyes tender.

"Well, it's come at last."

"Aren't you excited?"

"A little."

"Afraid?"

"A little."

"I'll say a prayer."

"Thanks."

They looked at one another for a moment. Again he remembered the image of something gentle and wild, poised on the brink of flight. She smiled a little. He turned away.

It was hard going, the upward climb. Soon his breath was coming in quick jerky gasps and, for the first time, he began to feel the effect of the long strain. He smiled wryly to himself, as he slipped and slithered on banks of rotting pine needles, remembering how pleasant it had been coming down. On hands and knees he dragged himself up the sandbank, and half tumbled over the fence. Once clear of the trees he could see the road again. . . .

The convoy had moved only a few miles.

The relief of finding that his timing hadn't been crazy was momentary. His agitation returned as the convoy crept nearer. He wondered if the men were in position. He had arranged that they work in pairs. Courage was so much a matter of showing off. He longed to be with them, but that was impossible. He wondered, too, as an afterthought, what the feelings of the convoy might be. Was their lumbering movement merely part of the traditional drill? How would they react under fire? It occurred to him, and the thought was troubling, that they too, each one of them, were capable of infinite suffering and infinite bewilderment.

The convoy rounded the hillock opposite the herd's house, about a mile and a half away. Time to change his position! He must see the impact of the first action and be within reach of the Second Section.

His course was slightly downhill and he made good progress. The path by the fence, rough but sure, afforded excellent cover. The Second Section was under MacCormack's command and, as Joe plunged through the undergrowth, he smiled at the thought of Skinner's pompous efforts to give an impression of composure. It was comforting though that in action MacCormack was unexpectedly ubiquitous, and utterly fearless.

The Volunteers had done their work well. A tree-trunk found itself deposited, as if it were by accident, across the road. Beyond this there was no sign of activity. As he gazed on the peaceful panorama of craggy mountain and wooded valley Joe could not help but shudder to think that the serenity would be so soon, and so violently, shattered.

The convoy breasted the hill a few hundred yards away and came trundling down the jagged road at reasonably good speed. Four of the escort were travelling in front. They would be the first to see the tree-trunk. It would be obscured—fortunately—until the last moment by a twist of the road. Joe's pulses quickened.

The first of the escort rounded the bend. With a harsh grating of brakes they skidded to a standstill. Their actions, as expected, were automatic. Turning in their saddles and shouting, the soldiers waved the convoy to a halt. There was commotion then, shouts and counter-shouts, dispute and explanation. Bewilderment begot confusion and confusion begot fear. Joe smiled. It was almost as though he rehearsed it. The lorry-drivers were remaining in their seats. That he could only have hoped for. The others were dismounting, gathering in groups, arguing. A few had taken their guns and stood, as it were, on guard peering into the undergrowth. But there was no stir from the Volunteers and the rhododendrons were innocent as prayer. Gradually the excitement diminished. Joe smiled again, a little smugly. They had decided to move the tree-trunk.

The bulk of the soldiers stood around shouting advice to the hardy souls who tackled the job. They appeared oblivious of danger, and interested only in seeing a job well done. It was a matter of seconds before the tree-trunk was dragged aside.

Even Joe was startled by the first volley. It shook the valley with a thunder-like boom that echoed from mountain to mountain. A second ear-splitting detonation followed. Within seconds the road was deserted. Now was the moment of doubt! The drivers were still in the lorries . . . For what seemed like an age Joe held his breath. . . . Another resounding burst . . . A moment later, in obedience to his will, he heard the faltering purr of an engine.

The exhilaration of success gave him new surety as he raced through the trees. With the Second Section he could play a more active part. Glancing back, after a further burst of fire, he saw that the lorries had made a slow getaway. But—and this he had not bargained for—two of the escort had followed suit. Joe's dismay was short-lived. This was the hazard that gave relish!

Now on a level with the bridge Joe could identify the positions of the various groups lying in ambush. But there was no movement. Flattening himself behind a boulder he eased out his gun, released the safety-catch and cocked the hammer. Looking up he was startled to see Sonny Coughlan racing across the marshy waste between the bridges. Crazy! Time and again he was warned!

The depleted convoy came steadily on at fair speed. The leading lorry bumped over the first bridge and turned. The second, lurching perilously, followed suit. The two motor-cyclists were almost across when the whole countryside was shaken by a deafening boom. Momentarily paralysed by blast, Joe took a little time to realise that Coughlan had blown the bridges prematurely. His plan now would require drastic alteration. The lorries were islanded between two bridges. How to get them away? A little shy laneway further along might be the solution. It meant replanning the escape route!

Through the cloud of dust he blundered down the hill. The lorries jolted to a halt thirty yards from the bridge. Joe took a risk coming into the open but, when the dust cleared, his action would be covered by the Volunteers. Besides, once in action, life took on a new rhythm where Reason was not so essential, and success was always more sure. About five yards from the first lorry he jumped on to the road bank, in position to cover both drivers.

"Get your hands up. Quick."

He could hear, further down, the bewildered shouts of the Volunteers. The air still was thick with dust.

With hands half raised the driver of the first lorry, a heavily built man, emerged from his cab. He had a gun in his holster.

"All right. Drop that gun."

Difficult to keep both lorries covered!

The lorry-driver lowered one hand, pulled the gun, dropped it on the roadway.

"Now turn around."

The second driver, low-sized and sullen-faced, moved more slowly. He chose to get out by the opposite door, which put Joe on the alert. Joe edged into position and put on first pressure. When he appeared again the driver had a gun in his hand. Without bothering to enquire, Joe squeezed. It was neat. The bullet pierced the center of the forehead. The man looked surprised and pained. He staggered a little before he fell.

Joe never knew whether the sound of the shot or the shock of seeing his comrade dead roused the other. He whirled round, made a wild rush, and drove a heavy fist at Joe's head. The blow was easily averted but the impact of the great bulk sent Joe sprawling on the mudguard. Huge hands gripped his throat and he felt the thumbs digging deep. Bulging eyes glared down, with the intensity of madness. The huge claws shook him viciously, crashing his head against the bonnet and gripping his throat again.

Bringing his knee up sharply Joe drove it into the other's crotch. The quick yelp told him that his effort had effect. The hands relaxed. Twisting sharply Joe brought the butt of his gun down on the big fellow's head. The blow, with the weight of his shoulder behind it, had little value. A well-aimed and unexpected left sent Joe flying. He still had the gun and, as he fell, he aimed haphazardly and fired. The driver had grabbed a gun too and when a second shot rang out Joe felt a twinge. He fired again, without effect. He saw the big fellow steadying his aim. In terror and desperation Joe rolled on his belly and flattened. Another shot rang out. Joe stayed still. He felt no pain. Skinner's voice broke the silence.

"Are you all right, Joe?"

MacCormack's gun was still smoking. The lorry-driver's body stretched half across the road.

"Yeh, I'm all right. Thanks, by the way, for saving my life."

Even Skinner had lost his complacency. His face was hard, his eyes frightened.

"Jeez, Joe, we're bunched. Coughlan panicked. The second lorry is out of commission. And them bloody bangs were heard in Drumcondra. We'll have the whole Free State Army out here in no time."

"That's all right. We'll manage."

"Manage? What are we goin' to manage? The second lorry's outa commission, I tell you. How are we goin' to get the stuff outa here with both bridges down?"

The Volunteers had straggled down from their positions and stood in uncertain groups along the roadway.

"How about moving the stuff from the second to the first lorry? Could she bear the load?"

"Don't know." MacCormack paused speculatively, then darted away.

"Bedammit I think it could, Joe. Bedammit I think it could."

He was away again.

"There's room all right, Joe. There's room sure enough. Will we chance it?"

"Have to be quick."

"Leave it to me, Joe. Leave it to me."

MacCormack was like a child. The Volunteers too, after the disheartening debacle, were eager for action. Skinner's good-humoured badinage soon had them moving.

"Come on, you sons of bitches. Get them boxes out— and quick. Form a line can't you. Crowley! You get in that lorry. Ryan, get in the other! Now, start shiftin'. Get the rhythm of it, men. Get the rhythm."

There was little he could do till the ammunition was transferred; so Joe took the opportunity to survey the scene. Both actions had taken place in fantastically short time, and the pale light had scarcely brightened into morning. An occasional bird, flying high, was the only sign of life. The roadway was a picture of chaos: earth, stones, heather and peat. He could still hear an occasional rattle of fire from up the valley. Across the vast plain below, the city stretched vaguely to the north. In the blind light of afterdawn it seemed like a great lethargic animal; but Joe knew how abruptly it could change.

126

"How's it goin'?"

"Not bad! Come on! Put some life into it, men!"

In the excitement Joe had been only half-conscious of his wound; a sudden jab reminded him. Removing his coat and jacket he let them slip to the ground. A flesh wound! As though in answer to his need Anna came hurrying from the trees.

"You all right, Joe?"

"Yeh, sure. Tear a bit off the sleeve and tie this thing up. It's only a scratch."

"Darling, you're wounded."

"Please! Don't make a drama. Get the bandage on."

"Let me clean it first."

"All right. But make it fast. What's new?"

"The explosions were heard in the city and Jack Lysaght reports two police cars passing through Terenure to Rathfarnham." She spoke quickly, but apparently without any idea of the import of her news. "He thinks they're headed this way . . ."

Joe didn't wait. Grabbing his coat he ran to MacCormack, shouting.

"All right, Skinner. That's enough. The Guards are on their way." He turned to the Volunteers. "Two lorries across the hill. Get over quick as you can. Take the road to Ballybrack and drive like the hammers of hell. Crowley, you get up to the First Section and tell them to retreat. Skinner! Anna! Come with me."

Before he finished the Volunteers had grabbed their rifles and were racing towards the woods. Anna made for the lorry.

"How the hell do we get outa here?" Skinner asked.

"There's a boreen down among the trees. Leads to the Tallaght Road. If we get on to that we're away."

"Jeez Joe, you're a genius."

"Come on. Jump in. You'll have to drive. My arm is a bit wonky."

MacCormack gripped the jamb of the door and jumped smartly. Joe hurried to the other side.

The lorry started easily and rolled down the hill. Through the binoculars Joe could see the police cars racing through Edmunstown, little more than a mile away.

"Careful, Skinner. Just here. Turn to the left. Turn to the left, man."

As they jolted under the trees Joe glanced back. The Volunteers had disappeared, dissolved among the trees as if by magic, leaving the road strangely lonely. Among the rocks and stones and tufts of grass the bodies of the two soldiers were lying where they fell. There was something ugly, incongruous—almost outrageous—about the untidiness. Further away was the other lorry. It too was strangely alien.

With MacCormack driving in lyrical fashion, the lorry jolted down the leafy laneway. Skinner seemed already drunk with the delights of victory.

"She'll be comin' down the mountain
When she comes.
She'll be bringin' sweet new rifles
When she comes.
She'll have arms and ammunition
For the ending of Partition
She'll have arms and ammunition
When she comes."

Far away Joe heard the sound of the police sirens. They screeched to a crescendo, then abruptly died.

He looked at MacCormack.

"I'm goin' to need a drink after this."

12

A Hair of the Dog

The Hotel Universe never made up its mind whether it was a refuge for transients, a home for old ladies, or a residential hotel. A terrace of Victorian houses, purchased for a vast sum, it had been ruthlessly mutilated, and disguised inside and out with obscene brown paint. Dermot Walshe and Joe Corcoran lived at the Universe. It had desirable features so far as they were concerned, not the least of which were the eight separate stairways leading to eight separate exits.

The Universe served breakfast in your room, virtually, though after a somewhat quaint fashion. In the region of eight o'clock the telephone rang and a flowery voice informed the guest that his tray was waiting. Rising drowsily he felt his way to the door and, miracle of miracles, it was true. The breakfast call was a device invented by "Lady Jenny" to keep the maids from the occasion of sin, but it suited Joe. He liked breakfast in bed; it enabled him to outlive the more shameful phases of a hangover.

His awakening on the day after the ambush was agonising. He had been sleeping on his right side and the pain was troublesome. His head, too, was throbbing, and seemed divided into several circular sections all separated one from the other and from his body. His eyelids, as was not unusual, appeared to be glued in position. But it wasn't the pain that troubled him most. It was the blackout! He had no idea how or when he got back to his room.

The thing was to try gathering the threads; start at the beginning, and one thing would lead to another. There had been a party, down the country somewhere; Anna was there, and Skinner. Memories of cattle running loose slithered through his mind; a bright-lit, smoke-filled bar, herds of drunken farmers lurching . . . Then somewhere else in a car: fast-moving, lights blazing, rushing and stopping; the talk was loud and doors banged . . .

It mightn't be so bad but for the apprehension! Terrors ordinarily laughed away enlarged now to nightmare horror. He talked too much maybe, insulted Anna, behaved obscenely in some way. In the whirling void of bewilderment the wildest speculation tightened to near certainty. His forehead was clammy and his breath came in gasps. He tried hard to still his brain, to freeze away the frenzy. But it wasn't any good. His mind went racing wildly, creating new conjectures, each one more horrifying. Fear that he had said or done something outrageous grew and magnified till all other thought was submissive. A quick chill rippled his body, leaving him trembling. . . . It was hopeless trying. . . .

The breakfast call should come soon. That'd give him a clue, tell him the time anyway. . . . In the whirlpool of images and abstractions one thought was dominant, the unshakable resolution never to touch it again. Every unhappiness he had known could be accounted for by that fatal addiction: impetuous actions that led to tragedy, friends insulted, deterioration of mind, and the pretensions that had lately become a habit. He had no desire for leadership—he lacked the character—but after a few drinks he was capable of any affectation. In his new role he would exploit his real nature, a kindly unobtrusive man; establish a reputation for charity.

If he could confine himself to wine it wouldn't be so bad. How pleasant to exchange the furtive ruthlessness of Revolution for the cheerful good-fellowship of the bon vivant . . . become a connoisseur . . . His presence would be coveted at dinner parties where belief in the gracious form of life had not entirely disappeared. . . . He would not, of course, flaunt his knowledge. If requested he might give an opinion, a little diffidently, concerning Chateaux and vintages. And the other guests would make acknowledgement.

To avoid the raucous friendliness of the public house was important! Guzzling whiskey in an effort to obliterate reality was the declaration of despair. Might be possible, of course, to have an occasional apéritif. No! He knew there could be (literally) no half measures. He must give it up. He must prove to himself and to others that he could be rigid, that no temptation of circumstance or environment could alter his resolution. . . . In the shadows he saw a dark figure standing apart, remote and unsmiling. . . .

The painful pressure of a full bladder had become uncomfortable, making it imperative that he embark on the perilous journey to the washbasin. Grunting wheezily he raised himself on an elbow, slipped one foot and then the other on to the floor, and with a further wheezy effort succeeded in reaching a sitting position. His reactions were

131

bleary and the light dim, but Joe could see that his clothes were scattered haphazardly, and that two chairs were lying in positions which could not be considered appropriate. With his fists down-pressed on the edge of the bed he slowly raised himself. Again he waited, distrustful, till the surges receded.

Joe was not surprised to find himself dressed only in his shirt (other hangovers made that acceptable), but when he tried groping forward he was disturbed to discover that he had small control over his limbs—that, in fact, he was still drunk. In someone else the gentle wavering zigzag would have been funny, but Joe didn't feel like laughing. When he succeeded eventually in reaching the washbasin he opened his eyes as wide as was prudent and peered in the mirror. The vision was not prepossessing, a haggard, ghost-like, grey, aged countenance. There was a gash on his forehead and the lower part of his face was splotched with blood. Again, it was the absence of explanation that was most disquieting.

The washbasin had not been placed in a position suitable to the purpose, and Joe found difficulty in establishing a convenient relationship. Despite the blackout Joe remembered in detail the events of the ambush and appreciated that the victory celebration was responsible for his present condition. In to-day's perspective the triumphs of yesterday were not so overwhelming. Optimism, he decided ruefully, was not so much a matter of success as a condition of health. He had an uneasy consciousness that once more his weakness was endangering the Movement. Had he been found yesterday by the police he would have been in no condition to prove an alibi. Joe tried telling himself it didn't matter, that a drunk can always slither out. But he couldn't somehow convince even himself.

He turned from the washbasin and stood a while savouring the relaxation. He was wondering if a libation of plain water would be too diabolically imprudent when the telephone rang. He fumbled across the room.

"Hello. Who's speaking?"

"Harry. This is Harry. Skinner MacCormack."

"Hello Harry. What the hell happened?"

"How d'you mean?"

"Last night. Did you take me home?"

"Take you home? I was ringing to find if you took me home."

"What was I like? Was I bad?"

"Not at all, man. In great form. A little lyrical, maybe."

"I didn't say anything, did I?"

"Not at all. Perfect gentleman."

"What happened to Anna?"

"She went off early."

"By herself?"

"Yeh."

"Oh hell! I hope she didn't mind."

"No. She was worried about you, that's all. I told her I'd look after you. Eh, did you see the papers?"

"No. What are they like?"

"Banner headlines."

"Fine. Better not talk."

"Great success. The whole country's in a panic. Policemen everywhere. We'll have to lie low for a while. You should see the headlines. Smashin'."

"By the way, what time is it?"

"Goin' on for six."

"Morning or evening?"

"What do you mean? Evening of course."

"Hell! I've only just woken up."

"Ha, ha! That's a good one." Harry chuckled delightedly.

"Why don't you give Dermot a tinkle? See if he's in. He probably has the papers. Might know how you got home too."

"That's an idea. What are you doin' later on?"

"Nothin' much."

"See you in Kelly's in an hour."

"Right. I could do with a drink."

"*You* could! *I've* a mouth on me like the bottom of a birdcage."

Joe put down the telephone and stood a while, leaning against a chair, looking vaguely around. His tongue was like a sponge, a dry sponge, a great big rough dry sponge, very dry. A drink of water would only set him off again. Porter was *imperative*. One luscious pint would send the blood circulating, irrigate the barren waterless sandy wastes. It wasn't that he was weakening. It was medicine.

Should he contact Dermot? Skinner's analysis was cheering but, of course, entirely unreliable. Dermot was shrewd, might throw some light on the blackout too. His tacit disapproval of Joe's drinking was embarrassing, but what the hell! He'd chance it.

Dermot was at his desk when Joe knocked. He had taken no part in the seizure and was not anticipating arrest; but it was his nature never to be surprised.

"Who's there?"

"Joe."

"O.K."

He rose leisurely and strolled to the door.

"Come in. Come in, Joe. Glad to see you."

"Hiya."

Joe had learned how deceptively healthy it was possible to look after a hot bath and a shave. He had polished his shoes too and his hair was tidy. The shirt in which he had slept had been replaced by something less abused, but he was still wearing yesterday's tweeds, and though it was evident that he had tried to remove the bloodstains it was equally evident that he had not entirely succeeded.

Joe had effected a transformation but in comparison with Walshe he was still an untidy eccentric. Dermot dressed well. His dark well-cut suit, stiff white collar and conservative tie were typical both of his profession and character.

"Sit down, Joe." He indicated an armchair by the fire. "Well, that was a great job yesterday."

"Thanks. I haven't seen the papers, what are they like?"

"Magnificent. Like a drink?"

"No thanks." Some inner compulsion prevented acceptance.

"How do you feel to-day?" Dermot's scrutiny was embarrassing.

"Not too good."

"You were in a bad way last night."

"Really?"

"I'll say." Dermot laughed lightly. "Yeah. Mrs. Jenkins knocked at the door early this morning, about two o'clock I think it was, in a shocking state. 'Come out quick, Mr. Walshe. I think he's dead.'" Dermot resorted to one of his braying laughs. "I slipped on a dressing-gown and went after her down the corridor. It was terribly funny! You were lying on the landing, your feet halfway up the stairs and your face in a pool of blood." His flesh was shuddering again. "I found your hat on the landing above and your coat on the landing below."

It was an amusing picture. Joe was glad to be able to laugh.

"That sounds healthy. What did you do?"

135

"Oh, there wasn't much trouble. Once I got you standing up it was easy. The only thing you wanted out of life was somewhere to pee."

"I see." Joe stood up. "I was wounded during the action, just a flesh wound, but you know how much blood you can lose. It was foolish to drink at all. Takes so little to knock you out when you're like that."

It was ludicrous. Discussion of his hangover seemed to take precedence over the national reaction to the ambush. Joe wandered idly to the bookcase and glanced at the titles.

"So you think the ambush was a success?"

"Oh yes, magnificent. Absolutely magnificent. Without doubt the most effective action so far." Dermot got up and went to the sideboard. Joe watched as he searched for the gin. He seemed to have difficulty in finding the tonic too—and the opener. "It has been particularly effective in giving international publicity to the Partition issue. That in itself is a tremendous achievement. Of course," he added as he returned, "there are some unpredictable elements. But on the whole it was magnificent. You're sure you won't join me?"

"Quite sure."

"The newspapers are a joy. Front-page inch-high head-lines. A sensation of this kind always catches the national imagination." He fetched a glass from the sideboard and a few slices of lemon. "It'll do a tremendous amount in re-storing morale within the Movement and, most important of all, it helps to build up our supplies. What are the guns like, by the way?"

"No idea. We had to get them dumped quick as possible when things started going haywire."

"Yes I know. Of course." Walshe was sitting again. He had the glass in his hand and kept raising it to his lips and moving it away. The blue-tinged sparkling liquid was vaguely hypnotic.

"Yes," Dermot was saying; "it's going to get respect for the Movement both inside Republican circles and outside. They can no longer regard us as undisciplined terrorists. Yesterday's operation proved that we are an effective fighting force."

"That's something."

Dermot paused to relish the flavour.

"It should have a good effect too on our recruiting campaigns, that is if we are still able to recruit. As I say it's the sort of action that appeals to young men, and of course it's the young men we want."

The glass was still having its mesmeric effect, but Joe detected something too casual in the facile flow.

"What do you mean, '*If we're still able to recruit*'?"

"Well, you know. That's possibly taking it from the most pessimistic point of view. The Government is using this 'outrage' as they call it to rush through the Coercion Act. It's being debated in the Dail at the moment. If they succeed it means we go underground. As you know, Habeas Corpus is suspended by the Coercion Act, which means that Volunteers can be arrested on suspicion. That won't be funny."

"I quite agree."

Walshe had risen, swallowed the remainder of his drink, rather unexpectedly, and was fussing around again with the bottle. He kept on talking.

"It's regrettable in a way that we were up against the Army and that there was so much loss of life. I shouldn't have wished to antagonise the Army." He poured a generous measure and topped it with the tonic. Joe was hoping he might be asked again, but the thought never apparently occurred to Dermot. He sat down by the desk, fixed his gaze firmly on Joe and gave a repeat performance of the mesmeric ritual.

"Trial by jury is suspended under the Coercion Act. The Government is setting up Military Courts. There is only one sentence—death. After yesterday's episode we can hardly expect much sympathy from the Army." He sipped his drink.

Joe did not reply. Dermot held his glass on a level with his eyes and stared fixedly at the breaking bubbles. "Unfortunate, so much loss of life. The Government is playing it up. *Tragic loss of life. Atrocity of this dastardly murder.* You know the stuff. Yes, unfortunate."

"So you think we were unwise?"

"Oh no. Not at all. I think the whole thing was magnificent. My only point is that if we are going to reap the benefits we must try to anticipate what reprisals the Government will take. Personally, for instance, I think it's most unwise for you to be seen around the city. There's bound to be a roundup."

"Don't worry. I can take care of myself. Well, thanks for everything." He moved to the door. "See you soon."

"Now look, Joe," Walshe rose hurriedly. "I don't want you to get me wrong. My only point is that we must expect and be prepared—"

Joe closed the door quietly. It was a deliberate rudeness, inevitably hurtful, which he regretted, but could not control. Dermot doubtless thought his realistic analysis had provoked the discourtesy. He was wrong. Joe just couldn't bear the sight of him guzzling gin any longer.

He turned to the right down the first staircase. The clock in Dermot's room said quarter to seven. Time for a gargle before Skinner arrived! Difficult to know what to have! Smithwicks and lime was good. A jorum of whiskey could be adjacent—the hair of the dog. But no. No. What he needed was a long drink, cool. A fill-up. Stout's too heavy, porter too thin. Mix them together, they're sweet as sin. Begod that's poetry, that is.

He sidled across to the window on the lower landing. As well to make sure before venturing out. More or less deserted! A white-bearded, hump-backed man edging along the footpath: a whore plying her trade: a bevy of neighbours in a pool of light. Innocent enough! Just to be safe he'd slip out the back and round by the alley.

It was a fine brisk evening, the air sharp. He regretted not bringing his coat. But there was scarcely any wind.

Joe agreed with Walshe's disenchanted analysis. The ambush had not been the unqualified success that Skinner would like to believe. Walshe's attitude was possibly over-pessimistic, but that was preferable to MacCormack's brand of optimism. Joe reproached himself for not having anticipated more accurately the effects of the seizure. He had concentrated too much on the success of the action to the neglect of its aftermath.

The laneway emerged at the corner of Kelly's. Joe slipped in the side entrance. His quick scrutiny was reassuring. He was the only customer! Ordinarily he selected his position with care but to-night he decided to be reckless, and sit on a high stool by the bar. There was a mirror backing the shelves. That should help.

"A fill-up."

The barman selected a pint glass and, without acknowledgement of Joe's condition, initiated the solemn ceremony. . . . Joe was happy to be back in Kelly's. It was a restful unpretentious pub. He liked the subdued lighting and the sawdust. He enjoyed watching the tall, lean, ascetic-looking barman; and he liked speculating what esoteric philosophy he might propound if he could be provoked into abandoning his monumental silence. He was a good crafts-

139

man. His pull was deliberate and purposeful. He glided slowly from tap to tap balancing the flow of froth and liquid. He let the pint lie then a while, until the overflowing froth had settled, before placing it on the counter.

He was stretching out his hand to take the drink when he saw the barman's brightening eyes. . . . Joe looked in the mirror. Four men were standing behind. One of them, the little fellow, had a gun in his hand.

"Are you comin' quietly, Mister, or d'you want us to beat the head offa you?"

13

A Change Is As Good As a Rest

It wasn't a cell. It was more like a high-ceilinged room, little bigger than the average drawing-room. There was a small square window high in the wall, opposite the hatch. The least expected feature was the double strip of fluorescent light that gave the intense daylight effect, killing shadow and seeming to filter into every corner. Even the space beneath the camp bed was denied its secret. There was neither chair nor table.

Joe's first reaction was one of relief, the illogical relief a businessman feels on boarding a liner. He had left behind a host of troubles, and no matter how much he might wish otherwise, he was no longer able to cope. There was the hope that, by the time he returned, they would have resolved themselves—or diminished. A lunatic on admission to a mental home gives a similar response. But unlike the lunatic or the businessman Joe knew that, as a prisoner, he would face a new set of problems.

He lay full length on the bed, his hand pillowed under his head. . . . The police hadn't sufficient information to prefer a charge or, if they had—the witnesses to support it. The Minister was probably engaged on a little slick anticipatory work—presuming the passage of the Coercion Act, and dragging him in for questioning in the hope that he might be able to prefer a charge later. His Excellency's police had a certain etiquette with regard to the proper accompaniment to an interrogation and had achieved a refinement in quick replies. McGuirk was all right, but that bastard Lehane would enjoy turning a knife in your guts.

The thought of Horgan was bothersome. It came sneaking into his mind at the most treacherous times, trailing a whirlwind host of phantasies, leaving tremors of self-accusation. Uncertainty was the root of his distress, uncertainty that stemmed from the impossibility of gauging Horgan's sincerity. It was possible that Horgan had engineered his arrest. If, on the other hand, he was sincere in his protestations he should facilitate his release. Again Joe felt the quiver of fear. Before he fell asleep he decided that whatever else happened he would on no account look to Horgan for help.

It took him a while after he awoke to overcome the surprise. He felt uneasy. The lights were still on, and there was the deathly stillness. He glanced up at the window, still curtained in darkness. . . . He lay quietly, listening. There was no stirring. A minute of watchful suspense assured him, despite his uneasiness, that there was no new danger. His vigilant anticipation had been instinctive. . . .

It had been foolish to sleep without a covering. Joe had all the aftereffects of a restless night, constriction, sweaty irritation, and utter exhaustion. His neck and feet appeared to have swollen. . . . He loosened his tie, dragged his feet from his shoes, and lay quiet again, listening. . . . Still there was nothing.

He looked at the ceiling, letting his eyes travel from corner to corner. Were they watching? His body was cold. He slipped on his shoes again and tumbled out of bed. . . . Walk quietly round. . . . And have a look at the walls. He moved cautiously, the tentative steps of a sick man. No sign! Didn't mean it wasn't there. Could be hidden up between the strips. His mouth was parched and his tongue swollen. He moistened his lips—and swallowed. . . . Distressing not knowing how long he'd been out!

It wasn't fair to leave him without even a drink of water. It occurred to him that they'd maybe forgotten. Stupid enough for anything . . . That kind of treatment was illegal. By what law and by what authority should they leave him indefinitely in solitary confinement? There was no justification. By what law and by what authority was he precluded from a reasonable amount of fresh air?

Joe went to the door. He knocked firmly—and listened. There was no sound.

"I say!" he called. "Is there anybody there?"

Still no sound. He knocked again, harder, and raised his voice.

"Is there anybody there?"

He pounded with his fists.

"Let me out of here! I want to get out, d'you hear? I want to get out!"

He was screaming now, pounding with his fists and kicking. The door seemed to absorb and diffuse the sound. He took off his shoes and banged on the jamb.

"Let me out of here, you lot of bastards! By Christ, when I get out of here I'll get my own back! Let me out of here!"

143

It was terrifying, the isolation, the sense of being cut off in the midst of a city, of being ignored, neglected, entirely forgotten. He rushed to the centre of the room. With the aid of the bed he could climb to the window, smash the glass and scream. Poised on the brink of decision, he sensed another presence. . . .

He whirled round.

MacGuirk was quietly closing the door.

"What's wrong, boy? Are you all right?"

Joe was taken aback.

"What d'you mean leaving me here without even a drink of water? Suppose I wanted to go to the jacks, what do I do? Hell, you can't treat people like that. That's not bloody fair." His voice was noisy, but the whiney note deprived it of conviction. "When I get out of here I'll get my own back on you, you pack of bastards."

"There now, there now. You're worryin' yourself over nothin'." MacGuirk had a red baby face and little eyes that seemed surprised. His voice was soothing, even sad. "Sure I left you a bottle of stout myself in the hatch. Didn't you get it?" He strolled to the hatch, looked inside and giggled. "Heh, heh! There it is right enough!" He came back smiling, the bottle in one hand and the glass in the other. "Sit down, boy, sit down. There's no sense in askin' your legs for support when a bed'll do it for you. Come on, boy."

Joe hesitated, then shuffled to the bed. MacGuirk plodded behind.

"How long was I asleep?"

"Asleep? How long were you asleep? Wait now till I see. What time is it now? He dug into a waistcoat pocket and came back with a diminutive watch. Nearly nine o'clock. You came in about half-seven, wha'?"

"I suppose so."

"You did! Ah shur, you musta been asleep nearly the half-

144

hour." MacGuirk towered overhead. He had tilted the glass and was pouring the stout. "Ah I'd say that. Nearly half-an-hour I'd say. There now, drink that down, it'll do you good."

Joe's hand was trembling. "Thanks." He gulped half the glass.

"Ah, you needed that. I say you needed that."

MacGuirk was gentling him like a baby. It was disturbing.

"A nice lot of bastards! Pulling me in with a drink in my hand. At least you might've let me finish it."

"I know, I know." MacGuirk chuckled. "Shur I know. That's what I was thinkin'. And afterwards I says to Paddy, 'Why didn't you let him have the drink? He looked like he needed it, poor divil. Why didn't you?' But *you* know Paddy Lehane as well as me. Decent man. None better. But he's got the kink. You know what I mean. He's got the kink."

"The kink?"

It was difficult. Joe was thinking about Horgan. He tried keeping a half-ear open just in case, but he didn't want to know too much about Lehane.

"What kink?"

Horgan was an enigma. In the old days he was easy-going. Hanging around after rehearsals waiting for what the sky would drop. Nothing he liked better than slipping into a snug for a bottle of stout. Now Joe was beginning to wonder if the hail-fellow-well-met was a blind. It wasn't a nice thought . . .

"Ah you know, the kink. On account of the brother, Jack Lehane, that was killed in the Trouble. You knew Jack didn't you?"

"No."

"Oh, a decent man, Jack. Beat him up first, before they done him in. Paddy's been tryin' ever since to get his own

145

back. Comical character. He'd walk a mile to get a chance to beat the tar outa someone. And you should see him with the childer. Shur he's a model, man, a model!"

"Is that so?"

He had been suppressing the thought of Horgan and the uncertainties his name evoked, and that suppression was stupid. He had probably been hoping that time would resolve the situation, but he realised now that the insecurity in his mind, caused by those uncertainties, had had a weakening effect on his decisions—and accounted, to an extent, for his drinking.

"The same torture is a wonder. Glory be to God, man, there isn't a beast in the jungle 'ud behave like human bein's when it comes to it. Funny! A man is a sight more kind to his dog than he is to his neighbour. D'you know that? And another thing! They make out that a cat playin' with a mouse is shockin'. Now! I agree, *but;* a cat playin' with a mouse is in the ha'penny place to the Bishops and Cardinals when they had their fling. Am I right? I say am I right?"

"I daresay."

"Roastin' and burnin', boilin' and bastin', tearin' them asunder and floggin' them to bits. An' the gadgets! The rack an' the wheel, the stocks an' the pillory, the cat-o'-nine-tails an' the stake for burnin'. You'd wonder how they worked them out, an' who put up the readies. Shur if they put only half the energy into sayin' their prayers the world 'ud be a better place. Am I right, Joe? I say am I right?"

"You're right."

Subconsciously, Joe felt, he had been exaggerating his guilt. His motive in having Coughlan arrested was undoubtedly not altruistic. Anna *had* asked him to see that Sonny didn't get in trouble. It was the means he used that were dubious—but then, of course, he had given the information when he was drunk. Once more he was reminded that everything he had done wrong in his life had been done after too many jars. . . .

". . . That's what I think about Paddy. He's a little fellow—d'you know? Always tryin' to be bigger than he is. It gives him a great kick when he gets some fellow twice his size rollin' on the ground highsterical. . . ."

Horgan was maybe telling the truth when he disclaimed responsibility for Clancy and MacNamee. But there was always the other, the frightening possibility, that Horgan was a subtle trickster who had betrayed his friendship. . . . Joe was pleased to have forced a showdown with his conscience. His evasion had not been mere cowardice. Experience had taught him the wisdom of allowing an uncertain issue to hover in the background in the hope that it would find its own solution; but he knew too how paralysing was the effect of unresolved issues, and how tempting it was to submerge truth in alcohol. Either the uncertainties became diffused or they must eventually be challenged. . . . Another thing about Horgan. He was always swearing eternal friendship and begging Joe, if ever he wanted help, to call on him. Curious he hadn't sent a warning! Hadn't even bothered to come down. If all his declarations were true he could only be pleased by the ambush; though of course he might be annoyed that he was the source of information. Either Horgan was or was not a hypocrite. . . . Having enjoyed the showdown with his conscience the thought of a showdown with Charlie was becoming more acceptable.

"Where's Horgan?"

"Who?"

"Charlie Horgan."

"The Inspector?"

"Yeah."

"Oh, the Inspector's down in Cork."

"Cork? What's he doing there?"

"What's he doin'? Shur he spends more time down there than up here. Whatever kind of a galoot took over his job must have a head on him like a turnip. Shur he can't go to the lavatory without the Inspector holdin' his hand! He has the poor man forever runnin' up an' down."

"That's as good a yarn as any. The two of them will be scuttered for the week, I suppose."

"Who? You mean the Inspector? Inspector Horgan? Are you in earnest! Shur he never touches it."

"He never touches what?"

"Never touches it."

"Ah go to God!"

"True Bill! They tell me in the oul' days he'd drink it out of a hoor's boot, but that's a while ago now." MacGuirk turned away and lumbered off towards the door. "I'm afraid Joe I'll have to be runnin'. They'll be after me blood."

"Just one thing."

"Yeah?"

"You won't be talking to Horgan on the phone to-night by any chance, will you?"

"To the Inspector?"

"Yeah."

"Talkin' to him on the phone. Well yes, I might. Right enough I might. Why?"

"You might give him my regards."

"Give him your regards. I'll do that. I'll do that Joe."

When he had gone Joe lay back on the bed. Horgan was an enigma. For a confirmed drunk to get a reputation for temperance was the achievement of genius. Too fantastic almost to be credible.

Joe was strangely pleased that Horgan was in Cork. He got up from the bed and paced around the room. There were too many inexplicable features in Horgan and his hirelings.

148

Joe glanced at the hatch. He remembered that MacGuirk had taken the bottle of stout from there. He remembered too that a few moments before, in searching for the spyhole, he had glanced into the hatch, and it had been empty. A small point, but it left him with an uncomfortable feeling.

14

Hughie Commiskey

Sonny Coughlan had butterflies in his tum, but he was not unhappy. He was glad of the long walk up the hill.

Sonny was pleased to be given another job. It meant that, despite the ambush incident, he had returned to favour. Sonny had explained to Dermot that his behaviour was not prompted by cowardice, that the arrival of the lorries accompanied by part of the escort had not been foreseen. He had tried to "cope" by disposing of the escort. In the excitement, it was true, he didn't realise that the lorries would be isolated but, after all, good old Joe took care of that. Walshe had been decent. He accepted the explanation, advised him not to worry, that nobody doubted his motives, and that in the circumstances a little hysteria was forgivable. Dermot had been decent but the others were still disinclined to be friendly. In fact, had he not been entrusted with this new assignment he would have had no alternative but to resign.

It was a lovely afternoon, the sky blue-grey, the sun reflected in pools of ice on the roadway; but the slight wind was sharp. Sonny enjoyed inhaling deeply the cold air, gave him a feeling of well-being. He was in good time, so he walked slowly. That too was enjoyable, enabled him to study the trees, the huge boulders on the wasteland opposite, and the small clouds that drifted occasionally across the sky.

Sonny resolved that his attitude to Commiskey would be one of undemonstrative subservience. He felt sorry for Hughie, forsaken by his cruel wife and left to survive in squalor. He wished so much he could do something to help. At the top of the hill he paused. The roadway was empty. Hughie had probably chosen that time of day when there would be few cars about, and fewer pedestrians. The walls were in poor repair—lots of footholds—so he had no trouble. He jumped down easily on to the mossy bank. Only a few yards away was the footbridge. He hurried across. There was no sign of Hughie. He whistled three times, and waited.

Commiskey's underground "hidey-hole" was concealed among the moss and rocks in the centre of the rath. He had almost completed his work when he heard the whistles. He was pleased, but he didn't smile. He continued parcelling the box. It was typical that he liked to think of people waiting, and could calculate to a nicety the lapse of time before he need appear.

Commiskey's face was tight, more by habit than necessity. During the War of Independence he had worked for a time in the engineering section and had become fascinated by the intricacies of infernal machines. He relished the meticulous craftsmanship, the delicacy of timing, and the final violence. Hughie had enjoyed his day's work, and he looked forward to the session with Coughlan. He liked

Sonny. The others had agreed that Sonny was an enemy agent, but that didn't influence his feeling. Though he lived in squalor Hughie was neat. He had procured an unused piece of brown paper, and he parcelled the box carefully, then tied it neatly with fresh string. When finished the package looked as though it had just been purchased. Hughie was content. He put the bottles back on their shelves, the soldering iron and tools in a drawer, and the spare pieces of wire on the rubbish heap. There was nothing left on the table but the neat parcel. He held it to his ear. No sound.

Hughie climbed the stone steps at the end of the shelter. On the platform at the back was an improvised periscope. A quick panoramic survey! Yes, everything clear! Coughlan was standing by the footbridge staring at the river. Hughie released the catch: a slight drag and the huge stone rolled aside. He squeezed through. The stone rolled back of its own accord.

Commiskey's abrupt arrival surprised Coughlan. Half-running, half-walking, he hurried across.

"No difficulty getting here?"

"No."

"Good. Good. You weren't followed?"

"Don't think so. I was the only one on the bus at the terminus."

"That's fine. Come with me. I want you to step from stone to stone like me. It's a bit tiresome but you get used to it."

Sonny hadn't the same animal agility but without too much loss of face he managed to follow in the steps of the master.

The afternoon sun slanting through the leaves gave an air of enchantment to the fairy rath. Sonny was charmed by the sense of wonder and mystery: the druidic circle of

152

stones, the mossy hillocks, and the sweet perfume of decaying leaves. He was especially happy to find Hughie in an amiable mood. Near the centre of the fort they halted.

"Notice anything?"

"How do you mean?"

"I want you to look round carefully. Notice anything unusual?"

Sonny was bewildered, but like a good Volunteer he did as he was told.

"No—I—I can't see anything."

"You're sure?"

"Certain."

Hughie didn't condescend to smile, but his eyes brightened. He bent down among the rocks, eased his fingers between two boulders, and pressed. The stone rolled smoothly back.

"Follow me."

Commiskey squeezed through.

"Oh boy! This is wonderful." Sonny followed more slowly. "How did you manage to build it?"

"You're the only one has ever been here. See those wires? Ordinarily when I go out I put them in position. Anyone forcin' an entrance'll be blown to bits."

Sonny was overwhelmed. In trusting him, where he had never trusted anyone before, Commiskey paid him the highest compliment. The dugout was sturdily built. There was a minimum of furniture: a worktable, some shelves, a cupboard, a chair and a bed. Sonny observed that the bed had no legs. It was supported at each corner by large cylindrical tins, loudly labelled "DYNAMITE." He wondered if they were full, but didn't like to ask. At the far end was a tiny door.

"That leads to the tunnel."

"Oh!"

"Yeh. An underground tunnel from the house."

Commiskey was putting on his coat. He slipped his hand in his pocket, took out a Luger Parabellum and checked it.

"You take care of that," he said, pointing to the parcel.

Sonny was stretching for the parcel when he turned.

"I haven't got a gun. Do you think will I need one?"

Commiskey thought for a moment.

"No! No, you won't need one."

The car, a ramshackle Austin Seven, was parked in a byroad.

"It has a good engine," Hughie announced. "By the way, have you got a watch?"

"Yeh."

"What time do you make it?"

"Exactly fifteen minutes past."

"Yeh, that's right. That's exactly right. O.K. Let's go."

Sonny's body was small and slight, but he found the Austin cramped. His knees were hunched up nearly to his chin. The springs in the seat had long given up any semblance of resistance, and a jumble of tools on the floor added their share of discomfort. The parcel balanced precariously on his lap.

"Be careful of that. Keep it clean if you can."

Commiskey drove as he lived, with a nice disregard for the rules. It was uncomfortable, but Sonny was not unhappy. The implacable diehard, whose reputation for taciturnity was nationwide, had entrusted him with secrets never before revealed. It was an honour.

Sonny was astonished at the speed they climbed the hills. Before long the high walls of the estates and the little walls of the small farms were far behind. Pine had replaced sycamore and withered gorse replaced pine. As they topped

Kinsallah Mountain the first shrouds of mist swept forward, and when it cleared again, they saw the rugged desolation of Cloonmore Valley stretching far ahead—a bleak barren treeless landscape. A stray sod of turf, fallen from a mighty rick, jolted the car. Commiskey laughed, but Sonny found the unchanging speed wearisome. The parcel was still in his lap, but that jolt had been awkward.

"What time is it?"

"Half past."

"I make it twenty-nine minutes past."

"Yes, you're right. Twenty-nine minutes past is right."

"Good."

The hill beyond Cloonmore was almost perpendicular, but the impetus of the downsweep carried them halfway up. Away to the east the grey-green valley, wide and deep, stretched bleakly to the sea. When the mist shifted, Sonny spied a casual cottage, far down, humble in its loneliness, and wondered what extreme of madness enabled anyone to endure that dismal splendour. He was trying to follow the line of the river when suddenly the mist crowded down and the valley was no more. On the other side was a lake, dark and brooding. Momentarily veiling the harsh cliff-face the mist swept down the mountain and crawled over the dark water.

The car didn't slow overmuch before they topped Drumany. Sonny was surprised again to note that within a half-hour of the city it was possible to reach so forlorn a wasteland: no walls, no fields, no trees; nothing within sight but an infinity of bog, sweeping slowly into cloud. There was small sign of life: a whirr of wings, a distant curlew call, an occasional ragged sheep crouched in a ditch.

On the level road the car gathered speed. Sonny wondered idly where they were going. Commiskey gave no hint and Sonny wouldn't like to be indiscreet. Down Wicklow way it would seem. For ten miles they would come on no sign of human habitation; but about five miles away, so far as he knew, was Drumany Gap, a centre of windy desolation where the road forked away to Wicklow, Wexford, and Kildare. They jounced over another bridge. Again Coughlan had difficulty in keeping hold of the parcel. He wondered what it could be, but it really wouldn't be nice to ask. A rabbit sprang from the side and raced in front of the car. Hughie took up the chase.

"Rabbit for dinner to-day!"

"Mind! Be careful! Don't run over him!"

"Why not?"

The rabbit swerved from side to side but kept to the road. Commiskey pursued relentlessly. He waited till it was within inches before he sounded the horn.

"Touché!"

Coughlan looked back. The tiny body lay still on the road, its head crushed.

"You didn't have to do that."

"No. I know. But think of the trouble I saved the poor bastard."

"What do you mean?"

"He's dead, isn't he?"

Sonny tried to laugh. But he wasn't amused.

"He wasn't doing anybody any harm. And maybe he liked being alive."

"Do *you* like being alive?"

"Of course. Don't you?"

"No!"

During the pause they stared into the mist. A raw wind rustled Sonny's hair. He tried closing the window. His arm and shoulder were stiff. And his ear was sore.

"If you feel like that why don't you commit suicide?"

"I haven't the courage. I haven't the courage to put my

156

head in a gas oven or swallow prussic acid. But, in a way, I am committing suicide."

"What do you mean?"

"Everybody"—Commiskey spoke slowly—"everybody on the Executive invites death."

"That's a new one."

"It's true but. Each and every member of the Executive is seeking death."

"Don't be ridiculous! I'm not!"

"I wonder. People sometimes, without knowing, want to die."

"Oh for goodness' sake don't be so silly!" Sonny never dreamed he'd be so outspoken; but he was irritated and almost angered with Hughie for claiming anything so outrageous. Really! Hughie'd say anything for effect.

They rocketed past a gaunt gash in the hillside, where hardy heroes of another era had quarried for rock. Silhouetted against the sky the giant turf-ricks had a sombre fascination—something eternal and primeval in their savage form. Sonny wondered vaguely who it was could own the turf and when they came to claim it. It seemed so much part of the spectral mountain it must be the work of wraithlike creatures emerging after darkfall. And when the mist came down it seemed that the wraiths were angered. Without warning it curled and whirled from behind the ricks, down the mountain and out of the sky. And it didn't come alone; it brought in its wake a heavy raincloud, thrashing pitilessly.

"Of course you're like the rest. Afraid to take them off."

"What?"

"The blinkers."

"What are you talking about?"

"Afraid to look and think, look objectively, use your reason."

"Nothing of the sort."

157

"Ah yes. Yes. Reality is too stark. Easier find a drug. Like religion. Right enough the clergy is the great exploiters. They know. They know the worthlessness, so they get you by promisin' a Paradise hereafter. It's canny. And if religion is wearin' thin you can always find another. Another drug. Another lie. Anythin' to escape."

"Escape what?"

"The reality."

"What reality? What are you talking about?"

"The reality of suffering, the fact that when you look without fear on the world there's nothin' but evil, nothin' but suffering, nothin' but pain. When we talk of good, son, we talk in relative terms. D'you folly? Good is a lessenin' of pain, that's all. The so-called pleasure of eating is the lessenin' of a craving. Love, a polite word for lust, is the satisfaction of a hunger. That's all. Man knows nothin' of joy, only degrees of pain."

Whether serious or not it was obvious, despite his denial of joyful existence, that Hughie was enjoying himself thoroughly. Sonny was certain that the Church had an answer to the points made and, given time, he would remember. But he wouldn't spoil Hughie's fun.

"Take the idea of Hell. We understand an eternity of pain—that's easy. But Paradise, Heaven, or whatever you're havin' is a joke. Not even the priests with their lovely faculty for spinnin' yarns can paint a decent picture of Paradise. The idea of oul' fellas and oul' ones with wings sailin' from cloud to cloud, playin' harps, is just funny, that's all. Just funny. Of course, the answer is simple. We can't picture Paradise because we never begin to know what happiness is. Simple! Our little dream at best is the same again—an absence of pain." Commiskey made it sound plausible, but Sonny felt certain he was shooting a line. He decided to get a word in.

"That's all very well, but most people I know quite enjoy life, think it's worth while. And, after all, so long as they think so, it *is* worth while."

"Most people don't think at all." Hughie's enthusiasm receded into deliberate bitterness. "Most people are animals. The life force is strong. The greedy grasp for survival is strong enough to ignore the suffering, the pain, and the evil. It's laughable the way people are codded. Even what we think of as 'beautiful' is designed to perpetuate pain. But in his heart every man knows the truth—that if children were the result of an act of reason rather than lust there'd be no survival. Aye. An' he knows too that the only Paradise he'll ever find is the escape from pain that comes with death."

They turned to the left at Drumany Cross and hurtled down to Carberry. The desolate plain cowered under the downpour. Deep roadside pools screamed and scattered as they plunged. A whirling mountain cross-wind staggered the car and lashed the windscreen.

"Surely you don't disbelieve in God?"

"I dunno. I don't know." His voice was strangely sad. "I've thought about God and tried to be fair. Maybe He likes lookin' at suffering. Maybe there's a reason, a reason we've yet to learn. Or maybe God, as we think of Him, is not All-powerful. I dunno. I don't know."

It was obvious tht Hughie was half-serious. Of course Sonny realised that such ideas were unbalanced and the product of a diseased mind. In a more amenable situation he might be tempted to cross swords with the old warrior, but just now he had no inclination.

"If you feel like that I don't blame you wanting to kill yourself."

"That's another thing." Commiskey maintained his melancholy calm. "Church and State, the priest and the politician, loathe a suicide. Why? Because he makes a truth public, he shouts out loud the open secret, that life's a liability. The priest, who murmurs of Christ's charity, will refuse him Christian burial. And the law loathes him too. A madman and a coward! The weaker the argument the louder they roar. Funny! If the suicide is unsuccessful they're even angrier. Instead of comforting his affliction they torture him in prison for lack of skill. Surely if a man has no other right, surely he has the right to do what he wants with his own life."

"Oh no. Not at all. His life belongs to the community. Man has duties as well as rights, you know."

Commiskey didn't appear to have heard. He looked at his watch again.

"What time do you make it now?"

"Nine minutes to."

"Nine minutes to. That's correct. Yes, that's exactly right."

Abruptly as it had begun the rain ceased; and the wind died. The change caught Sonny unawares. Commiskey's monotone and the mesmeric rattle of rain had been so stupefying that he had come to accept them as inescapable. Now, under a whitening sky, he saw the mountain mist dissolve. Proudly the earth emerged from its travail, and the sun smiled on the reawakening. Halfway to the heavens a fearless skylark carolled his praise. Even Hughie appeared to find relief in the resuscitation. At least his driving became less hysterical.

Beyond Carberry the road twisted and crawled, climbed a little and plunged again. In the trough of the first canyon a white-whirling stream spluttered under a tiny bridge. They had barely topped the hillock when Hughie braked and the car slithered to a stop.

"This is where we get out."

"Right. Where do we go from here?"

160

"All in good time."

It was pleasant to crunch the sand underfoot and inhale the fragrant air. The reeds by the roadside quivered gently, seeming ashamed to shake away the raindrops. Hughie looked back up the road, then slowly turned to scan the panorama.

"You see that building down there?"

"Where?"

"Down the hill. Near the lake."

The ramshackle place?"

"Yeh. It's a ruin. Used to be a herd's house, but it's not used any more. You're to take the parcel down there. A man will be waiting. You're to give it to him."

"What do I do then?"

"What do you do then? You come back here, of course."

"You'll be waiting for me?"

"Yes—I'll be waiting for you."

Sonny paused to think, but there didn't seem to be anything to say.

"O.K. I'll be seeing you."

Sonny looked a little silly as he moved away. He kept to the middle of the road, which was inappropriate for so puny a person. Against the background of harsh cliff and bleak bog he appeared so frail as to be almost negligible. For a while it seemed that he lost himself behind a hillock; but he appeared again, after a while, smaller and punier than before. Hughie watched patiently. Far away a sheep bleated and, in answer to its cry, the beginnings of a rainbow arched the sky. When Sonny had crossed the second bridge Commiskey went back to the car. He was opening the door when he heard the explosion.

It had been neatly timed.

15

Horgan's Hypothesis

He was lying down when Lehane came in. He didn't get up or turn around. MacGuirk, he thought, and the thought was not exhilarating! In the past few days MacGuirk had slithered in three or four times, smiling his good-natured smile. Mostly he stood beaming down, but sometimes, when he seemed to be consoling, he'd squat on his hunkers. . . . Lehane didn't speak. He stood inside the door, waiting. Joe was quiet too, expecting the high-pitched sing-song. The silence made him turn. Lehane was holding open the door, his face impassive.

"Come on."

This was the moment Joe feared, but after four days' solitary his mind was clear. Lehane too was tense. The stillness of the tiny body was an effort, and the controlled voice betrayed suppression.

"To the right."

The corridor was dark. Joe's brogues clattered on stone. Lehane padded behind.

"Up them stairs."

Joe determined to resist. After all, it wasn't the first time a Volunteer had to prove himself. The more physical he made the conflict the more expeditious would be the outcome. . . . There was a further corridor at the top. Joe marched on, his footsteps clanging on stone, echoing from roof to stairway. Halfway down the passage a chink of light edged under a door.

"Out o' the way." Lehane pushed past. "Here he is, Inspector."

It was a big, brightly lit office. At the far end, silhouetted against an outsize window, Charlie Horgan was poised behind a desk.

"All right. You wait outside." There was something different about Charlie, and it wasn't only the well-cut suit or the sleek hair. "Hello, Joe. I see you've been getting yourself in trouble." Joe ignored the outstretched hand. "Sit down. There. In that chair. It's comfortable."

Joe remained standing.

Horgan ambled back. Joe had braced himself for questioning. Now he diverted his resources into anger.

"You're a fine friend all right!"

"What've I done now, Joe?"

" 'If ever you're in trouble remember Charlie Horgan. A friend in need.' I suppose you've forgotten you ever said that or where you said it. It was in Kelly's. No, I don't think you forgot, because that's where you sent the G-Men."

"I'm sorry, Joe, I dunno what you're talkin' about. I never sent any G-Men."

"All right. Maybe you didn't. But you knew I was goin' to be pulled. Can you deny it?"

"I'm not denying anything."

163

"Admit it! You knew I was goin' to be pulled."

"So what?"

"You admit you knew but you wouldn't gimme the tip-off. 'If ever you're in trouble remember Charlie Horgan.' Oh, a hell of a friend you turned out to be."

With hands joined across his little paunch Horgan sat back complacently.

"Don't you think, Joe, that you'd be better off if you sat down? You're doin' yourself no good gettin' into a lather."

"You might at least have given me the tip-off."

"Friendship, of course, is two-sided. Isn't it now?"

"What do you mean?"

"Well, it wasn't very nice to take advantage of the information I gave you about the arms shipment. That wasn't exactly friendly."

Joe was confused.

"The arms shipment? What's that got to do with it? What harm did that do you?"

"It was my responsibility—"

"And another thing. What was all the blather about sympathy? Sure the way you were talkin' I thought you were ready to hand over the Government. What are you groanin' about now?"

"I could have lost my job."

"Your job. That's all you think about, keepin' your belly full. What about the country? Did it never strike you that you've a duty to the country?"

"Occasionally."

"But you take damn good care to turn a deaf ear, don't you? Oh, I know your kind, the little family man with his stake in the country. Yeh, it'd be shockin' to lose your job! Nothin' matters so long as the little nest in Wolsley Estate isn't upset. There's a gapin' wound in the body of the Nation, but that means bugger-all so long as the Missus has

164

her imitation fur coat and the childer their four square meals."

His voice was high-pitched, a tremulous whine he couldn't seem to control. It was good to let off steam; a pity though he didn't speak with more conviction.

"Take it easy, Joe. We won't get anywhere by shouting."

" 'Take it easy, take it easy.' That's the slogan should be written over Government House to-day. Build more factories. Establish more industries. Employ more Civil Servants. Make them fat and flabby so that the profiteers and the bureaucrats'll chorus in their sleep: 'Take it easy, take it easy.' Wouldn't it be a terrible thing if the voice of the dead was heard above the chorus, terrible if the soul of the people was revealed again still demanding fulfilment, demanding that all obstacles in the path of our country's destiny be cast aside. My God, isn't it tragic."

Joe's body seemed to crumple. He leaned forward resting the palms of his hands on the desk, then slowly eased down into the chair.

"Isn't it tragic. The betrayal. To think that men who fought in the Insurrection, that men inspired by the poets should set up a Satellite State still tied to Britain—that they should allow their brothers in the North to suffer on in servitude. What a transformation—that men who were prepared to die for the ideals I hold to-day are ready to kill me now because I still maintain those ideals."

Joe's body slumped. It was so melodramatic it was shameful. He hoped the Inspector wasn't too penetrative.

During the long tirade Horgan stayed quiet. Now that Joe had paused, he leaned forward, his hands still joined. A gentle smile played around his lips.

"That's all very eloquent Joe, very eloquent. But of course it's founded on no basis of reality. You will remember I told you that the Government was anxious as you to end Partition. And you will remember, too, that you agreed that we should work together to that end. In those circumstances, leaving aside the question of friendship, it wasn't very proper to use the information I gave you about the arms shipment without advising me of that fact."

"When did I agree? I never agreed to anything."

"When Lehane and MacGuirk brought you up to my place I suggested that we work together, and you agreed. Do you deny it?"

"I never agreed to anything. Did you seriously think that I'd be willing to sell the Movement to a crowd of British hirelings? If I agreed to anything it was only in the hope of getting information. Does that shock you?"

"Not exactly. It simply means, if I may put it that way, that you are willing to betray your friends to attain your ends."

"It means that I am ready to be as ruthless as my enemies. This country was held in subjection by laws made to maintain a ruthless conquest. To undo that conquest it is necessary that we too must be ruthless. Our enemies have the power, the money and the armaments. We come into the battle with bare hands." Joe had adjusted to the situation. The hysterical note was gone. He was on firmer ground now. "We need feel no guilt in using cunning and deceit to attain our ends, because we know that right is on our side, and to champion that right we have to be ruthless."

"Then all your talk about friendship was, shall we say, a little unreal." Horgan got up slowly, put his hands in his pockets, and wandered around the chair. With his back to Joe he stood looking out the window. "I'm very interested to hear you state your point of view. There's one thing I want to ask you, but. You claim the right to be ruthless. Do you allow a similar right to others who wish to achieve the same object by different means?"

166

"Certainly." Joe would have wished to feel as dogmatic as he sounded.

"Good. Good. I'm glad of that."

Peculiar to see Horgan all dressed up in his Sunday best. The suit, a kind of blue serge, had two natty vents. It was disquieting too, the change of personality: made Charlie seem remote, and so pompous.

"Yes, your theories are interesting. They are in line with most revolutionary thought. The underdog must be an opportunist; he must be ruthless in the use of assassination, and he must be cunning in the propagation of lies. Sounds horrifying when we say it in cold blood. Yes, Joe, I'm glad you have the intelligence to face reality. And I'm glad you're sufficiently civilised to allow that others with the same ideals have an equal right to be ruthless." He paused as he turned. "You do say that, don't you?"

"That's right."

Charlie was pleased.

"There must be something wonderful in this country to justify the suffering caused in bringing about her liberation. Tragic, isn't it, that our history should be one long story of misgovernment: massacres, famines, persecutions. One wonders how the country survived without producing a nation of manic-depressives. Maybe that's what it has produced! Maybe the willingness to sacrifice their lives is the subconscious death-wish of a broken people."

With hands clasped behind, Horgan paced slowly back and forth. Mostly his head was bent forward seeking on the floor for inspiration, but he paused occasionally, and the ceiling became the object of interest.

"It's magnificent, though, that through those centuries there were always a few young men ready to assert our sovereignty—and to answer for that assertion with their lives. In no other country has there been an Insurrection so

167

truly wonderful as that of Easter Week. The martyrdom of the poets had something of the mystic beauty of Christ's Sacrifice. Only a poet or a saint could have the vision to realise that the blood-sacrifice would awaken the conscience of the Nation, that from that gesture would come so lovely a flowering of national consciousness. But after the Rising the poets were dead! It was as well, perhaps. It's as well they didn't live to see the beauty of their sacrifice made a mockery by the horror of Civil War. If the Insurrection united the nation in one magnificent effort the Civil War threw it back into chaos. The morale of the people was destroyed. Their faith in themselves and their leaders disappeared, and they retreated to the protection of an apathetic cynicism. It doesn't matter who caused it, or why! It was a crime, a terrible crime."

Joe was willing to grant that Charlie had unexpected eloquence. What surprised him was the delicacy of his sentiment and its expression. It was so unlike Charlie it must be phoney.

"Do you agree, Joe, that it was a crime?"

"Yeh. A crime on the part of the compromisers that signed the Treaty."

"I think it was just a crime, Joe. But let's not argue. The men who threw down their guns and took up the reins of Government, whether of one party or another, were faced with a tough job—the rule of an apathetic and divided people. These men had fought in the Rising. They and their colleagues—of both parties—still had the same ideal, to make Ireland a United Republic. But they had known bloodshed—and they no longer believed in it. Besides, a situation had been created in which the shedding of blood was no longer necessary. They determined to fight on for the old ideal in a less glamorous way—by the drudgery of constitutional method."

168

The novelty of Charlie Horgan as professor of history was wearing thin, but Joe had no temptation to interrupt. Charlie's thesis was tendentious. It would be easy to point out that two successive Governments had done nothing either to restore morale or undo Partition. But what the hell! The anti-climax of Joe's anticipations had been a shock: and he hadn't yet found his balance. His opening attack had, of course, been a diversion, helped him to find composure; but he still needed to get things in focus. Charlie's oration wasn't for purposes of self-glorification. He wouldn't waste all that rhetoric. Joe must anticipate his direction.

"Now how does your band of terrorists fit into that background? Just as every dog has his fleas, every great movement has its imitators—the second-rate men—without the genius to be original, but with too much vanity to know they *are* second-rate. In the eyes of the Government your movement was the aftermath, the vibration of the echo: a huddle of crazy cranks and young extremists cashing in on the traditional adulation of the rebel. You'd never do anything constructive, because you had neither the genius, the integrity, nor the ability. Instead of ending Partition you'd help to perpetuate it. But because you had the sympathy of the Army you were a threat. Young soldiers weren't sure whether their allegiance belonged to the Government or to your nest of gun-slingers."

A steely core, suggestive of inner tension, had crept in. Charlie threatened to be dangerous.

"Now what did the Government do? Believe it or not they sent for me."

Joe sat back and searched his pockets. He didn't look at Horgan, but glanced round and at the ceiling. The thing was to half-listen, try thinking of something else, ignore the leaden weight of dread. He must deflect even his own at-

169

tention from the prickly sweat and the quickening pulse.

"As I saw it there were two alternatives, collaboration or extermination. Either we must find a formula whereby the Government and the Movement could work together, or we must create a situation in which it would be possible to destroy the Movement without antagonising the country. It was made clear that your organisation was utterly ruthless, and that if I was to succeed I must be equally so. Now Joe, I'm going to put a certain *hypothesis* to you, and this is where it begins. Imagine me in a situation like that. What am I to do?"

Charlie rested a pudgy thumb on the desk. His jacket was open and the trouser zip wasn't quite in order. With the plastered hair he looked more bald, Charlie did. His head was too big. His forehead was too big. His pudgy body was too big for his too-small legs. He had let himself go to seed, Charlie had.

"The only person on the Executive I knew really well was yourself. Now let us suppose that, as I saw it, the first thing to do was to provoke your organisation into conflict with the Army. How was I to achieve this? I could waylay you in one of your haunts, pretend to be drunk like yourself, and let fall some information about a fake arms shipment. Let us assume, Joe, that you swallow the bait, and that, at a later meeting the same night, I lead you into believing that you've extracted further information, in fact that you've secured all the necessary details for a successful seizure of arms."

The shapeless terror that hovered distantly was crowding forward. The dread he feared to name, the terror too frightening to define was shaping. From this nightmare there would be no awakening. It couldn't be that the wisp of mist had become a cloud, the gossamer a net, that the hint of a suspicion was becoming an overwhelming certainty.

"Let us suppose, Joe, that luck is on my side and that, for your own good reasons, you give me certain information: and that in taking advantage of that information we are led to the discovery of a pirate radio station and succeed in bumping off the new-found Leader of the Movement. As a result of this gentleman's demise you are elected Leader. And your first claim to glory is to ambush the arms shipment. In this, of course, you are playing into my hands. The shipment is composed of dud rifles and dud ammunition—which we are able, without difficulty, to recapture almost immediately. Four young soldiers are killed. But so far as I am concerned the ambush succeeds. The country is shocked, a proper atmosphere is created for the introduction of the People's Protection Act. Four young soldiers are killed, which means that a barrier of antagonism is set up between your Movement and the Army—which also means that we are enabled to set up Military Tribunals to deal with crimes of political violence, and that we have the co-operation of the Army in determining that the only possible verdicts shall be acquittal or death."

He was being watched for the telltale flicker. If Horgan's oration was more than hypothesis the Movement was doomed. Ghastly that he fitted so easily into the long line of patriot dupes. Joe was afraid to raise his eyes, afraid the despairing paralysis would show. Horgan's smooth control and affectation of kindliness would seem to suggest that he was not talking hypothetically. But there was the possibility that the thing was a bluff. The silence was uncomfortable.

"So you recovered the arms shipment?"

"Yes." Horgan smiled. "Ah, sure that wasn't much of job. One of the first places we looked was down in Paddy Glennon's. I believe Paddy put on a great show of innocence. The oul' training, you know. They had a bit of trouble finding it

171

too. It was clever the way he had the lorry and all hid in the barn, under the hay. An oul' trick, of course."

Horgan pressed the bell.

"And now, Joe, I don't wish to detain you. I know you'll want to think things over. I hope you won't think too badly of me, Joe. After all it was a fair fight, and I wasn't any more ruthless than you. But there's one thing I want to say. The offer is still open. The offer of collaboration, I mean. We still have the same objective, you know. And I don't see why two people with the same objective must destroy one another. We'll support you with money, and we'll give you all the arms you want. But every action must be worked out in collaboration. It's an ideal arrangement."

The door opened and Joe knew without looking that Lehane had come in. Horgan came from behind the desk and held out his hand.

"Well, that's all, Joe. I hope there's no bad feeling. Let's hope we're able to work out something together. I'd like that a lot. Now that we understand one another."

Joe stood up. His body was weak. Horgan still was gripping his hand and Joe was embarrassed, embarrassed because he could feel the prickly sweat: and Lehane was looking. He must get back to the cell. He must have time, time to examine in peace Horgan's horrifying hypothesis. He must concentrate his energy. It could be a bluff. He turned away. Lehane was holding open the door.

"I'll have a chat with you to-morrow," Horgan said.

16

You'll Die When You Hear!

He lay on his back on the creaking bed, his fingers joined across his eyes. The room was cold and the light hurtful, but he was not dissatisfied to let time hover indefinitely. The first frenzy had faded in the sleep-weary night. He was calm now, comparatively. The light was troubling. He rolled over, facing in to the wall, and tried again to put the points in order.

However humiliating it might be, he must acknowledge his stupidity. Evasion of guilt had led him into the morass. Fearless self-examination was essential to escape. The initial failing was drink. Horgan caught him off guard in a pub. If ever again he escaped there must be no equivocation, no irresolution. *Drink was out.* Absolutely! In his attitude to Coughlan too he let his feelings intrude disastrously. That wrong must be undone. Vanity was his frailty. He must never again be arrogant either in regard to his own or other people's abilities.

Horgan was shrewd. His contention that the Movement was second-rate had some truth, but could have been as easily said about the War of Independence. Success or failure was the margin between greatness and mediocrity. Joe rolled on his back and put an arm over his eyes. The throbbing was still there. He'd like to get up and wander round, but didn't somehow have the energy. Besides it wouldn't help. Imperative, in the little time available, that he cut through the maze of pain. By concentrating in detail on Horgan's hypothesis it should be possible to estimate the bluff. Didn't seem credible that anyone crude as Charlie was capable of such ingenuity. He was cunning, though. He provoked Joe to proclaim his ruthlessness before revealing that he too had been ruthless. In fact he had blandly encouraged Joe to strip his own defences. What could be subtler? It might be that, hoping to weaken him, Horgan was taking advantage of events to pretend himself cleverer than he was. If the arms had, in fact, been recaptured it would be a pointer, though not a proof.

Almost without being aware of it, Joe sprang lightly from the bed. . . . He couldn't but admire the masterliness, daring, and subtlety of Horgan's deceit—if deceit it was. However much of a surprise packet he might be, it was hard to credit Charlie with subtlety: still more incredible that the collection of yahoos in Government could be capable of such energetic intrigue. They disliked, apparently, having their complacency disturbed. Conscience made fanatics of them all.

He circled the room slowly. There was an unaccountable weightiness in his limbs, and the wound was jabbing. It couldn't be long now before the lock would click, and Lehane would come. He stood by the door, listening. With

174

only uncertainty in mind he couldn't face Horgan! Important not to allow the weight of confusion to paralyse his thought. Inevitably he would outlive this ordeal and look back in peace on his near-despair. He slumped back on the bed. He could ask help from God. But God was so remote and his predicament so immediate.

Charlie must know that collaboration could only be effective if put on a proper basis—a firm agreement between Horgan as agent for the Government and himself as Head of the Executive. His tactics, in stripping Joe of self-respect, were a dubious preliminary to partnership. Horgan was trying to stampede him. Otherwise he would appreciate that such a partnership must at least have a semblance of equality. Horgan, for some reason, was in a hurry.

"Come on. Let's go." The door had opened and Lehane stood fingering the jamb.

"Take it easy, Bright Eyes." Joe levered lazily up. "Well, that was nice. I do enjoy my siesta, don't you?"

"Make it snappy."

"Just a moment." From an inside pocket Joe disengaged a gappy comb. "We shouldn't forget our manners, should we?"

Lehane was silent. Joe tardily smoothed his hair.

"Yes. That's better."

"Come on."

It was a while before his eyes attuned to the gloom; but he marched briskly on, his footsteps echoing cheerily. Lehane prowled behind. Joe had no doubt any more. Basically he knew now that he never had. He would reject Horgan's proposal outright. At no stage had he been, nor would he be, willing to compromise the integrity of the Organisation. Such mistakes as he made were innocent of evil. Whatever wrong he had done would be rectified and the consequences of his stupidity acknowledged—and undone.

175

He must not be led by intrigue to think himself more guilty than he was.

At the end of the corridor he wheeled right.

"Downstairs."

It was not, then, to be the interview. They'd soften him up first with a little treatment. Lehane's big moment! No wonder he itched like a bitch in heat. Interrogation was the word. . . . Joe tripped jauntily down. That the final showdown would not be as yet was a disappointment. But life was like that. He was no sooner acclimatised to one agony than the door opened on another.

"All right. Hold it."

He waited while Lehane struggled with the door. After the gloom of the corridor the sudden glare was startling, almost stunning. But, unless he was much mistaken, unless his eyes were deceiving him, the stocky figure and fat beaming face could belong to none other than *Skinner Mac-Cormack.*

"How're you Joe oul' son? I've sprung you. You're free. Habeas Corpus. And now, if you don't mind," he beamed on Lehane, "may I have the corpse?"

It wasn't easy to believe. He should be crying out, proclaiming to the world that he had shaken off the shackles, surmounted the insurmountable, that he was free once more to shape his fate. Instead he glided down casually into the light. The street was thronged. Could it be true that while he wrestled in agony these people had meandered on oblivious of his pain? He must get to know this world again. It was delightful, so unbelievably buoyant, full of gay, quixotic, never-failing charm.

"Come on Joe, I've got the car." Skinner elbowed through to the Morris. "I've got a corpse," he proclaimed. "I've got a corpse. Shove up there, Dermot, make room for the man."

"Good to see you, Joe." Dermot smiled.

"Thanks."

"Get in, can't you, before they change their minds and ask you back."

"Begod Skinner," Joe settled contentedly, "begod you're a marvel. That's the second time this week you came just in time to save my bacon."

Skinner jerked the door shut.

"Aye, it's becomin' a habit. I'll have to watch that."

Walshe released the clutch and the car glided into the traffic.

"How did you manage it?"

"It's all Dermot's doing." Skinner radiated self-efface-ment. "He bemused the oul' Judge with Government acts and trapeze acts and sexual acts till the poor gom didn't know B from a bull's foot."

Yes, he liked giving credit to Dermot, but of course Skinner knew that he had been primarily responsible. Der-mot knew law, nobody denied that. He was methodical and so on, but when the time came for action Skinner knew all along that he'd have to step in. It wasn't that Dermot hadn't the best intentions, just that he got so stupefied by the dust on the law-books he didn't know in the end where he was heading. A great character for all that.

"It's simple enough," Dermot said. "They put through the Coercion Act. But it isn't retroactive. They had no right to hold you without preferring a charge."

"It's to be signed by the President to-morrow. This, I might have you know, is your final night of freedom. Make the most of it."

"Yes," Dermot concurred. "I'm afraid we must go under-ground."

177

They filtered into the delirious traffic-channel, round Trinity and into Nassau Street. Skinner kept a lookout. Seemed safe enough!

"Where are we for?"

"Anna's place. A few of the boys are there. We thought you'd like a drink."

"I'd give my left tit this minute for a ball of malt."

Only his brightening eyes betrayed Joe's incredulous elation. Sitting back quietly he savoured the joy. The city, with which he was so familiar, had multiplied its charms. The buildings were more graceful, the people more exuberantly uninhibited, the atmosphere gloriously carefree. . . . Skinner was surprised that Joe was subdued—but then, after all, Joe was never one to show his feelings.

"What was it like in there? Did they treat you badly?"

"Oh no. No. Nothing like that."

"You see"—Dermot swerved across the road—"the Christmas Recess is on just now and the Courts aren't sitting. But in a case of Habeas Corpus you can always go to a Judge and demand a Special Court. We went to Smyllie-O'Connor."

They pulled up outside Anna's.

"Tell him about Coughlan," Skinner urged. "Don't forget about Coughlan."

"Wait till we get inside. Go on up. I'll park the car."

"Yeh. Shove it in the lane."

"Think we were tailed?"

"No. Not a chance."

"They might as well wait till to-morrow and do the thing decent."

Skinner rang the bell.

"If I had to climb them stairs often I'd get a bad opinion of myself."

178

Anna opened the door. Her eyes were radiant.

"Joe!"

"Hello, Anna."

"Oh Joe, it's good to see you."

"What's going on?" The barrage from within was alarming.

"I just invited my three hundred best friends to a party, that's all."

The inner door opened.

"Joe! It's Joe! Joe's back!"

They surged into the hallway.

"Good old Joe!"

"Welcome back, Joe."

"We knew they wouldn't hold you long."

"Easy there. Take it easy." Skinner pushed through. "What about a jar? Where's the liquid sustenance?"

Joe ran the shoulder-slapping gauntlet.

"Good old Joe."

"Can't get rid of a bad thing."

Between the members of the Movement and their hangers-on the room was crowded almost to suffocation. The women were of the angular bespectacled type which sprouts on the fringes of the avant-garde. He gathered from the rollicking palaver that the party was well under way. Through the blue haze he spied a liberal gathering of bottles.

"What would you like?" Anna asked.

"A drop of Irish, I think."

"Don't forget to tell him about Coughlan."

"Help yourself, Harry. What would you like, Dermot?"

"Something similar."

Someone, to add to the clamour, switched on the radio and a frolicsome tune tumbled forth.

"Can't hear a word."

"Over here."

Again Joe suffered the ritual shoulder-slapping. He was guided, jerked, dragged, and manoeuvred to the seculsion of an alcove. Skinner followed, bearing aloft, in twin chalices of crystal, two golden libations.

"Here, give us a hand." Dermot adjusted the Chinese screen.

With mock solemnity Skinner presented one large jorum of malt.

"Here, Dermot. Stick that behind your jersey."

"Wait till I tell you. The problem, you see, was which Judge to select. I decided on Smyllie-O'Connor."

"You know him, don't you? Greasy little customer."

"Well, as soon as you'd been inside a few days myself and Skinner went out—"

"—late at night—"

"—to the house in Booterstown."

"Great gas," Skinner laughed. "Your man was in bed half-jarred. Came fumbling down without the false teeth, mumbling through his gums. Couldn't make out a word. Then off back up with him to get them."

"At first, of course, he did the high and mighty—"

"—Jesus yes—"

"—but I had the facts."

Despite the hubbub Anna and Crowley were dancing sedately in and out among the huddles, and Gerry Baker, self-effacing Director of Intelligence, was vainly cajoling a horsey-looking woman into doing likewise.

"Habeas Corpus, as I pointed out, is a very old remedy for the violation of personal liberty. And among other things I let slip that any Judge delaying Habeas Corpus forfeits five hundred pounds to the party aggrieved."

"That did the trick," Skinner chortled.

"At first he was struggling between his reputation for integrity and fear of the Government—"

180

"But when Dermot mentioned the spondulicks it was marvellous. The papers were out, signed and sealed before you could say six-to-four."

"Lovely!" Joe twinkled. "Must've made nice reading."

"Oh, the papers were smashin'."

"Government was livid."

"And the police don't know where they stand."

"That'll all change to-morrow."

"Aye. Enjoy it while we can. Hey, what are you doin' with your glasses empty? Gimme them here."

Skinner gathered the glasses and shouldered back through the crowd. There was nothing he liked more than a party, but that wasn't the only reason for Skinner's elation. During Joe's involuntary retirement he had deputised as Leader, and relished every moment. Responsibility agreed with him, and the dutiful respect of his colleagues stimulated his sense of authority. He wasn't a fool. He appreciated that it was dangerous having a party, but it seemed a fitting climax to his period of leadership: and in less congenial times it might be a sustaining memory.

Gerry Baker, having abandoned his ambitions where the horsey woman was concerned, was doing the honors as barman. Gerry, too, was in rollicking form.

"Three good dollops of Gold Label."

"Comin' up."

That they were about to be forced underground was no deterrent to Skinner's hilarity. He knew all along it wouldn't be easy. It was that sense of realism he had done his best to instil, and that blind belief in face of hopeless odds, which was the essence of his character and had enabled the Organisation to survive.

"There you are."

"What about a drop of water?"

"Shur, there's no water." The sedate Gerry had acquired

a permanent grin and a low-class high-pitched accent. "But I'll tell you what I'll do. I'll water it with another drop of malt. How's that?"

"Fair enough."

Skinner gathered up the drinks.

"Mind your backs, please. Mind your backs."

Three youngsters, with arms entwined, were trying without success to harmonise the "Adeste Fidelis." Their voices, though low, competed adequately with the general uproar.

"Come on, Harry. Make it a quartette."

"No time for singin' until drinkin' time is over. Mind your backs, please!"

"Make way for the man."

Gerry Baker put him in mind again of Coughlan. He must remember.

"All right boys. Grab your drinks."

"Thanks."

"Well, compliments of the season."

"Did you tell him about Coughlan?" Skinner asked.

"No. I forgot."

"I must tell you. You'll die when you hear." Skinner took a quick gulp. "When you were pulled we got thinkin' of one thing or another, and decided there must be a leak. Like you said in Clutcher Keogh's. Someone led the G-Men to the Studio. Someone made a mess of blowin' the bridges, so that the whole ambush was nearly bein' a fiasco."

"And someone gave the G-Men the tip-off where the arms were hidden."

"They got them the followin' day."

"Didn't matter, because anyway the guns were only trash."

"Someone gave them the tip-off where you were hangin' out. As you said yourself they didn't lick the information off the ground."

182

Joe was pale. And his lips quivered. He kept glancing over the room, across at Anna and at the door, as if he were only half-listening. His eyes too were funny.

"Would you like something to eat?" Dermot asked.

"No. I'm all right."

"Are you sure, now?"

"Yeh. Certain."

"Wait till I get you something to sit on." Dermot was off in search of a chair.

"But the funny part is this." Skinner's large lips up-turned, and his moon face bulged with glee. Everythin' pointed to Coughlan. So we decided to rub him out. Wait till I tell you! Wait till you hear!" He found it impossible, almost, to contain the chortles. "The funny thing was that at the inquest oul' Michael Cohen the Solicitor—you know Michael don't you?—Michael got up and accused the G-Men of havin' 'done this poor innocent boy to death.'" Skinner couldn't contain himself. He released the glee in great guffaws. "Wait till I tell you!"

"Here's a chair, Joe. Sit down. Are you all right?"

"I'm O.K."

"You should have seen the hullabaloo. And the papers the next day! 'Slaughter of an Innocent.' I thought I'd burst."

"Did Skinner tell you?" Dermot too was laughing. "They gave him a National Funeral."

"Yeh, Coughlan!"

"Gave Coughlan—"

"A National Funeral!"

"It was the best ever."

"Thousands at it."

"Last Post, Tricolour and all!"

"And when two G-Men appeared in the graveyard the shawlies went for them and stoned them out of the place."

183

"The best part of it all, you'll laugh when you hear, the best part of it, I can't get over it, was that we all had to turn up, with long faces on us—otherwise they'd have copped on that we were involved. D'you see?" the remembrance of the long line of mournful dials tickled his fancy, and Skinner's fat face joggled with joy.

Dermot too was enjoying himself. "It was terribly funny."

Skinner thumped a resounding thigh, and they doubled up.

"Anyone that didn't turn up was suspect. It was a scream!"

Only Joe had lost his sense of humour. His hand enclosed the glass as if about to crush it. And his face was pale.

"Don't keep all the fun to yourself." Anna moved lightly across. "What's the joke?" She linked Joe's arm in hers. "Or am I intruding?"

"Sonny Coughlan's dead." Joe put down his glass.

"Yes, I know. He was a wrong 'un."

"A wrong one? I thought you liked him."

"I was at school with his sister. She asked me to be nice to him. That was all."

The doorbell rasped.

"That'll be Hughie."

"Joe, we're goin' to have a quick meetin' in the dining-room. Anna says it's all right. Just a few minutes."

"O.K."

Commiskey appeared at the door.

"I'd better have a word with the ray of sunshine. See you inside, Joe."

"In a minute."

Skinner took an upstage position by the fire. Commiskey dragged a chair out from the table. The others trailed in gawkishly.

184

"What kind of carry-on is this?" Commiskey demanded. "Having a party! It's a wonder the police aren't in on top of you."

"What's wrong with it?" MacCormack's smile implied that the situation was well in hand. "Seems to me as good a cover as any. Make yourselves comfortable, men. There isn't much room. Joe, oul' son, sit up at the top. I kept the seat warm for you."

"If you don't mind I'd rather you'd carry on for the moment." Joe had lost his old verve. His voice even was tired, almost tearful. "You take the chair, Skinner. I've been out of the picture now for a while and I don't know what's happening."

"O.K., Joe. You just have it whatever way you want."

Skinner was pleased. Joe would see how well he could manage.

"Let's get on with it."

The chairs scraped and creaked. Walshe and Gerry fiddled with papers. Joe leaned forward, elbow on table, his forehead clasped in his palm.

"First of all," Skinner's cough was itself a portentous command, "I'd like to explain, for Joe's sake, that we had an Executive meeting yesterday, and that arrangements were made for the Organisation to go underground. This special meeting of the Military Council has been called at the request of Gerry Baker, Director of Intelligence, who wishes to make a report. O.K., Gerry."

Gerry stood up, still fumbling.

"At the meeting held on the 25th ultimo Mr. Nolan instructed me to prepare a report on the killing of Martin Coyne. It was agreed, at that meeting, that, as soon as we had detailed information, a Court should be held, and that the police officer responsible should be charged with murder."

185

"That's right," Skinner concurred. "I remember."

"As you know, the names of the officers concerned were suppressed at the inquest, but it didn't take long to establish who the killer was. It wasn't quite so easy to obtain evidence. However, recently I was able to increase my contacts in Headquarters, and I can now supply incontrovertible evidence. I have here a microfilm of a secret police report. It leaves no doubt who the killer was, and confirms my original information."

"Good work," Skinner said.

"Who was the killer?"

"Yeh, who was he?"

"The name of the killer of Martin Coyne is *Inspector Charles Horgan*."

"Horgan? That bastard!" Skinner's mouth tightened. "I know that gentleman of an oul' date."

Joe had suddenly straightened and, even in the half-light, Skinner saw that his eyes were alive. He seemed about to speak, but hesitated, averted his eyes, moistened his lips, and turned away.

"What's this about a trial?" Commiskey wanted to know. "Let's not start puttin' on legal airs. We know who done the killin'. The question is—who's goin' to shoot him?"

"Hear, hear."

"Just a moment." In cool consciousness of his position Skinner raised a self-important, all-commanding palm. "Let's not be hasty. There is always in these matters a certain procedure. And even though the situation may be critical we mustn't allow ourselves to be stampeded." He cast a baleful eye on Hughie.

"Balls!"

Skinner chose not to be aware of the whispered muttering.

"We have the minutes here." The pages rustled gravely.

186

"Yes, here we are. This is it, I think. 'It was agreed . . . obtain detailed information . . .' Yes, here it is. 'A Court shall be set up and the particular police officer charged with murder. If found guilty he shall be sentenced to death: and that sentence shall be expeditiously implemented.'"

"That's all me eye," Commiskey cut in. "Things have changed since then. We're only wastin' time. The evidence, as Baker says, is incontrovertible."

"I don't agree." Dermot Walshe spoke quietly. "We mustn't imitate the methods of our enemies. Horgan has a right to a fair trial. He should be brought before a Court and given the opportunity to defend himself."

"Are you mad?" Hughie's eyes widened in mock horror. "Are you stark starin' ravin' crazy?"

"I agree with Dermot." There was an implication of finality in Skinner's affirmation.

"I suppose," Commiskey drawled, "you're goin' to write him a letter askin' him to drop in for a chat?"

"Now look here, Hughie." Skinner was most authoritative. "There's no necessity to be sarcastic. There's no reason whatever why Horgan shouldn't be captured. I'm sure Gerry can give us a detailed account of his movements."

"I can do that."

"An operation of that kind is not at all beyond our capabilities, and might add considerably to our prestige—particularly at a time when the Government is taking the offensive. What d'you say Joe?"

"I'm afraid I don't agree." Joe stood up. Skinner noted that his colour had come back, and his eyes were shining. "From now on we'll be 'on the run.' It might be possible to capture Horgan. The difficulty would be keeping him prisoner. And if he escaped he'd be able to supply the Government with the information they need to cripple us. I think Horgan should be shot, and the job should be done quickly.

Gerry's evidence is more than sufficient. I doubt if Horgan had as much against poor Martin."

"I agree with Joe," Gerry Baker said.

"Very good," MacCormack graciously acquiesced. "That makes it decisive. Now the question is who should we get to do it."

"I wouldn't mind havin' a go," Commiskey volunteered.

"I suggest," Dermot intervened, "that we pick three lads from various parts of the country, completely unknown, bring them to Dublin, and let them do the job in their own time. We'll supply them with all the information they need. As soon as it's over they can fade back to their homes, and nobody'll be the wiser."

"Yeh. Sounds like a good scheme."

"I agree."

"It'll take time."

"What's the hurry?"

"Look." Joe was up again. "I wonder if I might ask something?" He was smiling slightly, and his voice had the old sparkle. It seemed when he leaned forward, his palms resting on the table, as though he were taking them under his wing. "I should regard it as a special favour if you'd let me do this job. I've a few old scores to settle with Horgan and nothing would give me greater pleasure than to put a bullet in his guts. I'm asking this as a very special favour. I know you're not going to refuse me."

17

Pop Goes the Weasel

"I hear the Peelers is rushin' everywhere in motors, draggin' young lads from their beds. Is that true, Joe? Is it true that the city is safe no more and the men of Ireland are headin' for the hills?"

"I wouldn't know. Hurry up, can't you."

"Be easy now Joe. Be easy. The Man that made Time made plenty of it. What class of gun do you want?"

"Enfield '38."

"You have the luck. I got one back an hour ago. Hold on now. Pull the curtains, like a good boy."

Bartley Moore's tenement, over Carney's Cafe in Luton Row, was a dump for local jobs. Bartley's supplies were limited but his room was convenient both for procurement and disposal. Joe peered into the murk. Down across the street, under a smudgy lamp, the hackney was waiting.

Otherwise the bleak expanse was destitute of interest or significance.

"There you are."

"Good man. The blessings of God and His Holy Mother rest on your head this night." He groped for a chair. With feeling hands and fixed monumental head he climbed. "It's up here somewhere." He fumbled behind the pelmet. "I put it there. Less than an hour ago. I could've taken my Bible oath. Less than—Yeh, here she is. Cold as a true-born Sassenach, and every bit as oily."

"I haven't got much time."

Precariously perched, gun in hand, high and mighty on his pedestal, Bartley showed no sign of budging.

"The priests is to blame, Joe. 'Tis they are the canker. Aye! And to think of the noble men that gave their lives for Holy Faith while the bishops caroused at the table of the tyrant! When Paddy Dirrane was an outlaw they hunted him. They did! From the doors of the Church of God! But now he has power they come crawlin' with their litanies. 'Give us this day our daily dues. Forgive us our trespasses that we may excommunicate them that trespass against ye.' Joe! Are you listenin' to me, Joe?"

"I'm listening."

"Three great enemies brought Ireland to her knees. Who were they, Joe?"

"I really couldn't say."

"The priests, the medicine men, and the teachers. All from the one lodge. How many rounds d'you want?"

"Half a dozen. I'll have to hurry."

Bending down he groped again for the chair-back and, foot searching warily, lowered himself slowly.

"Come here to me, Joe. There's your gun. May it bring peace to the dead. Now, take your bullets. Here."

"Thanks."

190

"I want to shake your hand, Joe. Yes! There's the spirit of gladness in you. You have to do a hard joyful thing, and you must do it alone. May the great God guide your bullets straight. And when you're loadin' the gun I'd esteem it a favour if on one cartridge you'd put the name of Bartley."

"Right. I'll have to go now. Good-bye."

"God go with you."

It was a relief to have a closed door between himself and that phoney. Joe could have dealt more harshly with the old man, but he was reluctant to have the evening begin on a sour note. As he came down the hallway, Joe's pace slackened. He paused a moment at the door listening, then eased it open. There was little sign of life. . . .

Joe had effected a transformation. A black suit and dark overcoat replaced the haphazard homespun. His calfskin shoes were gleaming, and his white wing collar was equally impeccable. But the Homburg hat and horn-rimmed glasses were the most effective innovations. They managed to invest him with an air of sobriety. With the change of clothing there had been, Joe perceived, an indefinable change of personality. And when he got the gun in his grip there was another, more emphatic deviation. Until he parted again with that simple, crude, ill-mannered weapon he would never for a moment lose awareness of its bulk. If he returned without using it he would not be happy.

"Well, Paddy, everything all right?"

"No trouble at all."

He heard the first distant moan of a foghorn as he entered the car. It was a good omen.

"Ashton's pub in Clonskea."

"O.K."

Paddy's driving was effortless and the car drifted smoothly

out of the laneways. Sitting at ease, with a chauffeur at his command, gave Joe a nice feeling of well-being. Difficult to credit that only a few days before he had tossed and tumbled on a prison bed. His miraculous release was followed, unhappily, by the revelation that Horgan's hypothesis was no bluff, that Sonny Coughlan had gone innocently to his death: and that he, Joe, could never elude responsibility. It was the nearest thing to a personal panacea when Gerry announced that Horgan was the killer of Martin Coyne. Joe was possessed immediately by an extraordinary exhilaration. His resurgence not only gave him power over his own will and that of his comrades, but appeared to command even the will of the gods. To-night the elements, in the shape of a thickening mist, had joined the conspiracy.

They glided along Stephen's Green East and turned left into Leeson Street. Since the moment of decision Joe's exhilaration had never receded, but as the hour of execution drew near he sensed a growing tension. It was not disturbing. It meant that his nerves were on edge for instant response: and his operation, as a consequence, would be incisive. He didn't have to kill Horgan that night, but he wouldn't rest easy until it was done.

The car soared gently over the canal, drifted smoothly downhill, and curved right. Bartley's plea, that his name be put on a cartridge, was a reminder. . . . Their speed diminished as they neared the crossroads. . . . The mist was thickening. . . . He broke the gun, inspected the chamber and gave it a quick spin. Nicely mannered as a virgin bride!

"One for Martin.

"One for Nolan.

"One for Bartley.

"One for Coughlan.

"One for Skinner.

"One for me."

He replaced the gun and, sitting back at ease, pondered the mutability of circumstance. When last he sped through Ranelagh things were different. With handcuffs on his wrist and two sadistic ghouls for guardians he cowered in terror, never for an instant suspecting the refinement of agony being made ready. He remembered that Ranelagh on that night, coloured by his fear, seemed a place of unquiet apprehension. Peering into the mist he smiled wryly. It hadn't changed.

The audience from Sandford Cinema surged across the road, and the car slowed. Laughing faces, under neon lights, showed up clear and sharp. From Banbridge Road a gentle blending of boys' voices sweetened the bleak air. Carol singers! At some rigid gateway, hymnals in their blue-cold hands, they bundled together, singing praise. The thought of Horgan was obtrusive. Once again Joe tried to encompass the vastness of the betrayal. . . .

"That's Ashton's there. Will I go down?"

"No. Pull in here."

"This all right?"

"Fine."

"Want me to wait?"

"No. I'm O.K. now."

"I don't mind."

"No. Thanks just the same. Better get back. Goin' to be a nasty night."

"It is that. Well, good luck, take care of yourself."

He watched the car glide slowly down into mist. Paddy was staunch, but just as well not encumber him with information. Joe would have wished to exchange a word with Ned Ashton, a decent man; but that pleasure too must be postponed. The lights in the pub were dim. A raucous voice rattled the chill air.

"Now gentlemen, time please! Aw gents, the license!"

193

Variations on the same theme, sung to a different tune, were carried up faintly on the night air from Nick O'Shea's. It was bitterly cold. Pulling his upturned collar close around his throat Joe crossed the road and sauntered down by the Hospital. His spectral breath plumed out before him, floated softly, and dissolved. His left hand, buried deep in his pocket, was cold; but the palm of his right hand, where he clutched the gun, was clammy. As he approached O'Shea's the high-strung after-hour babble became defined. Jack Crowley detached himself, unobtrusively, from a garrulous group. He followed Joe down the laneway, adjacent to the road.

"The bike's chained to the railings."

"Yes, I saw it."

"Here's the key."

"Thanks."

"Just been talkin' to Baker on the phone. Horgan's on his way."

"What time's he expected?"

"Twenty-five minutes."

"Fair enough. Better get back."

"Good luck."

Joe climbed the hill over the bridge and turned right along the laneway by the Foundry. The street light disclosed, in dim outline, a courting couple frozen in deathless ecstasy. The laneway itself was unlighted and, until his eyes became accustomed, he found trouble making his way. The resistant tarmac was no longer there, and his calfskin shoes squelched and splashed in mud and sludgy puddles. He heard from the millpond the flipflop scurry of rats, jumping to safety. They too, unsentimental outlaws, must work under cover. A pale moon reflected uneasily in the still water. Far away he heard again the shuddering, mournful moan of a foghorn, its echo hovering endlessly.

A left-hand intersection brought him out at the opening of Wolsley Avenue. The road was deserted and, as he crossed, the street lamps flicked off, one after the other. He turned left and left again, into the cul-de-sac. The frost on the grass in the gardens shone through the mist. His crepe soles were nicely silent! No. 13 was the only house showing light downstairs. The curtains were wide and, in the garden, a granite bird-bath was revealed in hazy silhouette. A dowdy unsmiling woman was seated by the fire. He continued soundlessly along the path. It curved to the right. He followed the curve to the completion of the semi-circle before he turned, stepped nimbly on to the road, and darted into the trees. The frost on the grass crackled, and the dead wood was tricky. Behind the sturdiest tree he found cover, with a view of the room. He paused to savour the bitter joy.

Joe liked the thought, on this exalted occasion, of not working to a plan. Fluidity was the idea! He could get him as he went up the garden! As he opened the door, maybe? In the darkness the range would be doubtful. He'd let him get inside, but the woman might snarl up the getaway! One window was ajar! Joe had two regrets, that he wouldn't see terror in the eyes that betrayed him, and that Horgan would, probably, never know his killer.

The light in the upper window of No. 17 went out. People all along the Avenue were going to bed. In little houses, all over Ireland, little people were going to bed. He was momentarily assailed by a lonely yearning to share the comfort of the gigantic ant-heap, sink his identity. Vanity was his frailty, urging the necessity to remould the world, blinding him to the truth that he was incapable of reshaping even his own character.

In No. 13 the dowdy unsmiling woman lifted herself out of the chair and stood, indecisive. Joe eased from under the shelter, and balanced on the cement surround. Putting

195

a guard on the fire! She glanced round, returned some scattered books to the shelves, and collected her handbag. The light in the room was out! A light appeared on the landing, and in the hall the light went out. The light on the landing went out: and the house was dark. Joe eased back under cover. If she was awake she could still snarl up the getaway; but her retirement was a simplification.

The last of the bedroom lights went out, and the avenue was silent. A chill breeze shuddered the branches. It was bitter. The cold insinuated around his wrists and closed over all his limbs. He tried opening and shutting his hands and gently stamping his feet.

One of the windows in No. 13 was ajar. Pleasant to surprise Charlie! The thought was daring and delightful. Why hadn't he thought of it before? He stepped nimbly out, crossed to the footpath and moved swiftly along the curve. The gate was open. Quietly he slipped inside and tip-toed up the path. The window was just sufficiently ajar. He groped till he found the iron catch, and manoeuvred it slowly up. The frame creaked sluggishly. Joe's hand trembled, and his heart was pounding. Suppose Horgan returned? He hooshed himself up till he knelt on the sill. A thin varnish of ice encompassed the brick. It cut under his nails, numbing his fingers. Slowly he edged one leg in. His foot touched what felt like a chair. He eased further in till he reached the floor. This was the moment, on the verge of success, when it was so simple to be foolish.

So far so good! He stood motionless by the window, his hand resting on the inside sill. There was no sound! First he must get back his breath, then plan his next step. He blew softly into his hands till his fingers were warm. Between the fireplace and the window was the wing-back chair. Beside it, to the right, was the small table. He tip-toed to the table, took out his gun, cocked it, and put it down, the butt-end lying convenient to the chair. Over the gun he placed his hat. Neat! He was taking off his glasses when the chill wind made him conscious of the window. He tiptoed back, and was sliding it shut when he heard the voices.

Three dim figures rounded the corner, walking briskly. Their laughing voices and loud talk obtruded on the stillness. They paused near the gate. More gabble! It would seem, from the excessive exuberance, that they were neighbours of remote acquaintance, and that the man was telling his funniest story. There were corrective interjections from the woman and obliging giggles. Joe held his breath. Suppose Horgan asked them in? The thought was not pleasant, and Joe was urged to panic. Before he had time the air was rent by an explosion of guffaws, led by the delighted story-teller: and, shouting their gay good-byes, the group broke.

"Don't do anything I wouldn't do."

"Cheery-bye, and if you can't be good be careful."

"Abyssinia."

Joe returned to the chair, made himself comfortable—and waited. He was glad his heart was pounding. Glad of the apprehension. In action he would have repose. Horgan's quick effeminate step resounded sharply. The gate creaked wide. . . . The footsteps faltered. . . . Searching for his key . . . The door opened. Faintly from above a woman's voice was calling.

"I'll be up in a minute," Horgan shouted.

The door of the sitting-room opened. The light switched on.

"How're you, Charlie."

The lower part of Horgan's face became distorted. His chin receded and his lower lip twisted. His face was ashen gray.

"It's all right, Charlie. It's all right. Sorry if I gave you a fright. I had to see you, Charlie. I just had to see you."

"You did give me a bit of a start right enough." Charlie's little laugh was the best he could muster. "I never expected it. You know what I mean."

He stood inside the door, fiddling. Seemed strange to stand like that, incapable. It didn't look comfortable, but he made no effort. In appearance he was little different from the Horgan who argued so ably a few days before about the right to be ruthless. His hair was neatly plastered and the white collar faultless. He didn't seem different except that he looked older, his shoulders sagged, his fingers would keep fiddling, and there was that look of terror in his eyes.

"I know. I'm sorry. I had to see you. It's all right, I'm not carrying." Joe got up and stood with his hands wide above his head. "Search me if you want."

"I'll take your word."

"I had to see you, Charlie. You told me you were goin' to see me, and then the other fellows came. Why didn't you tell me, Charlie? Why didn't you tell me that all the time the lads were tryin' to get me out? If only you'd told me, things would've been different. We could've settled everything there and then. Sure I thought I was goin' to see you in no time. I thought we'd have a chance to talk about things. Why didn't you tell me, Charlie?"

"I didn't know."

Joe was amused to find that, in his rhythm and urgent servility, he was mimicking Horgan's manner—on that other occasion they had met in that room.

"Is it all right, Charlie, if I sit down?"

"Sure." Horgan's colour was coming back. With an attempt at nonchalance he threw his hat on a chair; but didn't sit down himself, and made no effort to remove his coat. "Sure. Sit down, Joe. It's just that I was a bit shook when I came in—so unexpected—you know."

198

"It was the only way," Joe urged. "There was nothing else to do." He looked appealingly. "If I went to the Castle we'd both be in trouble. I don't know how it is with you, but the crowd I have to put up with is terrible. If they knew I was here talkin', Jesus, I'd be in awful trouble. You see, Charlie, they don't trust you. They think the police are just scum that'd betray their own mothers. It's true. They think every policeman is in the business for what he can get. And what's worse you can't convince them."

"I see what you mean." Horgan's mouth twitched and his fingers fiddled again, trying for something to do.

"You know," Joe laughed, "I was a right gom. I used to think the Government hated the Movement because we were takin' the leadership out of their hands. That's why at first I couldn't believe in collaboration. I never dreamed they had the old ideal still in mind and were determined as ever to end Partition. Honest I didn't. I know it was stupid. I know that now, Charlie. I thought they were just a lot of senile delinquents, after sellin' their souls to profiteers. That's what I thought."

"Oh, it's not like that at all."

"I know that now. But honestly Charlie I used to think they were a lot of tired oul' men, afraid themselves to do anythin' and bloody determined nobody else'd do anythin' either."

"It's not like that at all. It's just that the irresponsible use of force could easily perpetuate Partition. Before there is any threat of force the British should be given the opportunity to recede from their position."

"Of course I see that now. If only I had known. Why didn't you tell me, Charlie?"

Horgan gaped dubiously.

"Look, Joe, this is no time. I'll tell you what you'll do. Ring me in a few days and we'll have a chat."

199

"In a few days?" There was something excessively pathetic in Joe's disappointment. "You think that would be better?" Soulful eyes searched enquiringly.

"Yeh. In a few days. I'm very tired just now, and besides—"

"Very well, Charlie, if that's what you'd like. D'you think it'll be all right? You don't think it'll be dangerous? Jesus, I wouldn't want to get you in trouble. I wouldn't want that, no matter what."

Horgan turned to the door. "No. I think that's the best thing. It'll be all right. We'll have a chat in a few days."

With his left hand Joe reached for his hat and, with his right, simultaneously for the gun. It was dreamlike, it was so simple. There was a nice diffidence in his body as he padded across, the Homburg clutched over his belly.

Horgan opened the door.

"After you," Joe insisted.

Horgan unwillingly acceded.

"Oh, by the way, Charlie, I nearly forgot. There's something I wanted to ask you. I'll have to do something about this memory of mine, it's gettin' terrible. I nearly forgot."

"What was that?" Horgan opened the front door.

"There's a ridiculous rumour goin' the rounds that you were responsible for shootin' poor Martin."

"Who?"

"Martin Coyne."

"That I was—?"

"Yeh, I know. I know it's fantastic. But that's the way it is. They don't care what they say. I just laughed, when I heard." Horgan was out in the garden. Joe couldn't see his face anymore. "I know it can't be true and I want to be in a position—"

"Well, you see, Joe—"

"I don't want any equivocation."

"The trouble is—"

"Did you kill Martin Coyne?"

"You have no right to ask that question."

"The only questions in the world, Charlie, that are worth askin' are the ones we have no right to ask."

Horgan seemed never to grasp the imminence of death. The range was dangerous, so Joe aimed for the heart. The crash of the detonation trumpeted round the Dead End. Horgan looked stunned. He raised his hand, and his lips moved; but before he had time, his body drooped, toppled, and slumped. Joe looked down at the crumpled heap, and wondered. For safety's sake he gave him another slug in the brain.

Joe was prepared, if things were difficult, to make a get-away across the gardens. He cocked the gun again, as he slipped down the path, and held it at the ready; but even when he recrossed the road there was no sign of alarm. In the seclusion of the laneway he felt more at ease. The mist had thickened and the foghorns seemed never to cease wailing. Passing the millpond he would have liked to ditch the gun, but the fear that he might need it again was a deterrent. Besides, whether found on him or not it was evidence. Near the end of the laneway he slowed down, uncocked the gun and slipped it in his pocket. He attempted a debonair swagger, as he came into the light; but between the squelching mud and the puddles it wasn't too successful. The courting couple were still locked in death-less ecstasy. He was turning into the main road when, faintly, he heard a woman scream.

There was no reason why he should panic—but he did. Without bothering if the way was clear he raced wildly across the bridge, and hurtled down the laneway. He knew the stupidity of arousing attention but, nevertheless, sped recklessly along the declivity till he was almost at O'Shea's.

Passing the pub he relaxed to an uncertain walk—and searched for the key. The doors were tight shut and the windows dark. Nick was in bed, and his drunken clientele had staggered off in search of homes. A large car, with amber foglamps, came slowly down the hill. Joe flattened himself against the wall, terrified that the sweep of headlights would spot him. The great monstrosity purred peacefully by.

His hands were trembling, and it took him a while to unlock the bike. Panic fears beset him: it might be punctured, wasn't oiled, wouldn't go. In his mind's eye he saw a dowdy unsmiling woman bent over a crumpled heap on the blood-wet ground. He must get away quick. Dammit, he forgot about clips. Frantically he stuffed his pants in his socks, and jerked the bike to the kerb.

It was heaven. Crowley said the machine was in good order; but Joe had no idea. It gathered speed like an angel, soared up to Ashton's and shot like a light down Sandford Road. He had the glorious sensation of being airborne, triumphantly carried on the wings of the wind. At Eglinton Road a winking red light cautioned care! Not for him the mild admonishment! Between the lorry and the honking headlights he sailed regardless, sailed with swift serenity down Sandford Road, through mist and mud, on slippery cobble. At Belmont Avenue a fat policeman gazed on the flying figure, gazed and turned, turned and gazed. Past Sandford Cinema he swiftly sailed, onwards to the city, his coming heralded from afar by the grave notes of foghorns.

18

Trial by Fury

A four-roomed cottage standing alone, in defiance of blustering winds, on a shaggy headland north of the city, provided Joe with a cosy hideout. And when Anna joined him their sojourn was transformed into something of a honeymoon. Perched on top of a heathery hill the cottage promised security from intrusion; and endless walks along myriad craggy paths assured a rejuvenation of tired nerves.

A sprinkling of snow had fallen in the morning, investing the mountain with sudden magic. Crazy gulls shrieked and screamed: screamed, shrieked, and cascaded down the exploding waves. A flock of smaller birds, flurrying together, hurried through the air to the restful rocks: rested and flurried again away. Joe wandered lazily back along the path. Across the bay the heaped-up Wicklow hills gleamed, white-crowned, under a single sunbeam. Moving slowly, a graceless tanker set forth from Dublin on its stubborn journey.

203

Joe had learned that he was being sought by the police, 'to assist in investigations concerning the murder of Inspector Horgan.' He tried not to worry. The elation he acquired when Horgan's elimination first presented itself had never quite receded: and the implementation of his wish had cleared his mind of all its most benumbing worries. In killing Horgan he avenged the deaths of Coyne, Nolan, and Coughlan; and avenged too his own humiliation. He had given a reply to the suggestion of collaboration, and effaced all possibility that the Inspector would tarnish his integrity.

He could concentrate now on defining a firm policy, an active programme which would at once restore morale and be a proper reply to Coercion. The Executive had their idiosyncrasies, but were fundamentally sound. A clear-cut policy would provide the discipline to make an effective unit. The fight must be carried to the North. Skirmishes in the South only confused world opinion. By carrying the battle into the North the problem of Partition would again be high-lighted. With clear-cut issues defined by an active campaign there was no reason why real progress could not be made in achieving the national objective.

As he turned from the path Joe glanced up at the cottage and over the surrounding land. Yes, it was a good hideout. He had told himself so, many times. He had told himself that the death of Horgan had eliminated all his major worries. That helped too. But after the kill the killer is sad. Joy is in action and anticipation. He had told himself over and over that Horgan's death had reduced uncertainty, that his hideout was safe. But still there was doubt: fear of the careless word, the quick betrayal, and the silent gathering shadows. And there was another fear, more difficult to name, fear of the lack of fear, when his melancholy mind would collapse into questioning. The waiting was dangerous.

He kicked open the bockety gate and straggled up the

path. It was a traditional, thatched cottage. He liked the sturdy simplicity of the whitewashed walls and the restfulness of the asymmetrical windows. He liked the ever-changing contours with which perennial whitewash had surfaced the stone. Even the acrid smell of turf and the uncertain plume of smoke were inexplicably heart-warming. It was the nearest thing to a home he had known in years.

"Hiya darling."

"Good, you're back. Nice walk?"

"Quite pleasant."

Hunched over the table Anna was ardently engaged in pressing his coat. She fluttered round, touched his cheek lightly with her lips, and fluttered away again.

"We have to go into town."

"What's wrong?"

"Executive meeting."

"Oh no! Not another!"

"I'm afraid so."

He sighed excessively, slouched to the fire, and flopped on the settle. He had known a meeting was inevitable, but the summons was a shock. A moment before, any escape from aimless waiting would have been welcome, but now it seemed that he was exchanging one uncertainty for another.

"Why can't they leave us alone? Jesus, I'm tired. It's all right for them, but after all, the police are after me. It's askin' for it, goin' into town. Why can't they leave us alone?"

She came to him softly, gently laid her hand on his.

"I know why you don't want to go."

"Why?"

"Because you've been happy here. We've both been divinely happy. We're both afraid to leave even for an hour, for fear our Paradise might disappear."

205

"Maybe you're right." Gently he raised her head and gently kissed her. "Maybe you're right."

"My only true love! Let's go quickly, and get it over."

"O.K."

"Wait, I'll get my coat."

Why couldn't they come to him? He struggled into his coat, wondering if his melancholy was merely habit, wondering if Irish leaders of other days were condemned to the same stupid vigilance, had the same fear of being an imposter, an actor playing outside his sphere. He fingered again through the pile of papers. Horgan's death had certainly caused commotion.

"MURDER HUNT!" "POLICE AND ARMY SWOOP!" "POLICE HUNT FOR KILLER!" Editors shrieked for a drastic reply to the 'Terrorist Challenge.' Bishops shouted threats. Gunbullies, now in Government, cried out their horror. There was talk of curfew in the city area. Joe noted with glee that, though no leading Volunteer had been arrested, a handful of loud-mouthed hangers-on had won their martyr's palm. Photographs of the weeping widow and cheerless children were front-page interest. During the Anglo-Irish War, it said, Horgan had been a member of Collins's Secret Service. Strange! It was something Charlie never mentioned.

"Shall we go?" Anna had tidied her hair and burnished her make-up. "Don't forget your glasses, darling, and that ridiculous hat."

He smiled weakly and fumbled, searching his pockets. Turning, he wavered to the window.

"I think it's goin' to rain."

"Really? Looks quite nice."

"Always before rain I get apprehensive. Most people do! But I feel it more than most. It's a sort of depression, believe it or not, in which the will to live all but disappears. Un-

206

fortunately it's not replaced by a sufficiently strong will to die." His voice, though tearful, was saved from self-pity by a hint of humour. "But the worst thing is the apprehension, the feeling that something dreadful is going to happen. Ridiculous isn't it?"

"Darling, I don't ever want you to be unhappy. I don't ever want you to go away. It's just that they need you too, so much. Without you they're children, just children."

"All right, let's go. Let's get it over."

The wind had strengthened, and a mild gale was blow-ing as they trundled down the mountain. Across the bay the Wicklow Hills had hidden behind a wall of cloud, but overhead the sky still boasted a cheery patch or two. The fresh breeze helped dissipate Joe's fears. Before they reached level ground he not only was reconciled to his fate but had begun to outline his immediate policy.

Yes, Horgan's death had certainly roused the country. It showed that the Organisation had an answer to Coercion. The authorities, both Government and Hierarchic, together with their feudal lords, were screaming for vengeance. But whereas their shrieks were echoes of British predecessors, Horgan's death echoed many another deed of blood which had touched the heart of the people. A masterly inactivity, in the present situation, was the best tactic. The Government should be encouraged to exhaust its energies.

At Talbot Street the first feathers of snow caressed the windscreen. It was a good omen! The place was alive with police, uniformed and otherwise, but in the confusion of sheltering crowds the car was unlikely to attract atten-tion. The snow settled neatly on the tops and bonnets of cars, perched on the hasty umbrellas, and whitened dark shoulders. There was little danger that the police were checking vehicles, but the fact that they were on the alert, and that additional units were drafted, did not make for peace of mind. However, the elements, as usual, were helpful. Except for the inverted fanlights cleared by the wipers, the car windows were soon snow-curtained.

"The Keepers of the King's Peace are out in force."

"So I see."

Shops and shoppers alike, oblivious of all unease, had conspired to celebrate Christmas with traditional gaiety. Multicoloured lights sparkled gleefully in the windows, and garish decorations added their hilarity. The length of Henry Street, under a gracious gauze of snow, was canopied in twinkling stars, and in O'Connell Street the trees had blossomed in glittering colour. From the pillared portico of the General Post Office a chorus of heavenly voices carolled a sad romantic exhortation: "Adeste fidelis, vere triumphalis."

At Abbey Street there were more police than civilians. In white-blossomed uniforms they paraded officiously, crisscrossed the street, or cowered in the shelter of lorries. A few high and mighty ones were urging the traffic forward. The drivers ahead appeared to be slow. By dint of squinting through the windscreen Joe detected that roadblocks had been erected on the bridge. Cars were being scrutinised, and an occasional driver questioned.

"We should have circled round. This is madness."

"I'm sorry. We hadn't time."

Anna was pale, and her driving erratic.

"Take it easy. We'll be all right."

A treble line of soldiers, in battle dress, straggled across the bridge. They were excessively young, and uncomfortable. They carried their guns uneasily. The officers were more efficient—and officious.

Anna was flurried. Each time she inched forward the gears grated.

"Easy! Don't lose your nerve."

She dragged the gears again. The engine jerked, shuddered, and stalled. The car in front pulled away, and there was angry honking behind. Anna adjusted the gears and switched the ignition. With another rasping dissonance the car jumped and stalled. A phalanx of angry police bore down.

"What the hell's goin' on?"

"Get that car outa here."

"Come on, get her out of here! You're holding up the traffic."

Anna switched the ignition, adjusted the gears, and the car shot forward. The road was clear and, as they skidded through, the imperious officers waved them on. With soldiers acting as a Guard of Honour the spluttering engine ferried them over. As he passed an apoplectic major, Joe heard a muttered "Woman driver!"

"That was a near one!"

"You're telling me."

They turned left at Nassau Street.

"What will we do about getting back?"

"I'll ring you at Clutcher Keogh's. We'll arrange it then."

"What time?"

"Eight o'clock."

"O.K."

The Square was still and desolate. The shiny white mantle, under the lanky street lamps, had already achieved a nice serenity; and the rattling Ford, making mighty gashes, was an ungracious intruder.

Anna pulled in to No. 67.

"All right. See you later." She put out her hand; and he held it a moment.

"See you."

"Who is it?"

"Corcoran."

Dermot opened the door.

He had not seen them since the killing of Horgan, and it was with some self-consciousness that Joe swaggered in.

"How you fellows? What the hell made you drag me in? Jeez, the place is overrun with cops. I don't mind takin' a risk as you know. But this is a bit much."

The funereal curtains were drawn, and the anaemic lamp contributed a minimum of illumination. Standing uneasily behind the table, Gerry Baker and Jack Crowley were shown in pallid outline.

"I'm sorry. We wouldn't have asked you if it weren't important."

He sensed the tension. The anaemic lamp accounted only in part for the pallor.

"What's wrong? Something up?"

"We'll wait for the others."

Crowley and Baker were silent. They didn't move.

"Eh! What's goin' on? After all—"

He hadn't heard the footsteps; but as he spoke the door bounced open and Commiskey entered. He had a gun.

"Get them up!"

It must be a joke. Joe glanced round. The others had guns too.

"Put up your hands!"

"What the hell is this?" Joe tried laughing.

"Get your hands up and turn to the wall."

It was no joke. Commiskey's gun was cocked, his finger on the trigger, and his eyes were blazing.

Joe put up his hands. His sickly smile, as he turned, was meant to be derisive.

"Get your left hand behind you."

He lowered his hand. A length of wire was wound round his wrist.

"When am I goin' to know what this is all about?"

"Turn 'round."

His left wrist was elaborately bound with copper wire. "Get going."

"O.K." Joe tried laughing again, to cover his disquiet. "You fellows are goin' to look awful silly."

Dermot and Gerrry put their guns in their pockets. Commiskey threw a light overcoat over his—and kept Joe covered. They herded him out by the back. A glaring white cloak covered the garden, giving the trees a peculiar enchantment. Joe was intrigued to find himself savouring the loveliness.

A snow-covered car was parked in the lane.

"All right, get in. And don't try anything."

"Don't worry. I'll let you provide the fun."

Walshe and Baker moved quickly to the other side. Dermot took the driver's seat. Joe was entrenched between Baker and Commiskey.

"Got the scarf?"

A blindfold! This was melodrama.

"What d'you think you're doin'? Playin' a Chinese thriller?"

Baker folded the scarf, bound it carefully, and tied it tightly.

"Start her up. Everythin' under control."

Distant declivities of thought were clouded by fears too horrible to name. Horgan's shadow still lurked ominously. Coughlan's eager eyes and the baffled disappointment of Mr. Nolan intermingled remotely. There was an obvious upheaval, but whether the action taken was unanimous, or even a majority decision, was questionable. MacCormack's absence was conspicuous.

The imminence of danger ordinarily was galvanic, but Joe was rendered apathetic, he was so startled. They would

211

travel circuitously, but he should try to gauge the direction. The upward swoop and sickening fall meant they had crossed the canal. Travelling south! A nearby clock chimed. The jingle was familiar, but Joe made little effort. A benumbing melancholia had taken possession.

After about seven minutes Baker unknotted the scarf. The car pulled in, faltered, and stopped. Joe tried to glimpse his surroundings, but the windows were snow-blind. Baker and Walshe got out.

"This is the end of the Movement."

"You needn't worry. You have other worries. Come on, out you get."

Baker had opened a door at the side of a shop. He and Dermot stood waiting. They had their right hands in their pockets, and Joe gathered that an attempt to escape would not be advisable. Snow was still falling, and the street was empty. He glanced round. The snow made it difficult, but there was something familiar! Of course! They were in Rathmines, a seedy near-city suburb, parallel to Ranelagh. The town hall clock accounted for the chimes. It was typical that the blindfold should have been unavailing.

Baker led the way into a dark, evil-smelling hall. The others followed close. Joe tried remembering. Rathmines had been a select residential area in which, as the city overran the suburb, shops were erected in the front gardens. They climbed a short stairway and pushed through a door. There was a corridor to the right, leading to a dungeon-like kitchen and, presumably, a yard. To the left was a stairway. The cloying smell of dry-rot was oppressive. Baker still led the way. The rickety stairs were bare, and their footsteps resounded. Four flights, he counted, each about twenty steps.

"O.K., Gerry. Go ahead."

Baker opened the door.

The room was big. A rough table and chairs were the only furniture. Nick Roddy, an obscure Volunteer, was on guard. Skinner was at the table.

"Don't tell me you're part of this set-up?"

Skinner looked blank.

"Certain accusations have been brought against you. I've agreed, in the interests of the Movement, that they should be examined."

"What are they?"

"You'll learn." Commiskey unwound the wire and pushed him back on a chair. "Get your hands behind your back."

While Roddy bound him hand and foot the others took their places. Dermot was evidently President, with Crowley and Commiskey as colleagues. They perched pompously behind the table. MacCormack and Baker faced one another, wide apart, at either end. Joe was angled, a little away from the table, equidistant between. Once he realised that he was on trial, probably for his life, he could no longer pretend amusement. The vast, bleak, dingy room blurred into fantasy; enlarging, colouring, and contracting. He would have liked to protest against the injustice of being bound, hand and foot, while facing armed accusers; but for the moment he was too much engulfed in apathetic languor. It was, in part, protective. His speculation was so convulsed by terror that a defensive retreat was essential.

Dermot spoke first.

"This Special Court has been appointed to hear charges against you. Volunteer Baker is Prosecuting Counsel. Volunteer MacCormack will speak for the Defence. He turned to Crowley. "What are the charges?"

Crowley, in a flat hesitant voice, read from a typescript.

"The charges are:

"(1) That you, Joe Corcoran, conspired with the Free

State Government to obstruct the policy and impede the progress of the Separatist Movement.

"(2) That you, Joe Corcoran, are guilty of treachery by having deliberately forwarded information of a secret and confidential nature concerning the activities of the Movement to a hostile body, to wit the Free State Government."

Joe was too resistantly dull to appreciate the full significance, but he sensed again Horgan's lurking shadow. The room seemed to tilt ever so slightly, and the floor-boards creaked. When anyone moved, the boards whimpered, and when all moved together they chorused dissonant protest. The wallpaper once was pink, but the rushing sunlight had made it frightened, and the seeping damp had made it sad. There were purposeless picture hooks, lonely and absurd, and the bright shadows of frames.

"Have you anything to say?"

"This is a frame-up."

His reply was automatic, but the weight of depression made a mockery even of the pretence of belligerence. He heard Skinner demand his right to an interview, and Hughie's caustic negative. They argued, interrupted and squabbled prima facie and reserved defence, with Commiskey's interjections causing near chaos, until the whole thing took on the shapeless horror of a nightmare pantomime. A floor-board squeaked, squawked, and whimpered; and Gerry Baker was talking.

"Mr. President and Members of the Court."

It was ludicrous that these yokels should involve themselves in such hocus-pocus. Gerry pompously insisted on looking grave, and the others on looking pompous.

"Mr. President and Members of the Court! For some time now it has been apparent that there was a leak of information high-up in the Movement. More recently it became clear that in every action taken we were somehow playing into the Government's hands. It was only natural that some of us should become suspicious, and should attempt to seek out the traitor in our ranks. Within as many months three of our Leaders have been murdered: Brian Goulding, Martin Coyne, and James Nolan. Each one had a perfect hideout. Or so we thought. Each one had a hideout which would have been perfect had it not been revealed. Brian Goulding's dugout in the Dublin Hills, the location of which was known only to a few Executive members, was surrounded by G-Men in the early hours of the morning. Goulding was arrested, and subsequently hanged. Martin Coyne's hideout in Gloucester Street was known only to Executive members. It was judged to be perfect as any hideout can be. Coyne was shot leaving the house at daybreak. In revealing the whereabouts of Mr. Nolan the Informer should have received double blood-money. Not only did he betray his Leader: he also revealed the whereabouts of the pirate radio station. I want you to note that in each instance it was the Leader who was annihilated—and I want you to face without fear the awful reality that each Leader destroyed prepared the way for a traitor to take control—and so direct our dedicated energies into chaos and disaster. Fortunately we were able to uncover this foulness before it destroyed forever our precious national heritage. I am satisfied that I have sufficient documentary evidence and living witnesses to prove that Joe Corcoran was a Government spy, and that he gave information of a secret nature to the Government, through its Agent Inspector Charles Horgan."

A chair unsettled, a heel scraped, a board squealed, and MacCormack was demanding: ". . . no opportunity . . . not satisfied . . . not yet sent for trial . . ." And Commiskey, in most illegal language, was advising him to shut it. A draught from nowhere rocked the naked bulb, casting shadows. The snow was heaping around the window. Joe wanted to tell them. About the bulb. Someone would notice. He wanted desperately to let them know, that he wouldn't like them to get in trouble.

"I can prove beyond reasonable doubt that Corcoran met Inspector Horgan at various places throughout the city. In friendly collaboration they planned, among other things, the ambush of the fake arms shipment, and the assassination of our successive Leaders. This was part of a carefully thought-out plan to enable Corcoran to seize power and so reduce the Movement to a mere instrument of Government policy. We were the only Organisation dedicated uncompromisingly to the separatist ideal. And the Government was aware that, if permitted to grow, we must inevitably take control. Already the country, and particularly Nationalist circles and the Regular Army, was turning in disgust from successive political parties which were not only generally incompetent but had failed to face up to the problem of Partition. Realising their predicament the Government was not slow to appreciate what was required. They must entice, engineer or provoke the Organisation into such action as would lead it into disrepute. They must provoke the Movement into such action as would shock Nationalist circles by holding us up to ridicule, as a stupid, careless, and inefficient bunch of hoodlums. They must engineer a barrier of antagonism between the Regular Army and the Movement. Finally, they must create the atmosphere for the passing of a Coercion Act, setting up Military Tribunals to hunt down Volunteers, ruthless shooting galleries whose principal business would be to pronounce the death sentence. How did they achieve this? While Leader of the Movement, Volunteer Joe Corcoran conspired with the Irish Free State Government to ambush two lorry-loads of arms. In this engagement four Free State soldiers were shot dead. Though the arms were well hidden in the premises of a

216

trusted ally they were, nevertheless, recovered by Government forces almost immediately. They were recovered because Corcoran not only planned the ambush in collusion with Government agents, but also planned the recapture. It is noteworthy that the arms for which we risked our lives, and in the defence of which four fellow-Irishmen *lost* their lives, were, in the event, found to be useless. The depth and intricacy of Corcoran's treachery is seen most clearly, perhaps, in this episode."

Joe became aware, through tangled shadows, that without pretending they were watching. Secret glances darted uneasily, making him vaguely vain. There was a crack lingering in the ceiling, the grey paint was peeling and, in the high corner, three dusty cobwebs wiggled. He became aware that in his fear he was not alone; and it was comforting. First he was frightened by the magnification; but now, comforted by their fear, he perceived that if he could disprove the exaggeration, he could all but disprove all. He tried struggling out of apathy, tried desperately to coax a curl of derision. But it was better, easier, restful, more expedient to relax. Besides, he was tired. He let his spine sag. And then again he didn't care any more.

"Let us pass over the fact that Corcoran was willing to gamble with the lives of his comrades, and was willing to dissipate the dedicated energies of Volunteers in a useless enterprise. The aim of the Government and its agent Charles Horgan in collusion with the accused was more intricate. They sought, as I have indicated, to create the ready excuse and the proper atmosphere for the passing of a Coercion Act. The deaths of four soldiers in the ambush episode was successful, so far as the Government was concerned, in effecting a cleavage between the Regular Army and the Movement. Up to that time we were able to count on the tacit sympathy of the young mercenaries, and we were certain that in a time of crisis they would refuse to take action against us. After that episode the Government found no difficulty in setting up Military Tribunals, with attendant firing squads. After that episode they found no difficulty in using the Regular Army to hunt down Volunteers. The ambush of the arms shipment antagonised not only the Free State Army but created consternation in Nationalist circles where ordinarily the Movement was looked upon with sympathy. The immediate recovery of the arms held the Movement up to ridicule and permitted the Government to boast of its ability to cope with the so-called 'terrorist activity.' The depth and intricacy of Corcoran's treachery was best seen in the ambush episode, but his ruthlessness and cunning are more clearly appreciated by reference to the slaughter of Volunteer Coughlan which, in collaboration with Government agents, he cleverly engineered."

Chill fear again engulfed him. But the thought recurred that if he could disprove the embroidery he could disprove all. The bulb still was swinging, twisting jumbled shadows. In the convulsion of light and dark the faces grew and went. Crowley's moronic stupidity was horrific, an amiable fool transformed to a fearsome ogre. Skinner's hands intertwined across his chest, and his cheeks were purple. He wasted so much time outside, examining his performance, that he was incapable. The little scar on Hughie's lip was red.

"It became apparent that there was a leak of information. Realising this the accused decided to divert attention from himself by casting suspicion on another Executive member. Acting on information received—from the accused—the police had followed Volunteer Coughlan to the Studio. The accused took the opportunity to suggest, by innuendo, that this circumstance might be suspicious. Coughlan's hysteria during the ambush didn't help. But again the accused ex-

218

aggerated a minor failure with the deliberate intent of diverting suspicion. On the following day when the guns were recaptured it was accepted that Coughlan was responsible. We played into Corcoran's hands when we wiped out Coughlan. The subtle insinuation, the mild innuendo, were deliberately planted with the cold resolution that he be liquidated. Had he lived he would probably have become suspicious, and might have led us to the real culprit. As a result of Corcoran's cunning we have, each one of us, the blood of an innocent victim on our hands."

Dermot's mild detachment never wavered; but he did reach for a pencil, and it might be that his effort was a blind. Commiskey's little scar was purple; he wasn't sorry for Coughlan; it was just that his vanity was hurt. Baker's face was fat. A simple Dublin chiseler, he hid his background in a synthetic accent. Joe recalled that he had encouraged Gerry's promotion. He didn't expect gratitude, but the twist was ironic. Gerry's debt was maybe an incentive. Nothing his kind liked less than being under obligation.

"When I have proved conclusively, as I shall prove, that Corcoran collaborated with Horgan in the capture of the Studio and the murder of Mr. Nolan, when I have produced documentary evidence to prove that Corcoran collaborated with Horgan in planning the ambush of the phoney arms shipment and its subsequent recapture, when I have produced a living witness who will tell you of the various meetings Corcoran had with Horgan, both in and outside Police Headquarters, I think you will be more than satisfied that Corcoran was also responsible for the deaths of Brian Goulding and Martin Coyne."

This was too much. Skinner bounced suddenly into ferocious activity. "Circumstantial evidence! Living witnesses!" A pudgy paw pointed accusation. "Let's have less imagination and more facts."

"Sit down, Mr. MacCormack."

"Sit down."

"I'll not sit down!"

"Sit down and shut up."

"I will not sit down and I will not shut up. I'm not going to be muzzled by any crowd of misdirected imbeciles." Joe chortled inwardly. Once he had the bit in his teeth there was no stopping Skinner. "Before a Court of this kind sits, the first, basic, and obvious essential is that the procedure should be decided. The Prosecution has clearly devoted substantial time to preparing these *trumped-up* charges. I have been given no information as to procedure, nor have I been given proper notice of these ludicrous allegations. Furthermore—and this is completely ridiculous—I have had no opportunity to consult my client." There was a pause. Skinner allowed his hands to fall to his sides, and an expression of sweet reasonableness transformed his features. "Look gentlemen! Let's be sensible. It's too ludicrous to believe that the Leader of the Movement should be guilty of treachery. It's just impossible. One point alone will demonstrate the utter imbecility of such a suggestion. One single point! The main charge, I gather, is that Corcoran collaborated with Inspector Horgan. Isn't that correct? But every member of this Court knows that it was Corcoran was responsible for the demise of Horgan. Am I just a little obtuse or does it seem that these attitudes are mildly contradictory?"

Skinner sat down quietly, intertwined his fingers and waited. There was a pause before Dermot turned to Gerry.

"I agree with the Defence that the charges are fantastic. When the possibility that they were true was first brought to my attention I was equally aghast. But, as evidence piled on evidence, I had to acknowledge that they were unanswerable. I had to face the truth that my friend Joe

220

Corcoran is a traitor. It is not difficult to understand why Corcoran killed Horgan. The Defence will remember, as also will the members of the Court, that when it was established that Horgan had killed Martin Coyne it was proposed that he should be captured, put on trial, and if found guilty, that he should be executed. You will remember how eager Corcoran was to dispense with the necessity for capture and trial. He was obviously afraid that under pressure Horgan would confess his part in the conspiracy. It was simple as that. Corcoran realised that Horgan's assassination was inevitable. To ensure that there would be no danger of a last-minute confession he wisely insisted on doing the job himself. And we stupidly agreed. His behaviour in this instance fits into the pattern of his other actions. When his collaborator becomes dangerous he callously annihilates him."

"Where are your witnesses?"

"I can assure the Defence that before he is asked to reply to these charges he will be given every opportunity to consult his client." Dermot's smile of mild forbearance was overdone. "In the meantime I suggest that the Prosecution should get a fair hearing."

"Circumstantial evidence! Where are your witnesses?"

Gerry chose on this occasion to disregard the interruption. Selecting a foolscap sheet from the papers before him, he held it up for all to see.

"I have here a police report of a meeting between Inspector Charles Horgan and Joseph Corcoran in Kelly's public house. At that meeting the first plans were made for the capture of the arms shipment."

"Where are your witnesses?" Skinner was up again. He disliked being ignored and once he had an idea, right or wrong, no one was more tenacious. Time and again Joe cursed Skinner's pertinacity; but now it was proving a blessing. "I suggest that an open meeting in a pub between a Police Inspector and a Leader of the Movement doesn't fit into the conspiratorial pattern as outlined by Mr. Baker."

"Sit down!"

"I must again request Counsel for the Defence to give the Prosecution a fair hearing. I guarantee that his hearing will be equally fair."

"Produce your witness!"

Baker seemed in no way affected by the heckling. He resumed his seat till the conflict subsided, then continued in even tones.

"Members of the Court may remember that at a meeting on that same evening—the evening of the day on which Martin Coyne was shot by Horgan—Corcoran made an off-hand reference to his so-called casual encounter. This, of course, was a clever tactic. What he did not reveal was that he had a further rendezvous in Jordan's pub later that same night, at which he gave Horgan a résumé of the Executive Meeting, and at which plans for the ambush were first outlined."

"Produce your witness!"

"I have here documentary evidence—"

"Documentary evidence! Produce your witness!"

"I have here documentary evidence in the form of a police report that, on that same evening, the accused advised Horgan that Coughlan could be picked up the next day outside the University. Acting on information received, Detective Officers Clancy and MacNamee trailed Coughlan to the Studio. In the gun-fight which followed, our late Leader, Mr. James Nolan, was killed. And the way was cleared for Joe Corcoran to become Leader."

"Poppycock! Why didn't they go direct to the Studio?"

"You ask for living witnesses! I have a living witness whose testimony you cannot doubt: who will swear that Joe Corcoran was subsequently brought to Horgan's house.

The accused was picked up by Lehane and MacGuirk and escorted in a squad car to Horgan's chateau in the Wolsley Estate. It was a clever cover. At this meeting it is understood that plans for the ambush of the arms and their subsequent recapture were finalised.'"

" 'It is understood.' Produce your witness!"

"There was a further meeting between Joe Corcoran and Inspector Horgan on the day following the ambush. The accused was again escorted by squad car, this time to Headquarters, where it was possible, without arousing suspicion, to remain in continuous conclave. Yes, it was a nice deception: the pretence of arrest to cover discussions of further collaboration. Are we wrong in thinking that they chortled over their achievement? It would be natural that they should gloat a little before they proceeded to serious business. After all, they had something to celebrate. The Coercion Act was already before the Cabinet. The outlawed Movement was going underground, and it was a matter for conjecture if it would ever re-emerge."

"Mr. President! I appeal to you! Is my client to be condemned on a series of assumptions? Or are we, eventually, going to hear some facts? We have had lots of talk about documents. Personally I haven't yet had an opportunity to examine these PRECIOUS IMAGINARY FABRICATIONS. Still less have I heard any evidence that they are genuine. We have had endless talk about witnesses. WHERE, I ASK AGAIN, WHERE ARE THESE LIVING WITNESSES?"

The door had softly opened. Baker's line of vision never changed. But the others were staring. Even Skinner looked shaken. Joe twisted in his chair . . . A bitter little rat-faced man poised diffidently on the threshold. It wasn't easy to believe, he seemed so out of place. It was Paddy Lehane.

"I have my witness," Baker said.

19

Mind the Step!

An awakening urge, bored acquiescence, a fumbling of seed, and he was thrust without tails, enthusiasm or acknowledged invitation into the whirligig, scrambling among the herd, trampling infirmity, to snatch at the dainties. Then came the men with the explanations: wiser to acquiesce, join the Knights of the smiling Scramblers; beware the shame of the sore thumb. To wonder is to be afraid. It was futile to question the silence. It would have been well to believe, accept the cosy story. Miss Faith Anaesthesia Hope, Consort of Cardinals, undertakes simultaneously to seduce both the bewilderment of Pain and the pain of Bewilderment. Why should he not believe that Paradise would compensate? Why not accept the legality, the triumph of greed, the unctuous abracadabra?

Pity for disorder, a fault of vanity, had been his weakness. High above, at an angle of eighty-five, the Town Hall clock chimed. WHO-IS-THIS-MAN? WHAT-DOES-HE-WANT? THAT-MAN-WANTS-SILK! HOW-MUCH-DOES-HE-WANT? One . . . Two . . . The ponderous boom tolled out the death of yet another day. He would have wished to turn on his side but . . . no part of his throbbing flesh was free of pain; no muscle, artery, vein, ligament, or capillary but was an aching agony. The blood on his cheek had congealed, and under his eyes the palpitating ridges were two high hills.

Beyond the snow-circled window the cold world was silent. He tried picturing the gentle veneer of white magic glittering under the moon, virgin layers adorning roofs, window sills, walls, and weary branches. He thought of little birds, gentle in their joy, famished by the beauty, huddled hungry in the cold. The pale rays overflowed into the room, and their light was the colour of death. It seemed that of late he had spent too much time staring at ceilings, counting the cracks, waiting for spiders, or conjuring landscapes out of damp splotches. He listened again to the snores from within, the sighing outflow, and the quick rattling grunting snort. If he wanted he could escape, if he set his mind!

He never felt grateful for the "goodies," that was the trouble. He was too studiously conscious of the snare in the flower, the worm in the flesh, the dark of the sun and the fear in the darkness, the abject pathos of insignificance. Death and pain were a little akin, it was thinking made them terrible. He had hoped he might topple on the ridge of joy; a pity his passing should be shadowed in shame.

It was not as though he was the first to go. There had been others. His tentacled thought sought to encompass the street-lengths, old and young, who had blundered already into darkness, in tenements, townlands, cities, and mansions, over all Ireland, England, and the Isle of Man; jungles of giant animals, gentle fledglings and exquisite insignificant

225

insects: continent upon continent, millennium upon millennium of beasts, birds, human and inhuman beings all of which had already blundered reluctantly into darkness, none of which was any more troubled by the dreadful vagaries.

From the room within, the rattle and snort crescendoed to a strangled shriek. There was silence then. He glanced at the lighted fanlight—and waited, watching. The stillness was unnerving. Crowley had turned on his side! He waited, hoping too much the rattle would resume . . . and he had his wish. Barely perceptible at first, the heavy breathing amplified to a coarse comforting clamour. Who could be guilty of so unedifying a dereliction? Crowley! Where then was Hughie? It would be little trouble to climb up, and peep through. But why bother? If he wanted he could escape!

He had always hoped to think about God, come to an understanding; but even the knowledge that death was around didn't help. Since he gave up going to Mass he never somehow got things straight. He couldn't seem to budge the unspiritual convictions that had lodged in his brain. He didn't think it fair, though, being placed in a void where unhappy uncertainty was only reasonable. Belief in immortality was man's most blatant vanity. Belief in an immortality of torture was his condemnation of God. That the Divinity had revealed Himself was further vanity. Why, of all mortals, should man be chosen? The one indisputable truth with regard to a possible God was his admirable determination to remain remote. In the deep shadows he sometimes seemed to glimpse a plump, bowler-hatted, featureless Figure—philanthrophist, practical joker, sadist, or puppet-manager. Whatever happened Joe was certain that lots of people would be shaken, and in a vague way he pictured himself answering back and telling this joker off.

He looked up at the ceiling, and through the ceiling at

the white-clouded heavens. In the aery nothingness behind planets and stars he seemed to see, suspended without effort, an all-loving, all-merciful Being. "Dear God," he prayed, "have mercy on me. Dear, dear God, help me get out of here." A wave of self-pity watered his eyes. "Dear God, if I get out of here, I'll never drink again."

Crowley and Commiskey were told to keep guard! Were the others below or spread to their hideouts? It wasn't surely possible that the upheaval took place without some reaction. Skinner would ensure that word had got round. What of Anna? She must have been anxious. In the shadowed cloister of his mind he fancied a ferment of questioning faces, bitterly grimacing, angrily threatening. He thought of Anna, comfortable in love, and yearned to snuggle in the shelter of her affection. She would know, she would understand that he would make any sacrifice rather than harm the Movement. The compulsive idealism of the Volunteers was a pure, a splendid, and a holy thing. Anna would understand his incapacity deliberately to sabotage a thing so inherently good.

Reluctantly his mind went back to the trial. No horror, in life or after, could equal the agony of those hours when Paddy Lehane gave time, date and endless detail of the journey to Horgan's house, and the sojourn up in Headquarters. Step by step the fabulous case was built, till it was hard to disentangle fact from fancy. He wondered if Lehane believed his story. Strange he gave evidence! He wanted revenge, maybe; or thought he was giving the coup de grace which would kill the Movement. Could it be possible, as Baker suggested, that Lehane was, for some time, a secret agent of the Organisation?

In a moment he might jolt into wakefulness to find that

the grotesquerie had been fantasy, that in a dream his little fears had become monsters. Ironic that, in the end, it was his friends were his torturers! Even now he could remember only dimly the final horror when the bulky shadows gathered. He could hardly tell who was who, except for Commiskey who had the stick. It was Crowley who grabbed his lapels, and shook him like a salad. But it wasn't he who spoke. It was Baker wanted to know.

"How much did they pay you? What was in it for you?"

His hands and legs were still bound, so he couldn't hit back.

When they dragged him from the bed the wire cut deep.

"Come on, open up!"

"Who else was on the job?"

"Who else was workin' with you?"

"Were you talkin' to Paddy Dirrane?"

"Who were you squealin' to?"

It was Dermot, the slick unemotional one, who hit him first. He slapped him hard with the palm of his hand and, before he got steady, slapped him again. It wasn't so much that it hurt. It was the shock.

"Come on, who else did you split on?"

The others took a hand, jabbing his face with their fists till the blood was running, till he felt the taste of blood, and his eyes were blind.

"Who else did you give away?"

"Come on!"

"The truth for a change!"

"What did they pay you?"

He was not unwilling; he wanted to talk, to explain exactly, that he wouldn't want to do any harm, the Separatist dream was the one thing he knew to be good, that his guilt was small. He tried to, but Baker jabbed again, and the blood spurted. He went quiet then. What was the use?

He could bear the pain, knowing he need never feel guilty of a hundredth part of what they said.

He gathered that the pretence of formality had been abandoned, and that he was to die at dawn. His body, dumped on O'Connell Bridge, would be a warning. But first they wanted a confession, a written admission. He was able to stay quiet till Commiskey started with the broom-handle. He beat him first about the legs, then about the shoulders, and then about the face and head. Still he said nothing. He stayed quiet until that third jab in the kidneys. Then he screamed. And they got frightened. He hadn't thought of it before, how silly he was, that there were still people around. He didn't know they could be so frightened. He indulged himself in a shrill outpouring of pent-up agony. They jumped on him then, forcing their hands on his mouth. Still he screamed. Baker searched for a scarf, while the others dragged him back. . . . It was good to rest. It was ever so, ever so, good to lie back and watch the scurrying.

Thin lines of snow, delicately balanced on the window-bars, were high-lighted by the moon. Joe inclined to speculate how the Executive chanced upon so suitable a hide-out. 'Unfurnished house; select area; all mod. con.; many extras, including BARRED WINDOW.' The moonlight was painful. Closing his eyes he allowed himself to relax, muscle by muscle, joint by joint, to an almost total inertia. "Stone walls," he feebly murmured, "do not a prison make, nor iron bars a cage." The quotation was inapt. These particular walls achieved sufficient resemblance to be entirely convincing. To attempt to squeeze through would be hopeless but, if he got rid of the glass, he might do a job of dislodgment. To unload the glass would take hours! Besides, the bars were probably sunk in cement. At dawn, they said, he was to die! A matter of hours! To be the victim of nincompoops was humiliating. They'd botch the job for sure and leave his body a bloody mess.

With fists down-pressed against the bed he levered up. The pain was excruciating but, when his muscles adjusted, it would be easier. He edged his right foot on to the floor— and rested again. It was well, in a way, that his body was crippled. He must not hurry. He must attune his mind to work with deliberation, in utter silence. He brought his left leg slowly down. The constriction increased the weight of his breathing. He levered gradually up—till he was perched on the side of the bed. First he must take off his shoes. The laces were loose. It was tricky enough, even so, easing out without creaking the leather or scraping the floor. The thought of escape was refreshing!

A few coins in his pocket rattled, and their tinkle was like thunder. He paused to examine the room. Nearby was the tangle of wire with which he was bound, thrown on top of Commiskey's stick. His hat and coat were dumped on a chair. He probed his way to the window, testing every step. A floor-board shrieked. He halted, inched discreetly sidewards, and tried again. The window frames were steadfastly boarded, and the bars immovably sunk. He turned away, and with the same unhurried care stalked his way to the door. With feeling hands and questing eyes he searched. Neither lock nor handle was visible. He pressed with his palm. The wood creaked plaintively, but there was no give.

He crossed to the corner, lifted his coat, and lowered it soundlessly. The chair was heavy. Despite his utmost care it scraped the ground, and creaked. He placed it so that the centre back rested on the jamb. With a hand on the door-frame to lessen the pressure he brought one foot up. Now was the tricky bit! He must raise himself without causing a sound. This he effected with less than expected

230

difficulty: and it was with a mild sense of triumph that he stretched on tiptoe, and peered through the fanlight.

On the bed in the corner Crowley was puffing and croaking like a broken-down hack. Commiskey slouched in a chair. He too was asleep—with a gun on the table. Joe was amused. It had always been Commiskey's boast that he could stay without sleep for hours without end.

The fanlight, about eight inches high, was hinged at the top, and opened outwards. The catch was rusty. He exerted an even pressure, without result. He tried pushing the right-hand corner. It softened a fraction. He tried the left. It wasn't so easy. He heightened the pressure. It surrendered with a rattling gasp.

Crowley's regular rhythm broke. He fidgeted. Commiskey stirred, but didn't waken. Joe waited, for what seemed like an age, till the rhythm resumed. The catch had been dealt with. But the fanlight frame was still jammed. Using both hands, one to steady the catch, the other to loosen the frame, he started again. It was easy, except for the right-hand corner. He essayed a series of gentle jabs at barely separated points. It surrendered suddenly with an abrupt thud. He waited breathless, but his guardians didn't stir. The fanlight opened without sound, but only about seven inches. He couldn't possibly squeeze through.

Joe relaxed. The first job was to find how the door was secured. Gripping the top of the frame he raised himself on the back of the chair. He was now above the fanlight. To get a firm hold, he put an arm through and gripped the frame on the other side. He paused to let his fluttering pulse subside. Twisting his head to one side he gentled it tenderly through. His observation post was both precarious and uncomfortable, but he had a clear view. The door was secured, halfway down, by a large bolt-type lock, obviously new! He wangled his head gingerly back. The problem, in simplest terms, was first to reach the lock, and then to get it open.

He climbed down cautiously. He must find some means by which to withdraw the bolt. He glanced round. Except for the bed and the chair, the wire on the floor, and Commiskey's broomstick, the room was distressingly bare. His eyes dwelt on the wire-entangled broom-handle. That the instruments of torture should be agents of escape would be ironic. He padded stealthily across. The wire was pliable, but not strong. The broomstick was perfect.

The job of disentanglement was tedious, but with a definite plan taking shape he could suffer the monotony. Using a splicing technique he put a double loop of wire above the head of the broom-handle. This he fixed in position by coiling the remaining wire neatly around. He held the wire taut and made sure that each encircling coil was close. Having exhausted the wire in about twenty circles he effected a knacky bit of tying off.

He climbed on the chair again, stretched on tiptoe, and peeped through. Commiskey's head was deep in his chest. Crowley didn't stir. It was best to find a proper balance on the chair-back before putting the broomstick through. With the least shift of stress the chair groaned and the door-frame crackled. The sharp wood dug deep in his flesh, and the drag on his bones was torture. Keeping a wary eye on the sleepers he rested a while, to let the pain deaden.

He rested his right hand on the frame. Steadying the stick, like a billiard cue, between thumb and forefinger, he slid it through smoothly. Like a giant gun-barrel it stretched endlessly away. For safety's sake he held it horizontal until his head was through too. By slow degrees he brought the broomstick down until the loop was level with the bolt. It was difficult keeping it steady. Slowly he brought the loop

232

nearer. His hand was shaking. Millimetre by millimetre he drew it nearer. He glanced at Commiskey, terrified the tension would reach him. With the loop almost touching the knob he rested again. Steadying his hand was an effort. Every tremble was magnified. Resting the end of the pole on the bolt he edged the loop closer. Another tiny twist, and the knob was encircled. He waited a moment, breathing heavily, till the triumph subsided.

First he tried a gentle upward pull, without avail. He let the pole drag a shade on either side. There was no give. He chanced the upward pressure again, increasing the pull till the wire was taut. With a low rasp the knob jerked. He waited, watching the sleepers. Commiskey groaned and settled. Crowley was lost in dreams. Joe depressed the knob, exerting at the same time a subtle sideward pull. There was grating again, and he halted. He tugged the bolt and it came without sound. He depressed it again. The grating was gone. And the bolt was loose. Unhurriedly, he continued, pulling and pushing, releasing and tugging, dragging sideways a little each time. His elbow was cramped, but what did it matter! All the pain he ever endured was lost in the joy of seeing the bolt slip from its socket. The door creaked open.

He withdrew the broom-handle and clambered down. Where he gripped the stick an acid stain of sweat had darkened the wood: and his forehead was stinging. He moved with surety now, stuffing shoes in his pockets, shoving the stick and the wire on the bed. He turned to the door. The familiar undiminishing grunt and snort, still resounding at full pressure, were joy to his heart. He pushed gently. The door swung back with a flimsy creak. He crept forward, testing each step, still on guard for the treacherous board. He was circling Commiskey's sprawling feet when Crowley chose to disturb the world with a merciless moan. Hughie stirred, and Joe froze. If they woke now, he could at least make a fight. It would be better though to get clean away. Crowley snuffled and turned on his back. Commiskey slackened. Joe continued his deft navigation till the gun was under his hand. His fingers touched the hard steel. He strengthened his grip.

With the butt of the gun in the deeps of his palm he backed away. The door to the landing was open. He faltered a while. There was an attic above that led to the roof. On the landing below was a window, on to the roof of the annex. It was possible too to make his way down and out through the hall. The attic was risky, and there was no knowing whom he might find down below. With a farewell look at the sleepers he dashed down the stairs and heaved himself on to the sill. The window squealed like a duck in despair, but what the hell! It was joy to taste the cold sweet air.

The roof was white-shawled, ivory satin in the shining light. The surface was brittle but, as he slid down the gully, he felt no pain. There was a wall below the end of the roof, and an outhouse underneath. Wriggling round to let himself down he saw the house go suddenly bright. And he heard the first shot. It ricocheted off the chimney, spraying snow in the air. Slipping and slithering down, he hit the ground with a bump, as the second shot shook the snow.

The long garden was cluttered with shrubs. Keeping well down, he blundered away through the dark, impeded by weeds, whipped by the branches, startling snow from sleepy hedges. There was a tiny clearing near the end. He glanced back as he pulled on his shoes. The lights were on all over the house: and criss-crossing shadows darted from window to door. The wall, about seven feet high, was little trouble, the footholds nicely marked by snow. The frozen layer on top wasn't quite so inviting, but he managed all right. The

234

clock chimed as he clambered over. Another shot cut through the ice.

The wall on the other side was steep: and in the excitement he muffed his footing—and sprawled in the snow. He found himself in a spacious compound—one hundred yards of immaculate snow, bordered by scattered sheds. His trail would be clear. He must double back and lose his tracks in the slush of the street.

He turned to the left and, still crouching low, dodged around some open sheds. In the space beyond he found what he sought, a giant door leading to a lane. The wicket was open. He squeezed through, and sped silently down. He paused at the end. The street was deserted. He came on a level. No sign of life. It seemed safe enough! As he splashed across through the slush he glimpsed a newspaper placard, daintily lit by the moon. "POLICE HUNT FOR GUN-MAN."

20

Death Is So Kind

The world and his wife were aware of his thought. Not only the Executive, but Police and Military too, had divined his intention of seeking sanctuary with Anna. When he glanced behind, at Boland's Hill, he spied a grey figure backing into darkness. Commiskey was already stalking his prey. Joe twisted left, ran halfway down, and crossed the street to the shelter of an archway. There was a fair getaway, but better let Commiskey ahead. Crouching in shadow, he pressed hard into the stone. The joints of his left hand, sunk in his pocket, were stiff; but the palm of his right hand, where he gripped the gun, was moist. Nice, though, to have Commiskey for a target.

He was beginning to think that his eyes had been lying—when Hughie at last came slouching round. That quick glance was an alert survey. He sauntered on, peering into porches. At one shop window he paused and, as he

236

turned away, his swift appraisal was again complete. When he came level Commiskey slackened. Joe pressed closer, and drew the gun. But Hughie suddenly changed his mind— glanced down the street, and turned quickly away. Joe heard distantly the hurried shuffle, and wondered who had saved whose life.

He slid quietly out of the shadow and doubled back. At the corner he turned. He was level with the Market Arcade when he heard the car. It was far off, but the circling searchlight meant a police prowl. Joe glided in among the scattered garbage cans, and crouched on his hunkers. The squad car drifted slowly nearer, the circling light searching, digging deep into doorways. Joe rested a finger on the trigger. If there must be a fight, might as well be a good one. The far corner was a blaze of light, every crevice stripped of pretension. The car prowled closer. The surrounding area was drowned suddenly in the glare. Joe was tempted to blast the circling arc but, abruptly as it came, the brightness receded. And the car moved on without pause.

The far end of the Arcade opened into Dunraven Place —a wide thoroughfare, leading on to the main street. By dint of manoeuvring among the stalls Joe got a reasonable view. Shop windows were still alight, and neon signs glared and winked. There was an abundance of light on the corner, but it was hard disentangling the movement. The arc lamps shed their glare on a party of soldiers, loitering among roadblocks. Searching hands frisked a tall figure. A quick head turn, and Joe saw it was Dermot. He chuckled as the dark figure was led unwillingly away.

The direct approach to Anna was not feasible. He must send a message . . . Bartley was the man! Bartley could navigate the roadblocks. . . . Joe crept forward soundlessly. The street was empty.

Despite the cold and pain, despite the moments of terror, Joe's spirits were high. His escape was a victory, and the thought of his triumph was, in itself, an exhilaration. Plans were already shaping in his mind to rally the rank and file. He must contact Skinner! With the backing of the rank and file he would obliterate the present bunch of hoodlums and nominate his own Executive. It would be amusing to turn the tables, charge the Executive with false imprisonment, make them aware that their action had all but sabotaged the Movement. Tolerance of stupidity was his trouble. Events had proved, as they often did, that kindly encouragement of lame dogs led to catastrophe.

Joe had lived since his escape on a high pitch of exhilaration, but he was aware, subconsciously, that by provoking the upheaval he had participated in the guilt. And beneath the web of self-delusion he was conscious too of one sincere regret—that the idealism of the younger Volunteers had been shabbily abused. . . . Anna would understand. Anna would penetrate the complexities. With Anna he would find peace. They would go together to the hills, and on the slopes of Lugnaquilla the perplexities would fade. He needed only a little time, a little time with Anna to re-create his thought, evolve a plan, and go forward hand in hand with her.

It was a comfort to escape the bright lights. Luton Row was in the older section, deep hidden in a confusion of seamy side streets. The lighting was not lavish, and unaccompanied policemen had found that a casual stroll was inadvisable. In Luton Row Joe could relax among people who lived as he did, on the edge of desperation. The musty odour of decaying brick was sweet and the grace of fallen grandeur comforting.

Carney's Café was the only building showing light, and that scarcely discernible. The single bulb, high in the window, was hooded in heavy cloth. The sagging half-curtain was designed to defeat the inquisitive, but the grime had already achieved that effect. Joe knocked on the door. . . . He heard, distantly, a faint rumble of talk. The "Café" was in the basement. A shebeen frequented by pimps, prostitutes, and drunks, Carney's figured regularly in the press when "Danno," the proprietor, was fined for selling unlicensed liquor. Joe heard no sound, but, as he raised his hand again, the door jerked open.

"What d'you want?"

"I'm looking for blind Bartley, the ballad-singer."

Danno, the big bloated man, hesitated—then stepped aside.

"Come in. What's your name?"

"Tell him Joe wants him."

"Jaysus now I hope you're not gettin' me in trouble." He banged the door. "There's more police round to-night than you'd fit in Croke Park."

It was a drab, low-ceilinged room, almost dark; but he could see the damp wallpaper peeling. There was no furniture.

"Tell him I want to see him a minute."

"Come on so."

He followed down the ladder-like steps. There was neither banister nor handrail, and the only light came from the door below. Joe heard a rattle of applause, and Bartley's voice topping the talk.

"Come on in. Sit down there. I'll send him over."

"O.K."

After the unprepossessing foyer the basement seemed the epitome of normality. It was well lighted. Rough tables lined the walls, and there were chairs for those who fancied them. The majority crowded in the centre, laughing and chatting. Bartley stood by the fire.

239

Danno gripped the old man's arm. The statuesque head bowed, listening. He groped for his stick.

"Come on boys. Fag a' bealach. Make way for the old man."

"Is that you, Joe?" Searching fingers gripped the chairback.

"Yes."

"Are we safe here to talk?"

"Safe enough."

"What brought you here, Joe?"

"I had to see you."

"It's dangerous."

"I know."

"What's wrong?"

"I want you to go to Anna Quin's. You know it, don't you?"

"Yes, I know it."

"I want you to go now and bring her here. It won't be easy. The police are everywhere."

Bartley was silent. Joe studied the gaunt, bearded face; but the unseeing eyes gave no hint.

"All right. You stay here." Joe rose, but the old man pushed him back. "I'm all right. It won't be easy, but I'll do it." He moved to the stairs. "Look after my friend, Danno. See that he doesn't want for anything. Look after him till I get back."

"Right, Bartley."

Danno's assistant, a moronic youth, shuffled over. Danno followed Bartley up.

"What are you havin'?"

"Large whiskey."

"Right."

"And a packet of fags. What have you got?"

"Sorry. Not a cigarette in the house!"

A blousy slob detached herself from a nearby group. "Did I hear you askin' for a cigarette, dearie? I'll tell you what— I'll divide me last one with you. I wouldn't do it for everyone, mind yeh. Only you look like you need it. What happened? Yeh look like yeh were dragged backwards through a ditch. Here!"

"Thanks. I got in a bit of a scrap. A couple of bowseys down the Quays tried to beat me up."

"The lousers!"

"Won't you sit down? Like a drink?"

"I don't mind."

"What'll you have?"

"I'm not particular."

"Hey, Sonny! Make that *two* large ones."

The face of the whore was kindly. Unlike her sisters she was unmarked by any consciousness of shame or degradation.

"What's your name?"

"Maisie."

The adolescent shuffled back. In the down of his cheeks a cluster of pimples was sprouting. He was shuffling away again when the knocking started. The youth came alive. He dodged through the bickering mob to the far end, pulled a curtain and vanished. The knocking sounded again.

"Who is it?" Danno roared from above.

The moronic yob reappeared.

"It's only Mickser Hayes."

Joe savoured the whiskey. It was delicious. He took another sizable gulp, and felt the warmth spreading.

"Hey! Sonny! Another couple of the same."

"Right y'are, sir."

"And now, Maisie, tell us about yourself."

241

"There's nothin' to tell." Maisie's face was fat, and her clothes stank. She might, if necessary, provide a convenient lodging.

"Do you live near?"

"Not far. I used to live with me sister, Lord've mercy on her."

"Is that so?"

"Wasn't a bit like me. Thin little thing. A small breeze 'ud knock her over. She did smashin' in the business, worked hard too till she was *got at*. Many a time when I brought a fella back, as soon as she came in I seen he was all for a change of partners."

A fiddler, playing traditional airs, had taken Bartley's place: and a white-haired man, with the sad kind face of a drunk, was dancing. The others took little notice. Like corralled cattle the men elbowed round. The women crowded the tables, comparing notes.

"She was *got at* all right, be two Passionate Fathers down from Mount Argus. Promised her a job at the Nursin' if she'd go to England. Mind you I warned her. 'Teazie,' I sez, 'Teazie, you'll get no luck goin' to a pagan country.' Might as well be talkin' to the wall. This time last year she went. Off with her on the mail boat of a Tuesday. She wrote to me too, like she promised. She was happy, she said, workin' for some oul' nuns. It wasn't a week later, runnin' across for a package of fags, she was knocked down an' killed be a car. She couldn't say I didn't warn her. I often thought it was a judgment, so I did, a judgment."

"Well, the Lord have mercy on her. Hey! Sonny! Bring us two more large ones."

Whiskey was the perfect drink, warmed his body, heightened his mind, dragged him up out of the mire. The diminutive lush was still cavorting round. Joe would have liked to join him.

"Well, all the best."

"Good luck."

"The trouble with this world," Joe pronounced, "is that to live in it at all you have to be half-shot. Did it ever strike you that everyone, that if everyone was born half-shot, and lived half-shot, that everyone would be nicer to everybody? Everybody'd be in a good humour, not fightin' always and arguin' and killin'."

Another resounding knock! The boily boy elbowed through again, and disappeared.

"What's he keep dartin' in there for?"

"There's a grid. He can see who's knockin'."

"Who is it?" Danno called.

"It's Bartley back. Someone with him."

Bartley was back too soon.

"Excuse me."

Joe manoeuvred deftly through. The drab curtain cam- ouflaged the entrance to a cellar. The light came from an overhead grid. He looked up. Bartley was waiting at the door. Commiskey was with him.

Joe backed away quietly. He mustn't panic, or cause alarm. He manoeuvred gently through.

"You'll have to excuse me, Maisie. Back in a minute."

"That's all right, dearie."

"Don't go away."

"I won't."

Danno's heavy footfall clumped across. And the ceiling trembled. Joe was at the entrance to the yard when he heard the door open. He didn't wait. There was a high wall at the far side. With the aid of a friendly packing-case he scrambled over, and dropped deep into darkness.

The white lane wriggled between dark high houses, twisted around garages and the backsides of factories. The frightened snow, startled from his toes, arched before him like a white mountain, and died. He ran as fast as he could, but the houses ran faster, and it seemed that the snow underfoot was the same. He listened, but there was no sound, not even the splash of his feet in the slush. He didn't want to say it even to himself that the dark was his enemy, that the cold doors and gaping windows were seeking to clutch him. He would like to look back, but that would be madness. The tall dark places were seeking to hold him, the fingering chimneys, the groping windows, and the yawning doors. The stretched-down fingering chimneys failed, and the places collapsed silently, fell in a mountain of dust. He listened. But there was no sound. Behind him the houses were falling, but the only sound was the tiptoeing rat at the back of his mind.

Overhead was the luminous moon and the shy little stars shining behind. The moon was his friend. It ran, this side and that, over the roofs urging him on for all it was worth. What matter that under his feet the runaway earth was dragging him back. If he went on trying, the moon kept saying, he'd find the light. In a lull in the silence he heard the wind howl. It spiralled around in sinuous twists whispering threats, urging him all the time back. His heart was pounding but he heard no sound. Overhead the cloud-entangled moon deadened the silence, for fear he might hear the tiptoeing rat at the back of his mind.

He stopped dead at the end of the lane. The lights in the street were watching, watching and winking. Neon signs glared. Over-dressed windows sparkled. Even the supercilious lamps made little effort. They waited, watching, to see would he venture, daring him cross the mighty arena, daring him challenge the phalanx of darkness, daring him hurdle the serried spears. Above the hedge the white-blossomed trees held out enticing hands. He walked without fear and the lights were amazed, amazed to hear the sensible crunch of the snow underfoot. The winking lights were amazed to watch him climb the rampart, straddle the spears —and fall into darkness.

He lay for a while in the shade of the wall, breathing a sigh. It was good to snuggle in the burning snow.

The trees looked down with disdain. He didn't mind. He was glad to walk in their shadow, pleased to rest in the womb of the trees. He eased under the heart of an oak, and then he saw that the trees were weeping, that bitter tears were flowing out of the eyes and fingers, from the outstretched arms of the trees, that the trees were crying with no sound, and that their tears were bitter. The trees were weeping sorry tears for a bitter world.

Their sadness made him angry. He cursed the frenzied man whose melancholy seed had given him life, and cursed the acquiescent womb that thought it fun. They gabbled the prayers, poured the holy oils, lit the blessed candles, paid the priest his price to tell the Universal Lie. They darkened their eyes and deafened their minds, hurried away as fast as they could from the whispering voice insisting that what they had done was wrong. Sad to see the whole wide world living a lie, pretending a thing was good that was rotten! The weeping trees were tired of pretence and wanted only to sink into stillness, fade deep into lifeless clay. Only the trees were unashamed to tell the truth, that it were better a thousand times had he been never born.

Languidly he climbed the black wall, clambered over and dropped down sprawling on the path. Anna's place was opposite. He made no effort to hide his footprints.

He pushed in the apartment-house door, laid a wearied hand on the banister-rail, and dragged himself up. He wasn't in a hurry. There were fears in his mind, distant spectres haunting the outskirts, but he wasn't too troubled.

He mustn't make noise; it would wake the neighbours: and that wouldn't do. In a while she'd come, she'd open the door in her silk pink nightie. They'd talk for a while, talk for a little, with a locked door holding the world, keeping uneasiness out. Then they'd sleep. He would rest his head deep in her breast: and they'd sleep deep till the year after tomorrow.

He rang the bell. He must remember to tell her that the bars were a danger. A death-trap! He tried again, and heard her patter. She opened the door.

"I'm terribly sorry," he said pushing past; "I'm sorry to come at this hour, but it couldn't be helped." He stumbled on, and she followed after. "You've no idea what I've been through. You wouldn't believe it could happen. I must tell you the story, right from the start." He turned around. "You wouldn't believe it could happen in this day and age."

She was standing by the mantel and her face was pale. Her face over the pale pink silk nightie was pallid as lard. And her eyes were cold.

"I'll tell you what happened, right from the start. They arrested me first, Commiskey did, and the others as well, down in the Square. They bound me with wire and brought me a prisoner up to Rathmines. You wouldn't believe it. And me after workin' like hell for them all, breakin' my heart to keep them in order. D'you know what they said? D'you know what they told me? That I was a traitor, would you believe it? That I was a traitor! Jesus, I'll believe anythin' after that. I'll tell you what happened."

She stood by the mantel and her face was pale. He'd like to finish quick as he could, and kiss the coldness from her eyes. The line of her lips would relent, and her smile would break like the sun on the sea.

"They took me up to this house in Rathmines and put me on trial. Baker, Gerry Baker, got the job of doin' the dirt.

D'you know what he said? That all this time I was workin'
with Government agents to cripple the Movement, to bring
the Movement down on its knees. Would you believe it? He
said that I was to blame for Martin's death, and Goulding's too, and poor Mr. Nolan's. He said I was to blame for
havin' them shot. And the ambush as well. That was a plan
to cripple the Movement and I was the one that thought
it all out. And me after workin' like hell to keep them in
order. And me after tryin' so hard."

He'd have liked her to speak. But she didn't. She stood by
the mantel, her eyes cold as the snow. If she spoke it would
have been better. He could talk to her then, tell her how she
was wrong. But she stood where she was, and her eyes were
as strange as the coming of snow: and her lips as hard as
December.

"I know what happened. It was all the fault of Charlie
Horgan. You remember I said I'd be able to use him. Well, I
did my best. But he was too clever, that was what happened.
I thought I was great, coddin' him up to the eyes, but all
the time he was leadin' me on. I admit it! He made me a
fool—but not an informer. You know that, Anna, don't you?
That no matter what happened I'd never betray the Movement. No matter what happened I'd never let down the
lads."

He wanted to tell her, but somehow it didn't matter. She
didn't believe. He knew from the look in her eyes and the
line of her lip. It was the way he put it, maybe, was wrong,
or the fact that he didn't pretend. He told her the truth. But
Anna, his love, who always believed, was standing as cold
as a mountain of ice. He must have forgotten. It's hard when
you can't remember how best to tell the truth.

She turned to the phone on the mantel and lifted it up.
"I want the Police."

He walked slowly out, and down the stairs. There was

something back there that he should, or should not, have done. But he couldn't remember. There was something he left behind that got lost, that time he couldn't. He had hoped to go back; but now he couldn't remember what it was that was gone. It was something he lost that day in the field when he turned to the right. If he didn't go home he'd be beaten, and then he'd be beaten again because of the thing that he lost. Every wrong that he'd done in his life had been done after too many jars. He'd give it up. When this was all over. Once he was clear he'd never again so long as he lived. It was just that most of the time he was so much afraid, and never pretended.

He pulled open the door, and staggered out, into the slush. The squad-car was there. He poised a moment on top of the step, wondering. A shot rang out. And he fell. Three men in plain clothes came over the road. The two at the back were tall, but the rat-faced man with the gun was small. They came warily over and the rat-faced man had a new cigarette in his mouth. The thing to do, it occurred to Joe, was to pull the gun and fight. But what was the good? His blood was already staining the snow. And what did it matter? He looked up at the rat-faced man.

"Would you ever give us a pull of your fag?"

Paddy Lehane thought for a little, took the cigarette, and handed it over.

"Thanks." Joe took a long slow pull. "That was good."

Lehane raised the gun and fired another shot. Joe stiffened, and then relaxed. There was blood on his face, and blood on his clothes, and blood on the place all around. He didn't look neat. He didn't look tidy. But, for all that, there was a satisfied look in his eye.